T0374333

The Fallen

Samuel Coher

iUniverse, Inc.
New York   Bloomington

iUniverse books may be ordered through booksellers or by contacting:

iUniverse
1663 Liberty Drive
Bloomington, IN 47403
www.iuniverse.com
1-800-Authors (1-800-288-4677)

ISBN: 978-1-4502-1155-0 (sc)
ISBN: 978-1-4502-1156-7 (ebook)

Printed in the United States of America

iUniverse rev. date: 03/05/2010

Dedication to:
Mom and Dad
My three editors
and last
To all the fallen ones out there

CHAPTER ONE

I NEVER KNOW HOW MUCH POWER ONE PERSON COULD have. I guess it all depends on what the person has on the inside. Mostly his soul can tell you everything about a person, if they are greedy, power hungry, and hateful. I guess I did not have any of those when I died. My soul was pretty squeaky clean for the job that I was given. Somehow I was chosen for it. The name is Ethan Rush.

As I lay on my bed slowly waking up, I looked outside my window. I saw the bright yellow sun slowly rising in the east and hearing a couple of birds that wanted to mate. Some cars buzzing by on the street below and the bright blue sky was clear expect for a single cloud hovering above.

A loud knock on the door and a voice saying "Ethan, you up yet?"

"Yes mom, I am up." I answered in groggily voice. I got up slowly and took a look in the mirror. I'm just like an average 16 year old teenager, about five feet nine, around hundred and thirty pounds, blond hair and deep blue sparkling eyes. Standing there in my Joe boxers thinking to myself, why do I have to go to school on such a beautiful day, oh well I guess I need to start getting ready.

I walked into the bathroom and started to take a nice hot shower. While in the shower, I heard my mom's new boyfriend pull into the driveway. I really have not gotten the chance to talk to him but he does seem pretty cool.

"Bye Ethan." she yelled as I heard the door slam shut and the car slowly drive off. I got out of the shower and looked at the clock. It was blinking 7:30, so I thought to myself that I have about half hour before I need to get to school. I grabbed some boxer briefs and a pair of cargo shorts. While shuffling threw my shirts to make the perfect outfit, I found this black shirt with big smiley face in the middle.

I threw everything on and slowly walk downstairs. I walk into the kitchen; grabbed a Pop-Tart and the phone rang. "Hey" I said as put the Pop-Tart in the toaster.

"Hey Ethan, it's me Josh," the voice said.

"Hey Josh," I said back to him excitingly.

"What you doing tonight? I was thinking of throwing a bonfire on the beach and wondering if you can get permit for a bonfire on the beach tonight," he asked me.

"Well I got work from three to eight but then I am off. I will see what I could do about getting you that permit so you can have a bonfire on the beach tonight," I told him.

"I was wondering if you need a ride to school today?" he said quickly.

"Sure. That would be great," I answered.

"I'll be over in ten minutes. See ya then," he said and then hung up the phone.

I hung up the phone and grab my slightly burnt pop-tart and started to space out on the dream I had last night. Thinking about it really didn't help me make any sense of it, so I finished my pop-tart and got my stuff ready. I walked outside and saw Josh turning the corner.

Josh turned around the corner in his jeep wrangler, that he got only a couple of months ago. He pulled into my driveway with his black wavy hair blowing in the wind. He is little shorter then me and weighs a little less too. I jumped into his Jeep and threw my backpack into the back seat of his car.

"How you doing," I asked as we drive off.

"I am doing great. It is such a beautiful day out, wish we didn't have to go to school." He replied while looking out his window. Then I just started looking out the window and started daydreaming again. I heard him turn on the radio.

As we were cruising down the street about three blocks from the school, I saw this girl. She had the hour glass figure and hair that was solid black and flowed down her back. I did not get a good look at her because Josh was driving really fast. We pulled in to the student parking lot and I excitedly asked," Did you see that girl? She was totally hot."

"Why didn't you tell me to slow down?" he said to me. "Hey keep an eye out for a parking spot?"

"There's one right next to the blue truck," I pointed out to him.

As we were parking, I grabbed my stuff from the back seat and we heard the bell ring. "Shit we are already late for class," I said to him and jumping out of his Jeep.

"Yeah, but it is easy for me to sneak in to my first period. Besides I do nothing in my first period anyway," he told me with big fat grin on his face. Then we both started walking up to the doors and while walking to the doors, I dropped my backpack and books. Then I heard Josh yelling back at me, "See ya."

Picking up my books, I looked up and saw that girl again. She was slowly walking into the main office building. I wondered if she was a new student here. Quickly, I got up and ran through the doors just as the tardy bell rang.

The tardy bell rang and I was running to get to class. Finally getting there, I tried to sneak in but the teacher caught me. She marked me tardy on the roll sheet as I took my seat. It was English class, so I really did not pay attention too much of what was going on. Mostly I was thinking about that girl as I spaced off again.

The bell rang and everyone rushed out of the classroom, I went directly to my locker to put some books away. As I was opening my locker and a hand grab my ass. I turned around and saw my friend Rachael standing behind me with a smile on her face.

"Nice ass. I see somebody has been working out." she said with a smile.

"Thanks. How have you been?" I ask her as I went looking through my locker.

"I'm doing just fine. So what did you do this weekend?" she asked.

"I did nothing much. I worked all weekend. What about you? Go to any parties and get wasted?" I asked with a big grin on my face.

She hit my arm lightly and spoke, "Just hanged out with my boyfriend. No wild parties this weekend, but might be some next weekend."

"I hope so. I could use one right about now." I told her. She said goodbye and walked off. I whistled at her as she was walking away and she just turned around and blew me a kiss followed by an evil grin. I finish grabbing my stuff from the locker and went off to my next class.

Making my way through the crowded hallways, I reached the door just as the bell rang. It was history and we were learning about the civil war. My teacher was out sick, so the sub just put on this old flick about the war. I was so glad Josh was in that class or I would have fallen asleep. Josh brought out his deck cards and we started to play while the movie was going on.

"Hey, I saw that girl enter the main office this morning. I wondered if she is going here or what? Are you going to deal or what man?" I looked at him with this puzzled look as he shuffled the deck.

"Maybe you could point her out next time you see her. What is the name of the game we are playing?" he said while shuffling the cards.

"The name of the game is poker," I said. He passed the cards to me and I dealt them out and pretty much lost every hand that was dealt to me. About halfway through class, I had to use the restroom. So I asked the sub if I could go. I slowly walked out the door and down the hallway, looking into each room that I passed. I did not see the girl from earlier today which is what I looking for.

I got to the restroom, unzipped my pants and started to take a piss. I finished up and went to wash my hands. As I was walking out of the doorway, I saw her walking towards me.

As she was getting closer, she had a very short skirt on with a nice top. She must have been about five feet five. She walked up to me and said, "Hello. My name is Heather. I was wondering if you might be able to show me where my room is."

"Sure. It is right this way," I said with a shaky voice. She started talking about herself and where she came from. We reached her room and she grabbed my hand. She wrote something on it and went inside.

I looked at my hand and her phone number and a message was written on it. The message was to: *Call her right after school and we will do something later on if you want. Thanks for the help*. I slowly walked back to my class and the movie had finished when I got there.

Josh asked with a puzzled look, "Where have you been? I had to watch the movie since I had nobody to play cards with."

I snapped out of my daze and responded, “I got that girl’s number, the one from early and she wants me to call her after school.”

“Man you get all the girls. I wish I went to the restroom and came back with a girl’s number written on my hand. So are you going to call her up after school?” he asked with some anxiety in his voice.

“Yeah, I think I will call her. See what she wants to do tonight?” I told him.

He patted me on the back and said, “My little friend is growing up and leaving me in the dust.”

I punched him on the arm and then the bell rang. Josh and I walked to the P.E. locker rooms. I started to change when Josh asked, “So you going to let her play with your tool tonight?”

“No, I’ll leave that up to you,” I replied. We both laughed and finished changing.

We walked into the main gym. Joking around with each other, we noticed that the P.E. teacher was running late. He came in and we skipped the warm-ups and went directly into our basketball games.

I was playing against Josh’s team. We were playing really hard. The coach came over to watch our game. The final score was 36 to 35. Josh’s team won.

As we were walking back to the locker rooms, I congratulated Josh for the nice win. Some small talk was going on inside the locker rooms. I changed real quickly and went over to the soda machines. I got my favorite soda Mountain Dew.

Josh just then walked up behind me and asked, “Hey, can I borrow a dollar. I want to get a soda?”

“Sure, man,” I answered as I reached into my pocket and pulled out my wallet and gave him a dollar.

"Thanks. I owe you one," Josh said to me. He grabbed his soda and we walked out of the locker room to head towards our next class.

I said bye to Josh and see you at lunch time. I walked into my math class and that girl was in that class as well. When she saw me, she came over.

"Hi, thanks for helping me out this morning. I hoped we had a class together. I really think you're cute. By the way, I did not get your name this morning?" Heather asked with a smile that would stop you dead in your tracks.

"My name... My name is Ethan," I said a little dumbfounded.

"Nice to meet you Ethan, where do you sit?" she asked.

I pointed to my desk and slowly walked over to go put my stuff down. She walked with me and took a sit right next to mine. Just then the teacher walked in and said, "Good morning class. I hope everybody had a nice weekend. Did everyone do their homework?" he paused and looked at the roll sheet. "I see we got a new student. Heather, I hope you like Santa Cruz and now let's open are books to Chapter Seven."

The teacher went off on something about circles. Heather tapped me on the shoulder and handed me a piece of paper. I opened it up and it read; *I really like you and I hope you call me after school. I will not disappoint you so maybe we can go out and you can show me around town.*

The ball rang and I nodded at her. She giggled and went out the door with a little bounce in her step.

Slowly I walked to my locker to put my books away. Putting away my books and taking out the books that I need, while doing this my stomach started to growl. Then I head out to the normal spot with my friends. As I was walking up to them I saw Josh talking to some other friends under the big oak tree and then he made his way over to me by the fountain.

"Hey Josh want to go get some food before lunch period ends?" he asked.

"Ok," I told him and we walked to the lunch lines where we waited about ten minutes. We got to the little window; I ordered a Togo's sandwich, bag of chips, and Mountain Dew. Josh ordered a burrito, curly fries, and Pepsi.

As we walked back to the spot where we ate lunch, the normal crowd was there. Rachel, Jimmy, Travis, Jessica, Vicky and Mike yelled, "Hey guys, how is everyone doing today?"

We said back, "Ok, the same as yesterday." Then we all just started talking and making small talk and jokes about each other.

I asked Travis, "How was the baseball game you played over the weekend?"

Travis replied, "It was not that bad. We won five to three. The pitcher for the other team got nail in the nuts in the fourth inning. He was fine after they iced him."

"Really, sounds like that hurt," I said as I grabbed my nuts and squirmed a little.

"Yeah, it did. He could not play for the rest of the game. He had an ice pack over his crotch for the rest of the game," Travis told me while trying not to laugh.

Rachel asked, "Hey Vicky when do you get your new car? I want to drive it to this new club opening up next week."

She answered, "I get it this Wednesday. My dad is going to take me to pick it up."

"Cool. So when do I get a ride in it?" Jimmy blurted out.

"Never, if you do not kiss me right now?" Vicky demanded. Jimmy walked over to her and planted a big kiss on her lips.

The ten minute bell rang and Josh told them about the bonfire. "Hey if you need a lift after school, meet me at the Jeep," yelled Josh.

We said goodbye and walked off to our next class which was T.A. Nothing big was going on that class. All we did was a watch a movie on some weird science show.

The bell rang at two and I packed my things and left. I was walking to Josh's jeep when I remembered that I needed to go to my locker. Quickly running to my locker and out of the corner of my eye I saw a piece of paper on the ground. I picked it up and it read: *Are You Ready?* I just crumpled it up and threw it in the trash bin. I reached my locker and grabbed the book that I needed. I bolted down the empty hallways and out into the parking lot.

CHAPTER TWO

JUST AS I GOT TO JOSH'S JEEP AND WAS LEANING UP AGAINST it he was exiting out of the doors. He finally made it to his car and unlocked it. I threw my stuff in the back and jumped in.

"Hey Ethan," said Josh with a big grin on his face. "So are you going to call her when you get home?"

"Yeah sure," I said anxiously.

"Call me after you finish talking to her. I want to hear everything that you two talked about. Do not leave me out of this one," Josh said to me.

"Ok, ok. I will not forget my good buddy Josh," I said to him. After that we talked about class and school. We finally arrived at my house; I grabbed my stuff from the back and jumped out of the car.

"I'll talk to you later tonight," Josh said as he was backed out of my driveway.

I slowly walked up to my door and pulled out my keys and unlocked the door. My mom had left me and wrote that she will not be home until late and left some money for dinner. After reading the note and taking the money, I went over to my phone and started to dial Heather's number.

"Hello," Heather answered the phone.

"Hey, it is me Ethan," I said trying not to sound too dumbfounded this time.

"Oh hey Ethan, how are you?" she asked.

"I am doing just fine and how are you?" I replied.

"I am doing fine. I wanted to thank you again for helping me out on my first day at school. Are you free to night?" she answered.

"Well I got work till about eight and then I am making an appearance at a bonfire but after that I am free," I told her.

"Well how about you meet me at my house about nine-thirty tonight. It will give you some time to change and go to your friend's bonfire," she told me. Then she told me directions to her house, which happen to be pretty close to my work.

"Ok. Well I guess I will see you later tonight. Hope you have a good rest of the day," I told her with a little excitement in my voice.

"Ok. You have a good day and I will see you later tonight," she said then hung up the phone.

I hung up the phone on the charger and then I remember that I need to call Ethan. I picked up the phone again and dial his number. "Hello," he answered.

"Hey it's me Ethan," I said to him. "So when does that bonfire start again?"

"It starts around seven till whenever you feel like leaving. Speaking of the bonfire, do you think I can stop by your work to get the permit early?" he asked me.

"Sure but I will only be there for about an hour because I am going to meet her at her house later on tonight. Since you want to know and I'll be going too," I said to him all proud and confident.

"Good for you. Hope you have a good time. I'll be stopping by your work tonight to pick up the permit for the bonfire. So guess I'll see you tonight. Oh by the way did you need a lift to work?" Josh asked.

"No thanks. Think I'll walk today since it is a great day outside. So catch you later." I said to him and hung up the phone.

I went to the phone rack and hung it up. Slowly walking up stairs of my house to my room, I started to think about everything that has happened so far today. The door to my room got stuck so I put my shoulder into it. I went flying into my room and noticed that it was about forty-five minutes before I need to be at work. Quickly I grabbed my uniform and a change of clothes, which I stuffed into my backpack for after work.

I changed into my work uniform which was black slacks and a green Santa Cruz Boardwalk shirt, ran down the stairs and out the door. I was not able to have the leisure walk that I wanted to. While running down the street, the wind was blowing past my face and the sun heating up my body. It felt like I was almost flying off the ground.

Finally I reached the Boardwalk and walked up to my game booth. The clock hit three and I started my day. The day went by pretty slow until five when my friends came by. Josh came up to me and asked, "Hey can we get that permit for the bonfire tonight?"

"Sure guys," I answered. "I will be back in a sec. I just need to ask the boss for it."

"Ok," Josh yelled at me while I walked into the back.

I walked into the back room of the booth and saw Ryan my boss just sitting there. "Hey Ryan, I was wondering if I could get a permit for a bonfire tonight?" I asked him.

Ryan replied, "Sure but I thought you have a date with that girl name Heather."

"I do but I will hang out with my friends before I have to go to Heather's house," I told him.

"Oh ok. Let me go fill it out and you can sign it before you get off work," Ryan said and then walked out of the backroom.

"Thanks, I owe you one for doing this," I said and I went back to the front of the booth and told the guys, "I will bring it to you guys once I am off work."

"Thanks and we will see you out there," Josh said and then his girlfriend and her little brother all walked away.

A couple of kids came running up to my both screaming, "Daddy, daddy can you win that for me?" then looking up to their dad with puppy dog eyes. Then the dad asked me, "How much to play the game?"

I answered him, "It is two dollars for three balls." The game was to break two plates and then you will win a prize. The prizes were a giant Taz doll.

"Do you want to give it a shot, mister?" I said to the dad all coy.

"Sure, why not. If I do not spend my money on this, I will defiantly spend it somewhere else in this park," he told me with a grin.

So he handed me two dollars and I gave him three balls. I walked off to the side so I would not get hit. The guy threw his first ball and it hit the holder of the plates. Next shot broke the middle plate. It had a nice smashing sound to it when it shattered into a million pieces. With his last shot, he kissed the ball hopping it would smash one more plate so his kids would be happy. He threw his arm back and in a quick forward motion the ball was released from his hand.

All I heard was the smashing sound of the plate behind me. "Nice shot," I told the guy as I grabbed one of the giant Taz doll.

"Thanks, it was nothing but luck," he said nonchalantly. I handed the Taz doll to the little girl and she had the biggest smile on her face. Her eyes were all shiny and brighter then the sun. She gave her daddy a big hug and a kiss. Then they slowly walked away.

Just as I finished re-racking the plates and cleaning up the floor, Ryan walked up behind me.

"Hey Josh, how have you been," Ryan asked.

"I am doing fine, just working and school," I replied back to him.

"I wish something would happen around here. It is so boring just sitting in the office or backroom of the booths doing nothing," he told me.

"You can always come out and run the booth for a little while or just walk around seeing if everything is ok," I said with a laugh.

"Well you get back to work and stop doing nothing," he said and handed me the permit and went into the backroom.

I was looking out onto the beach and noticed that Josh was walking up to the booth. I went into the backroom and told Ryan, "Is cool if I take off now?"

"Yeah that is fine, go enjoy your party," he said in a soft voice.

"Hey, did you want to come to the party?" I asked him as I was about to leave.

"Well, sure but are you sure that would be cool with Josh?" he asked me.

"I am sure it will be just fine," I said and then vanished around the corner.

Josh walked up to the booth and I sneaked up behind him. I reached out my hand and grabbed his shoulder. He quickly turned around and saw me behind him.

"Hey," he said little out of breath. "What are you doing out here? You're supposed to be working till eight or so I thought."

"Yeah but my boss let me have the rest of the night off. It was slow and he said to go enjoy yourself at the party with your friends," I paused. "So where is the nearest restroom so I can go change?"

"How should I know you're the one that works here? Shouldn't you know the answer to that question," he said with a little laugh. He followed me to the nearest bathroom and told me, "I will be down at the party, so hurry your ass up."

"Yeah, I'll be there as soon as I change into some better clothes," I yelled from inside the restroom.

As I entered the bathroom and a few boys were taking a leak in the urinals. I walked to the last stall and went in. Locking the door and hanging my backpack on the back of the door, I started to unzip my backpack as I heard some of the teenagers walk in. They started to check each stall by kicking the doors in and making a lot of noise. When they go to my stall they stopped and left in a hurry. I heard them say, "Yeah he is in there. Want us to give him a message?"

The other voice said, "Tell him to hurry his sorry ass up."

The teenagers came back in and yelled, "Yo Ethan, hurry your sorry ass up."

I yelled back, "Ok. Just hold you pants on ok." Then the teenagers left and Josh was still waiting outside for me to change. I went back to grabbing things out of my backpack. I threw on some black khaki shorts, gray wife beater and black button down shirt. I threw my work clothes into my backpack and opened the door to the stall. I walked over to the mirror and checked myself out. After finishing making sure I was looking good, I headed out towards the bonfire.

Walking towards the light of the bonfire, I could hear the voices. As I slowly walked down the steps, I heard the music blasting through the quiet night air. While getting closer, I saw some people dancing around the fire, others jumping through it. Just outside the ring some couples were making out or just sitting there talking about who knows what.

On the other side of the fire was a long beach table covered in a nice cloth. On it was drinks, food, the stereo blasting tunes at full volume, and a bucket full of water and apples. I guess later on we will bob for apples or something. Shadows dancing with the movement of the flames, the wind was spreading the heat from one end of the beach to the other. The fire must have been a good eight feet high. I looked up and saw Josh walking towards me.

"Did you like your surprise that I left you?" he laughed.

"Yeah, it was really funny. Them scaring the crap out of me and all," I paused to punch him in the arm. "So here is the permit and do not lose it. I am heading out in a while and I will see you before I leave." I handed him the permit and walk off in a different direction. It was about eight when I decide to make toast to my best friend.

I stood up on the table and started to speak. "To my friend Josh, without you this party would have never happened. You have been a great friend to all of us and will be one in the future. Best wishes in everything you and your girlfriend do. Hope you guys never break up." A big cheer from the crowd rose up.

Everyone started chanting "Speech, Speech, Speech."

"Ok, Ok." Josh said and got up next to me on the table. "Well I could not have done this with out Ethan, my best friend, and Sarah, my girlfriend. Babe, come on up here?" he paused and wait for her to join us on the table. "Thank you Sarah for being there for so many years and being my girlfriend. Ethan you're the one who has kept me out of trouble over the years and if not for you guys I probably end up in jail. My hope for all you guys is so great and I am still waiting for someone to knock me off my throne." Laughter filled the still night air. "Well thanks to my friends and my girlfriend to make me who I am today," he finished and then an up roar of whistles and clapping disturbed the calm murky night.

When I got down from the table, I hugged Ethan and told him, "Hey it is time for me to go meet Heather and I will see you guy's later." I made my way through the crowds of people and then towards the Boardwalk.

Slowly feeling the night air flow around me, I started to think of what might happen when I got there. I was wondering what she would be wearing and if I was in the right clothes for her taste. Still wondering if we might get into something more then I wanted to. If we do, would I just walk out on her because I think that I am not ready.

Just thinking to myself about what might happen when I got there was bugging me. I looked at my watch to check the time and it was eight fifty-five as I entered her yard.

Her house was two stories, white. In the front yard was a couple of red rose bushes and the grass was nicely trimmed. It was surrounded by a small white picket fence.

I walked up to the door and use the knocker. About a minute later she was standing there in some short jean shorts and a white shirt. The shirt was somewhat see through and underneath she was wearing a black bra.

She said, "Hello, would you like to come in?"

"S... Sure," I said with a small confident in my voice. She shut the door as I walked in. We walk into the living room which had a big screen TV, a five speaker entertainment system, a big leather couch and a nicely woven rug covering the hard wood floor.

"Have a seat, make your self at home," she told me and pointed to the couch.

"Ok," I answered back. She walked outside the room and into what seemed to be the kitchen.

She yelled, "Would you like anything to eat or drink?"

"No, thanks," I yelled back.

She came back with some water in her hand and set it down on the table.

She said, "Thank you again for helping me out in school today. Do you want to watch a movie? I got a whole section of different type. You can pick the movie if you want."

I pick some movie that was really boring. I don't even remember the name of it. Then I felt her move closer to me.

About fifteen minutes into the movie, I felt her hand move towards my lower region. She unbuttoned my shorts and then started to feel my dick through fabric of my shorts and boxers.

I heard my zipper being undone. That is when I stood up and my shorts fell to the floor. I was standing there with my Joe boxers all tented up and I told her, "I think we're moving to fast. I should go."

I pulled up my shorts and started to go for the door when she ran in front of me and blocked it. "I am so sorry, I thought that might be the right way to thank you," she said sincerely.

I told her, "No, I do not like the way you thank people."

"I am so sorry. How can I make it up to you?" she asked with sniffle.

"How about going on a date with me tomorrow," I answered her with smile to hopefully cheer her up.

"Sure," she said bashfully.

"I really do like you," I said. After we settled back on the couch, we decide to finish that crappy movie. It was getting late and was thinking about how the bonfire was going. "I know this bonfire that is going on right now and I was wondering if you would like to go."

"No. Thanks, I think I would like to just stay here and get some rest for tomorrow's date," she told me.

We walked to her door and that is when I gave her a kiss on the check and told her, "I look forward to seeing you tomorrow."

I walked outside and then she shut the door behind me. I started walking down the street and I heard voices behind me. "I think it is almost time to awaken him. I can not wait to finally awaken him from his slumbers," the voices said.

It freaked me out, so I started to pick up my pace and did not look back. Finally reaching the Boardwalk, I turned around just to see if there was anyone there. Nobody was behind me. I walked through the now darken boardwalk and made my way towards the bonfire. Josh noticed me and he looked at the time. It was a little past eleven. "Man you were gone for a very long time. What did you do?" he said giving me a little nudge with his elbow.

"Yeah I will tell you everything in full details as soon as I get something to drink," I told him and walked over to the table to get some water. I took a drink and started talking again. I told them everything that happen even the two voices that I heard on the way back.

CHAPTER THREE

TIME FLEW BY AND THE FIRE NEVER DIED OUT. MOST OF the guest stayed till two in the morning and after two the party started to dwindle down to seven people. Josh, Sarah, John, Justin, Mike, Cathy and me just sat around the fire and told stories about each other.

"Hey how about we play truth or dare?" Justin yells out.

"Sure," we replied back to him.

"Since you suggested it, you get to go first, Truth or Dare?" Josh asked Justin.

"Truth," he answered back.

"What is your darkest fear?" Josh asked him.

"My darkest fear is that I am afraid of heights. I can not go on tall buildings at all," he told us with a little fear in the tone of his voice.

"Truth or Dare," Sarah asked Josh.

"Dare," Josh told her.

"I dare you to go swimming in your boxers," she told Josh.

"Ok, but I will want someone to come with me on this dare. Is that ok?" I asked the group.

"Sure, but who will be the one that goes with you is my choice," she said devilishly.

"Truth or dare," I asked Sarah.

"Truth," she answered me.

"Who was the first person you had sex with?" I asked.

"It was Josh. He asked me so politely when it was our first time and I just could not say no to those green eyes," she told everyone with a sly grin. Josh blushed a little bit.

"Truth or Dare," John asked me

"Dare," I replied.

Sarah spoke up. "You're going with Josh on a midnight swim in your boxers as well."

"Ok," I said while standing up. So Josh and I stripped down to our boxers and started to walk towards the ocean.

"Yo, Ethan let's stay together in the water. I do not want to get lost or something," Josh said.

"Yeah that sounds like real smart idea," I replied.

So we hit the water and just stood there so we could get use to the coldness. Everyone ran down to the tide line to watch us as we took a nice cold swim.

"Go further," everyone yelled.

"Ok, ok," we yelled back.

We walked in further and the bottoms of our boxers were getting splashed by the waves. Josh looked over at me and I was shivering. Then I noticed that he was too.

"On three we both dive into the water so we really don't freeze to death," Josh said.

"One, two, three," I said. We both dived in and splashed out of the water like dolphins jumping for fish, both of us freezing our ass off, when a giant wave came up behind us.

"Watch out," the group yelled.

Josh and I turned around but it was too late. The current pulled us both under the water. We tried to get out of the current but no luck. Our bodies floated back to the shore. John, Justin and Cathy ran over to me. Sarah and Mike ran over to Josh. Josh was ok but started to cough up some water when Sarah and Mike reached him.

CHAPTER FOUR

After I saw Josh was ok, everything went black. I did not know what was going on but all of a sudden the blackness was gone and it became a blinding white light. I felt like I was blind. I started to walk and use my hands as guiders. My hands found a pole and once I touched the pole the world seem to be less bright. I was able to see again and noticed that I had on a completely new outfit. I was dress in all black. It was black dress slacks with a tight black undershirt and a buttoned down black shirt.

The pole that I touched had writing on it. It read: *Welcome to the trails for your soul. Walk forth if you want to move on.* I thought to myself wow it seems someone has a sense of humor. Well what do I got to lose. This could just be a horrible dream and I must go through the trails to wake up.

I walked through the gate and was whisked away to the top of the Empire State building. "Welcome to the trails my son. It is time to become awaken," the voice bellowed.

"Who are you?" I asked but got nothing in response. Ok I looked around and all I saw was the word jump on a billboard down below. "If that is not a sign then I don't know what is?" I thought to myself.

So I leapt off the building. As I was flying through the air the only thought was what will happen. The ground was coming up fast but I did not close my eyes and a black hole opened up. I fell through the hole and ended up in the next place which was the bottom of a lake.

I didn't struggle to swim up; I just casually swam to the surface. Then I made my way to the rocky shores. When I got to the shores, I flopped down on my back and was looking up; when I noticed a human like shadow in the sky. The shadow started to move towards the middle of the lake. I made a guess that it wanted me to follow it. It took me across the lake to a small cave on the other side. It vanished into the cave and I was still a little worry about where this shadow was leading me.

"Well I guess forward is the only way left to go," I thought. There was no light in the cave expect for the light coming from the outside. "Ok I am going into a cave and there is no light. How can I make light from nothing?" I said out loud to myself.

"Like this," a voice rang out.

"Like what and who are you?" I asked into the darkness of the cave. Then the darkness had become a little lighter and then I saw this creature down on the ground. "Thanks for the light little guy."

"Your welcome, I don't get many visitors and you the first person that talked back to me. I guess I'll help you with your little quest," it said. "What is your name?"

"My name is Ethan Rush and yours?" I asked curiously.

"I do not have a name. Since you can talk to me why not give me a name," it said.

"Ok, well let's see you light up the day and seem to be happy most of the time. So I guess your name should be Caron. Do you like that name?" I asked it.

"That does sound cool so I guess I like it. Ethan, I thank you for giving me a name, now I will help you out Mr. Rush." Caron said. Caron looked like a frog but was a little smaller and it seemed that the light was glowing from its skin.

I picked it up and put it on my shoulder. We started walking down the path and a folk in the road was coming up. One path lead down and the other lead up. "Do you know which way to go?" I asked.

"Well I have never gone this far into the cave. Sorry I could not be more help." Caron said.

"You have been plenty of help so don't be sorry. You can gave me light and company when I was alone, so I think that is a lot better help then picking a way in a cave," I told it.

Caron smiled and then the lower path lite up and Caron said, "I guess we are going down."

"I guess so," I said and started walking down the path. After a few minutes of walking down, we got to a large cave that was lined with different kinds of doorways.

"I see you pass the first test and made a new friend. Congratulations now you must guess a doorway," the voice said and then nothing else.

"You know something Caron, I do not know who that voice is but it is really starting to bug me," I told Caron.

"Yeah I heard that voice when people pass by but they never even bother to help me out," Caron said.

"Sorry to hear that, but I am helping you out so I think we should pick a door together," I told it.

We looked at all the doors; each one just had a number and seemed to be on a track. The tracks lead to the circle in the middle of the room. I figured that we must push the door to the center to open it but first which door should we pick. There were eight doors all together. All formed a half circle in this room.

"So do any of these doors jump out at you?" I asked puzzled.

"Nope so I think we should just pick a door at random and hope for the best." Caron said.

"Well my favorite number is eight and it seems to be the number that is bolder then the rest so I say we pick that one," I told Caron.

"That sounds logical to me," it said.

We walked over to the door numbered eight and started to push towards the center. We got it into the center circle and then I heard a click and a handle on the door appeared. I grabbed the handle and turned it.

It opened to darkness. I thought we picked wrong but then a hand came out of the darkness and grabbed me. Carbon jumped on off my shoulder and said, "Congrats you passed and hope you do well on your next test."

The door closed as I went through and was in complete darkness again. I just waited where I stood. I could not see anything and did not know which way to go. I was not willing to try just in case there was no real way. It was tricky but I knew that I needed to do something or I might not get out of here. I searched my pockets and came up empty.

I went down to my knees and started to feel the ground that I was standing on. I felt two things. One felt like a switch and the other was a button, each on opposite sides of the ground. My first thought was to hit them at the same time but I could not reach with my hands but then I lay down on the ground and stretched out. My feet could hit the button and my hands could throw the switch.

So I tried that and then lights went on. Quickly I looked around. While still laying flat on my back, I took my foot off the button and half the lights went out. "Ok, my dreams like to puzzle me," I thought. So I took off both my shoes and stack them on the button. It worked and then I stood at the edge of one side of the platform.

I was in the middle of a room which was paint a solid forest green. The platform was dead center and nothing leading to or from it. There were no holes and as I looked down it had nothing to grab on to. It seemed like no way out but then something came to my mind.

It was something someone told me a long time ago. Your eyes are not always trusting but your heart will always lead you in the right direction. If you don't trust it, your life will just be a mess from the start.

I closed my eyes and started to listen to the beating of my heart. While my eyes were closed, my heart was echoing off the walls making a vision in my head of the room. It kept flashing and I was turning a little bit each beat. Then it flashed a path in front of me. I started walking towards the path and kept my eyes shut. The path was a zigzag up and then I hit the ceiling of the room with my head.

I opened my eyes and was about twenty feet above the platform that I was standing on. I pushed on the ceiling and it didn't move. I put one hand in my pocket and there was something there. I pulled it out.

It was a black marker. I thought, "How did that get there?"

Well if I can not see a way out, I might and try to draw a way out. I lay on my back and started to draw a doorway that was just big enough for me to fit through. I finished and lifted my marker off the ceiling. The door came to life and I opened it.

Jumping through and on the other side of the newly made door was the black shadow, that I saw in the sky before, he was just standing there. I walked over to him.

Before I reached him, he moved and started running straight towards me. I moved out of the line that he was running. He went straight passed me but he did get a quick punch to my right arm while I was standing there. I went flying a little to the left and then we both stopped. He came back around and I thought I must do something.

He was flying at me with clenched fists. I started blocking his punches and backing up. "I don't want to fight you," I said to the figure. He just kept punching away. I got one good kick to sweep him off his feet and the figure fell. Quickly it got back.

"You just don't give up," I said a little out of breath. "Well if you want to fight then I guess I'll fight back."

"Well finally you decide to fight back," the figure said. Then the black shadow melted away from his body and it was me standing in front of me. "Well come on, you little worthless piece of shit."

I went running towards him and start to fight him. The fight went on for a couple of minutes. Punches and kicks were flying all over the place. We blocked each others attacks and then we both punched each other in the chest, which sent both of us falling down to the ground. "You fight well," I said to myself.

"So do you," it said to me.

Then we went at it again. Pieces of our clothing getting ripped and small amounts of blood flying from our bodies, then I landed one good kick to his shin and put a little more pressure then needed. We both heard a snap. It went down but still wanted to fight. It tried to stand up but was not able to.

I ran over to him and asked, "Now that I won, let's get you some help to get you fixed up." I picked him up under his armpit and start to have him lean on me. I didn't know where I was going to take him but I knew not to give up even if we were just fighting.

Just as I was walking to a wall his leg got fix and said, "Congrats on passing your final test. Please go and meet the person that wanted you here."

He faded away and where he stood was a black hole. I jumped into the black hole and appeared back in front of the pole from the beginning of this dream. A figure of pure light and figure of pure black were walking my way.

They stopped at the gates. They didn't have any bodies just figures of what light and darkness looked like.

The white one talked first, "We can see that you have greatness in you. Your compassion and selflessness will take you far in life. We are sad to say that you are dead, well your physical form anyway. We tested you to see if it was time for you to be awake and it seems that it is."

The black one spoke next, "Well guess it is time for us to tell you who you are. You are the one son of the Gods. There is one other but you will meet him later on. Now we will wake you up from your sleep." Just then the black and white spirits floated towards me and went inside my body. I fell to my knees and my shirt ripped open and two wings came out one white and one black.

They quickly became under my control and then I heard the voices of the two spirits, "You may help or destroy what you see fit. Yet when we need you to do something we want you to do it then and stop what you're doing. Help with the task that is giving to you."

"Ok so what are my tasks," I asked them. Then I started to fly off as they told me what I needed to do.

CHAPTER FIVE

A FEW DAYS AFTER I DIED AND FOUND OUT I WAS THE SON of the Gods, the Gods talked to me.

"Hey son," they said.

"Hey guys, what s going on?" I asked curiously.

"Well we have some tasks for you to do," they answered.

"Ok what are they?" I replied.

"What do you know about the Black Zodiac?" they asked me all seriously.

"I do not know much about it. I have heard about it once but that was it." I told them.

"Ok. We'll fill you in on it. The Black Zodiac is just like the regular Zodiac but it's more towards the Wiccan and Satanism faith. It has thirteen different symbols but the only difference is that if you collect the power of all thirteen; something strange happens. We don't know what comes of it because every time we try to collect the thirteen, we seem to fail every time so we haven't completed it. The 13 signs of the Black Zodiac: Fallen Angel, Witch, Werewolf, Undead, Nameless One, Vampire, Life Giver, Life Taker, Broken Spirit, Spell caster, Wanderer, Ultimate.

"Wow, looks like I got my work cut out for me. So which one are you guys having trouble with?" I asked.

"Well the first half of the Zodiac is easy it is when we get to the Life Taker, Life Giver, and Ultimate is when we run into trouble. See the thing is that there are no more ultimates that we know exist on earth. The Life givers and takers are also rare but they do exist here. So we just need your help to locate them and get their powers."

"Ok and the next task that you need from me," I asked wait for something fun hopefully.

"The next task we will send you on is more of a treasure hunt. It is said in legend that there were four old ancients that lived long ago, each of them was as wise as the next and would be able to control anything they wanted. The thing is that each of them didn't want power or fame or wealth. They like living the quiet life," they paused.

"Ok so I guess they seem to be happy with their lives the way they wanted to live and not to rule anyone else," I said while waiting for them to continue.

"Your right, people from all-round came for their wisdom. Then one day the four of them decided to meet up and write down the most important means and wisdom that they had gathered through-out the years. They meet up and talk about this. Each of them decided to put in an equal share. The number they decide for each person was ninety-one and to write them down on scrolls. One for each day of the year and then when they were finished they would meet up again to share this wisdom with the others," they told me

"Let's me guess something happened," I asked and rolled my eyes.

"Well it took about three months for the four ancients to finish their work. Then they message the others when they were done and they picked a spot to meet up. When they met up for sharing their wisdom, there was a fifth waiting for them. He demanded that he must have the wisdom of the ancients. The Ancients told him no. The gentleman got upset and started fight with the Ancients. During that battle one sent all 365 scrolls away as he did that they also vanished with the scrolls. The gentlemen stopped fighting and wondered where they went. After that day nobody was able to find any of scrolls from these Ancients," they finished speaking.

"So you want me to find these scrolls and what?" I asked a little puzzled.

"We want you to find them and learn their secrets that they hold. We did find one but the strange thing is that it has a date on," they paused and the scroll appeared in front of me. "We tried to open it with spells and incantations and it does not want to open."

"Have you guys tried opening it on the date that is on the scroll? You did say they were wise and crafty so if they also just wanted to hide their wisdom, then they must have done something to protect it from falling into the wrong hands," I paused. I looked at the scroll and it had tomorrows date on it. "So it looks like I can test my theory out and open it tomorrow. One more thing how am I supposed to find the rest if I have no clue where to look?"

"Well, we hoped that there is a clue on the scroll once it opened up, but if there is not, just try to think like them. We got to go and good luck on those two tasks," they said and then left in a hurry.

"Well guess I am on my own to find these two things. I will have to wait till tomorrow to open this and start this journey. So I guess I need to start looking for the signs of the Black Zodiac. The first one easily because I am the fallen angel or at least that is what the Gods call me. I think finding the people for the Zodiac will be easier then the 365 scrolls," I said and then went on my way.

I decided to go on a Witch hunt. I remember that a few of my friends practiced Wiccan and was going to wonder how I should go down there since I did not get my body yet. So I got a long black trench coat and then noticed that I need to cut out long slits for my wings to come in and out so I would not destroy the coat. I grabbed a knife and cut the back of the coat and tested it out. It covered my entire body and the hood hides my face. I pushed my wings through and it worked perfectly.

I started my way down to earth in my new outfit and landed in the middle of one of the Wiccan ceremonies. They were channeling a warlord so I guess I decided just play along with them.

I came down with my wings out and even had the voice and everything; I landed in the middle of their channeling circle. "Wow we did it and this guy looks so cool. What is your name demon of the underworld?" they asked me all excitedly.

"My name is the Darc, lord of darkness. Why do you summon me?" I asked them in a low scruffy voice.

"We summon you to help us out with a task at hand," they say with a little fear in them.

"What is this task I must help you out with and in return I must ask you to help me out with a task of my own," I told them.

"The task at hand is that we want a little revenge on someone. What task must we help you out with?" the leader of the group asked.

"I must harvest your energy for the Black Zodiac. I must collect the powers of each, to form something great. So do we have a deal?" I asked in a low voice and extending my now bloody deformed hand.

They huddled up and wonder which one of them I would want to take there energy. "We do have a deal and which one do you want to harvest the energy from?" the leader asked.

"Well I take it you're the leader and will have the most spiritual energy so I would choose you." I told him. "So what do you need me to?"

"Ok that does sound fair. So I need to scare this jock that keeps picking on us," he told me.

"Ok so I do this favor for your and then I will drain your of your energy when the time is right. So tell me what you want me to do, my young friend," I told him and got down to his level.

He told me the plan and he wanted to be there with me to make sure it worked. The plan was to put fear into him. It was to stop making fun of people that are not like them. I took him to the jocks house and we entered through his bedroom. I enclosed the room off so nobody could hear us.

The gothic boy went walking over to the jock's bed and woke him up. "What the hell you doing in my bedroom?" the jock asked.

"I am going to teach you a lesson, my muscle head jock," the Goth kid said.

The jock got out of bed and was wearing some gym shorts and no shirt. He went for the door when he realized there were no exits. Then he went to let his angry out on the Goth kid. He took a swing at the kid and I blocked the punch. I came out of the ground and was now standing between the two. The Gothic kid spoke, "See this is my demon spirit and I can control him. Right now he will protect me and hurt anyone I want to. So I would not pick on me or my friends or I will send him after you." Then we both just vanished back to the summoning circle. "Do you think that worked?"

"I bet it did and you have nothing to worry about from him any more. Now it is time to keep you end of the deal," I told him.

"Well it hurt?" he asked.

"No I am just going to make a link to you so that when the time is right I can use your power, I will not have to fly down here to get you. Please walk into my wings so I can get a spiritual link with you," I told him. He walked in and then I enclosed my wings around him. I made small mark on his neck and then vanished. The next day, I watched to make sure he was alright and that the jock did not bug him. Nothing happened to the Gothic kid. The jock just passed by him and didn't even look at him or say anything.

CHAPTER SIX

After I watched over the kid just in case, I realized that I need to test out to see if the scroll would open up. I pulled the scroll out of my pocket. The date was glowing so I push down on it and the scroll rolled open in my hand. It read: *If you're reading this you must have found the first one of 365 scrolls. In each scroll there is a meaning and clue where the next scroll is hiding. Once you start just to let you know the next scroll can only be open the next day since they are dated in order. To find the next scroll it will be next to you when you sleep.*

As soon as I read the scroll, the two gods appeared behind me. They were looking over my shoulder. I turned around and asked, "So what do you guys think it means when it says next to where you sleep?"

"Well most people sleep in beds and next to the bed is a drawer. It is in a drawer," the white one said.

"By the way, where did you guys find this scroll?" I asked them curiously.

"It was found at the bottom of a lake. I do not remember which lake since it was a long time when we discovered that scroll," the black one said.

"Well I guess we got to wait and see what appears when I sleep tonight but I understand the lesson is that I must take the first step and start fresh each day. Each journey starts with a single step and this scroll is just the first step. Just got to wait and see what happens when I sleep tonight." I said to them

Night came and I went to bed. The next morning I awoke and was not surprised that the next scroll was just sitting there on the dresser that was next to me. Over the next couple of weeks I went back and forth with each scroll. Traveling throughout the world, even to places where humans couldn't reach.

While I was traveling, I remember my next stop was Paris and needed a Werewolf for the Black Zodiac. The Werewolf was quick and I had trouble catching it since I didn't have the speed to keep up with it. So I did the next best thing and waited for it to come to me. I sat down in the middle of the woods and started to mediate. It finally came back around and was circling where I was sitting. I had my wings out and ready with the link up. It lunged for me and as it was just about to land on my wings, I trapped it within. Quickly I linked it up. After I trapped it within my wings, it transformed back into its human form. She was cute but I had no time to help out this one so I left her in the woods and was off to get the next scroll.

I found the next scroll on the ground next to a plant on the side of a hill that was close to where I got the Werewolf. I opened it up and it read: *Do not look at everything the same way because you might miss out on something that was not there. The next scroll is hidden in valley that is not a valley but will be shown at sundown.*

I understood what the scroll wanted me to learn and I was really good at looking at things in a different way or light as they said. Yet a valley that is not a valley but will be shown at sundown got me puzzled. It must have been Las Vegas. The valley of the setting sun, when you look down the strip and it is like a valley at sundown.

I made my way down to Vegas and waited for the sun to go down. As the sun was setting, I sat on top of one of the casino's looking down into the valley. Sure enough I notice a small glittering thing on the strip. I went down to pick it up and meet him.

"Hey that was mine," I said trying to get it from him.

"Well I got to it first. If you lost it and I found it you must really need it," he said.

"It is not that I really needed it but I am on a quest to get that thing in your hand. By the way my name is Ethan," I said to the man.

"My name is Chance. I just wander around this town hoping to meet the next best thing or find something that would be great. I think you sir are that next best thing to come along in a long time," he told me with a grin.

"How about I tell you something, I am not human and I really need that scroll of the Ancients but I also need you," I said to him.

"Why do you need me?" he said.

"Well I am on two quests one for those scrolls and the other to harvest the energy of the Black Zodiac. I would like you to be the one of thirteen signs as my wonderer. Let's go have dinner and we can talk it over," I offered him.

He agreed and we took off to one of the finer restaurants in town. We got there and we order. As we waited for our food to come, he started talking to me. "So Ethan, I know this is going to sound weird but I know I have these extra powers to change the outcome of everything. I was able to change the luck of any game I play. Every time I thought really hard about it, it would change in my favor. So when I turned eighteen, I moved out here and use my powers to win big. I won enough money to survive; got a house out here and money to live the rest of my life," he paused.

"Sounds like you got it all set but I guess all good things must come to an end," I said.

"You're right. All good things did come to an end. I got bored of just making money and winning with nobody to be beside me. I stopped going to the casinos and just wandered around the town seeing what it has for a young guy like me. Each day going around finding new things, and then I meet you and this scroll you're after," he finished and held up the scroll. Just then our food had arrived.

We ate our food and then talked a little more about each others adventures. Then he said, "It was nice to meet you and I hope we can do this again. I'll link up with you and give you back the scroll. Here you go," he said. As I was grabbing the scroll from his hand and I linked up when we touched.

"The link is done and we can talk whenever you want. I'll always be there for you," I told him then vanished without a trace.

"Can not wait to meet you again, Ethan," he said and raised the glass to toast our meeting.

CHAPTER SEVEN

THE NEXT COUPLE OF MONTHS WENT SMOOTHLY AND I linked up with an undead and nameless one. They were real easy to get on my side since they don't put up much of a fight and really do not care too much. The scroll's riddles and locations were getting harder to figure out but I always was up for a good challenge.

It was about four months and six days from the first scroll and had made everyone since then. I opened the next scroll and it read: *Even the greatest warrior will lose once in there lifetime. You will not find the next scroll.*

I understood the lesson that every one in there lifetime is not able to do everything and will lose if you don't try but it made it sound like the next scroll doesn't exist. Well I guess I will have to wait and see what happens.

With that scroll, it took me to New York City. Well I thought to myself that since I am not going to find it, even if I try but since I'm here I might as well just relax and have a good time.

The night before that day I lost, I was visited by someone very interesting. So I thought I would find those for the

Zodiac but instead this one found me. She went flying into my room and was just about to bite me when I moved out of the way.

"Who the hell are you?" I shouted. No answer from her and she went after me again. This time I let her bite me in the arm. She was trying to suck the blood from me but nothing was coming out. "It won't work since I'm not human."

She let go of my arm and clamed down. Her fangs vanished and her mad demeanor diminished and was replaced with a sense of cool and clam. "Sorry for that. I was just really hungry and I saw your light on. You said that you're not human? What's up with that?" she asked while fixing herself.

"Well my title is son of the gods but most call me a fallen angel. I have been sent here on a couple of quests. One is about the Black Zodiac and the other is the scrolls of the Ancients. Each is about finding the right people and places. I might say that you're quite interesting and I would like to ask you to be my vampire in the Black Zodiac if you do not mind," I said to her.

"I will make you a deal. You hang out with me all day tomorrow without worrying about your quests and I'll join you. If you even think about you're quests and I will know since I can also read minds then I will not join. Do we have a deal?" she asked and extended her hand.

"So it is date then and what is your name anyway?" I answered and shook her hand to seal the deal.

"The name is Victoria and please do not call me Vicky. I just hate it when people shorten my name because it is easier to say," she told me then turn into a bat and flew back out the window she came in.

I went back to sleep but thought of how I was going to find her tomorrow for our date. I finally fell asleep and was awoken by the sound of the phone ringing in my room.

"Hello?" I answered the phone while still waking up.

"Hey sunshine, you ready for our date?" the voice on the other line said perky and cheerful.

"Morning to you Victoria, just give me a few moments to get dressed. I take it your waiting for me downstairs in that lovely black shirt and tight leather pants. By the way you look hot. So I guess I got to match you or at least wear the same color," I said with a laugh.

"You cheated. You're supposed to be stunned when you come downstairs," she paused. The phone went silent for few seconds when she came back on. "Oh well I guess it was all fair since you do look hot in just your black boxerbriefs," she laughed and hung up the phone.

I got up and passed a mirror. I did quick look at the hottie in his underwear and now to put on an outfit to match hers. I looked through the clothes I had with me and through some on. I walked down the staircase to meet her and got to the ground floor.

When I walked out of the stair case, her jaw dropped when I opened the door. I was dressed in all white from head to toe. My hair was platinum and I had a white trench coat with a white button down shirt underneath with white slacks to complete the outfit. The only thing black on me was my underwear. I walked up to her and said, "I take it you like the outfit and think you might want to pick you jaw up off the floor."

I grabbed her by the hand and lead her out the front door of the hotel. We decide to walk to our first destination. It was a nice little coffee shop in downtown New York.

"Well you look stunning, Ethan," she finally told me after the shock wore off.

"So do you, Victoria," I replied back giving her the once over.

We started talking about this and that and how we got our powers or found out about them. We reached the little coffee shop and got drinks. We sat down at one of the tables outside. We continued telling each other our stories.

She started to cry a little bit when I told her my story but told her, "It will be alright because now I can see my friends any time I wanted."

She smiled and looked at her watch. She said, "We are late for out next thing we are doing today."

"Ok, so where are we going?" I asked as we walked out of the coffee shop.

"You'll just have to wait and see," she said and grabbed my hand this time and dragged me into a taxi that she called. The taxi was taking the long way to wherever we were going on. I thought this might be a chance to get to know Victoria a little better. "So what do you do, Victoria?" I asked.

"Well I work at a blood bank for the Red Cross," she paused and looked at my face. It had that look like are you serious. Then she just busted up laughing. "No I work for the stock market, on the floor as a buyer and seller, but the look on your face was priceless," she said and imitated the look that I had.

"Ok. Ok you got me. So how is the job then and shouldn't you be there right now?" I asked with a smile.

"It's ok, I like the feel of everything happening at the moment and not waiting around for the next thing to happen. See I was always taught to live, live for the moments that we have and the moments that we lose. When I saw you on the street, I wanted to meet you, so I took today off and here we are," she told me.

"Cool. Sounds like you have a very interesting past to tell and I hope I can hear about it," I said and then looked out the window of the taxi.

We talked a little more about our jobs and the present life we are living. The taxi cab finally pulled in front of this really tall building. It expanded about five blocks in each direction and only one doorway in. We got out of the cab and then I just had to look again because it changed.

The size didn't change but more windows and doors started to appear. I thought it was a little strange so I put my guard up. Then she told me, "It is alright your eyes are not playing tricks on you. This building is a special one. It belongs to people like us. The gifted humans of the world can be trained here and just relax and be themselves. There are no leaders or anything like that but I think it is funded by the government or some rich guy," she told me as we walked through the door.

As we walked through the door everyone stopped what they were doing and just stared at me. My wings came out and they have gotten bigger since the last time I used them. They filled up most the wall that I was standing next to, the black wing was become more of midnight black and the white one was become like pure white.

"Sorry to interrupt, Victoria brought me here and my name is…" before I could finish one of the people came and started talking.

"We know who you are. You're Ethan Rush, son of the gods; your legend is what made this building come to life. We been training to help you out with your quests but first we will not help you till you come back since your not ready to lead us fully. I know you will come back but till that day you are welcome," the kid told me.

"I guess I feel honored or something, also take it that when we enter the building, our human forms vanish and that is why my wings came out so instantly. Well I hope I can help you guys out as much as this legend is foretold. Well it was nice to meet you all and I'll see you around," I said that and turned around and walked out of the building.

Victoria followed me out of the building, she saw me sitting on the curb just a little shaken. She sat down next to me and rubbed my back. "Sorry I didn't know you where the one from legend and I wouldn't have taken you here if I knew," she said to me.

"It is not your fault. I just didn't realize how much I had an affect on this world. I thought I would just help out in small ways and make a small difference in this world," I paused and stood up. "I guess I am a legend and will not let them or anyone down."

I looked up and noticed it was almost time for my surprise that I was doing for her. I grabbed her by the hand and we flew off. It was just after dusk and we landed on the Statue of Liberty. We rested on top of the flame that she holds. I told her to look over there and she did.

I started an incantation which made the sky start to light up. The spell that I did was one to make fireworks appear and have a blast. The entire sky lit up and so did her eyes. I knew she enjoyed it and so did I. looking down, I noticed that everyone else was enjoying it as well. I kept it going for a few minutes and then did one big finale.

After it was over she just turned around and gave me a hug. She whispered in ear, "Thanks for the good time and here is your next scroll you may have lost the day but you did not lose your quest and I would love to be apart of your team." She bit me on the neck which linked her up with that bite. After she left her mark on me, she turned into a bat and flew off.

When I got back to the hotel, I pulled out the scroll from my pocket. I looked down at the scroll in my hand and wondered what the next place will be. I opened it up and it read: *Sometimes it is good to take a break and sometimes you just need to learn to relax with the help of others. The next scroll will be waiting for you in the eyes of a beholder.* I looked around the room and found one more thing that she left behind. It was tomorrow's scroll. Her eyes must have been the beholder of the scroll and we were destined to meet here in New York.

CHAPTER EIGHT

A couple of months had passed; it was just over eight months since I started these quests. I linked up with a broken spirit in Japan. The spell caster found me in Greenland and the scrolls kept leading me around the world. The only three I was missing from the Black Zodiac were the life giver and taker and the ultimate. I stop trying to find them and started putting all my focus on the scrolls.

The next scroll I read took me up into space. It seemed like the Ancients knew or saw the future. It took me to the space station and I was able to help them out with a broken down satellite which also held the next scroll.

I waited till the next day to open it up. It read: *Now that you been on top of the world it is about time to see it from the inside. The next scroll was made from the earth itself.*

Well it could be in a volcano or at the sea bed where crust meets the water. I was thinking hard to find the answer. Then I remember something Caron told me about Tahoe. It came back to me and then I was off to see Caron.

"Caron where are you?" I yelled into the cave.

"I am right here. You don't have to yell I can hear just fine," he replied.

"It is so nice to see you again my friend. I need your help again with these scrolls. You told me once that Lake Tahoe was the beginning and the end of the world. I was wondering if you knew that if anything was created here," I asked.

"Well it is nice to see you to but I don't see the point of asking me that question. Nothing was made here since the late 1980's. This town is still the same now as it was back then," Caron said to me with a strange look on his face.

"Would you like to take a trip with me then?" I asked.

Caron face lit up and said "Sure I would love to see what you're so excited about."

I picked him up and put him on my shoulder. I took off and went flying to the historic walking grounds. In this place they had Indian teepee's, old style colonial housing and everything was so precise and neat. Each house had some wax mannequin dress up in old style clothing and doing something that they would be doing back in the day.

Caron asked curiously, "What are we looking for?"

"We are looking for something that does not fit into the scene or something that was made from earth," I told him.

"Oh ok so it's like a needle in a hay stack. Since it is important to you then it's important to me," he said with a smile.

We started looking through the windows of the houses and nothing popped out at us. Then we went over to the Indians teepee and searched around there as well. We came up with nothing but then I remembered that the Earth rotates each year so we need to go back to where it all started inside. Off the historic site was a small graveyard for the fallen.

I started looking at the tombstones and one name popped out to me. It was an old Indian name. It was Totemic

Wind Shores. I looked at the date and it was about the right year. "Hey Caron, I think we need to dig this person up and see if he has the scroll I am looking for," I yell to him.

Caron came over to me and started to help me dig. About an hour later we hit a box. Out of the hole we crawled with the box in hand. "Hope this is what we need," I told Caron.

I opened the box and inside was more dirt. I did not know what I needed to do. I dug through the dirt and nothing came up. Then the wind blew through the box and it start to get solid.

Caron told me, "Look the wind was making it hard." Caron blew on the dirt and it started to get harder. I brought out my wings and made small gust of winds on the box. The scroll was starting to form. More wind and then it all formed into the scroll.

"Thanks Caron for helping me out and it was nice to see you again. Guess I got to go now but till we meet again have a great time," I told him and flew off after I dropped him back in his cave at the end of the lakeshore. I flew up into the sky and waited again till the next day to come.

Two more months pasted and I still could not find a Life giver or Taker, I tried at all the places the scrolls took me. Yesterday's scroll took me back to New York and I thought I would find one there. I read the scroll and it told me to find what I was looking for and don't give up. For everything will be found sooner then later.

Well it is a Taker and Giver of life would be easy to find I guess but then I guess one does not want to be known because their talents we be use too much. Then I thought ok if I was unique and had to hide my powers where would I work. It hit me like a ton of bricks. The hospital is a great place to hide it from the world.

I went to the most crowded hospital in New York. I was posing as a doctor and they were paging me in and out all day. Then I noticed a nurse that seemed a little too young to be there. "Hey nurse what is that girls name over there?" I asked and pointed.

"That inter over there, I think her name is Wilma. She has been working here for about three years and keeps to herself," the nurse told me.

"Thanks," I told the nurse. I looked up and she started to walk away. I noticed that she had this aura around her that seemed to scream that she was different. I followed her down the hall to one of the patient's room.

"Hello mister Gann, My name is Wilma and I will be taking your life away tonight. It will be quick and painless," she said to the patient even though the patient was in coma.

I walked in and said, "So you do have the power to take life away. Sorry to barge in on you but I could not notice there is something about you that screams I need to talk to you. My name is Ethan Rush and I'm not really a doctor, I'm the son of the gods. I was wondering if you could also give life back," I said and waited for her answer.

"Oh, I didn't know anyone heard that. I guess I can give life back with my powers. My name is Wilma. I knew that I had these powers but it seemed that I didn't want any one to know that I had these powers. That is why I came to work for the hospital since life and death are common here. I would be able to practice my talents and hide them to the world," she told me shyly.

"Do you know if it is time for them to live or die before you take them?" I asked her.

"Well I just get these feelings and I follow them to the room. It is like a light I see. When I enter the room, it is dark and cold that means the person is about to die, so I take them or if it is light blue or white and warm that means to help them get better and well," she told me. Then I looked around and noticed what she was talking about. The room felt dark, empty and cold.

"I see. Well I'm here on a quest to link up with people of the Black Zodiac. What I need is a Life Giver and Life Taker. I am sure there is no rule saying that it had to be a different person for each sign. Would you like to link up with me?" I asked and extended my hand.

"I don't know. How do I know that you are who you say you are? It seems like your intentions are pure but I still need some form of proof," she replied to me hastily.

"Well how about I meet you on the roof in about an hour, I'll show you everything you need to know," I told her and then walked out of the room.

An hour passed and I went up to the roof. I opened the door to the rooftop and she was waiting for me.

I took off my coat and finally they had giving me a permanent body to us when I was here on earth. Then I brought out my wings and she took a step back. I think I saw something in her eyes that told me everything. She started to speak, "I have seen those wings in my dreams. You're the one that is going to become powerful and change the world for the better. I must not deny my destiny and neither can you."

"I know what you mean. I felt the link between people and the ones like us. It is like we are destined to be able to help and even take away what is there or not. So would you link up with me?" I asked again.

"I will," she told me and then she ran into my arms. I made two links with her. One on her right arm and one on the left, she then asked me, "I know this is strange but I was to meet you up here and give you this."

She reached into her pocket and handed me three scrolls. Then she left and as she was leaving she said, "We'll meet again and at that time I'll show you something more then just my powers."

I smiled at the thought of what it could be and sat down on the rooftop. Looking at the scrolls, I had two more months before the last scroll would be found. Then I did the math ninety-one per Wiseman that only comes up to 364 then I looked down at the three scrolls. One was dated for tomorrow, the next one had a date for next month and the last one just had the numbers 365. She gave me the last scroll, she must know more then I do about these things.

CHAPTER NINE

THE NEXT TWO MONTHS WENT BY QUICKLY. I GOT TO the last scroll and it leaded me to Stonehenge. I opened the last dated scroll. It read: *This is the last scroll. You should have had a great journey and meet a lot of fun and exciting people. One of those people that you meet along the way would have given you a scroll with numbers 365 on it. That is the last scroll and you will need all the scrolls. Since you are here the back of the scrolls will light up and instruct you further.*

I gathered up the scrolls and read the back of them. Each telling me to do something else, it took me all the way till sunset. Just as the last ray of light vanished from the horizon, the scroll with the 365 number on it lit up and I ran to the center of Stonehenge to open it up.

I opened it up and it was blank, nothing written on it. Just as I set it back down, four spirits popped out of it and they flew around Stonehenge. They were laugh and talking to each other like it was just another day. Then one stopped and noticed me in the middle. The four of them went and lined up in front of me.

"Thank you my friend for freeing us. It has been too long since we seen the light of day. It was a long time ago," one of them said.

"What is your name traveler?" one of the others asked.

"My name is Ethan, the one that was tested by your scrolls of wisdom. What are your names or is it just the four Ancients?" I asked.

"Well it has been a long time and that one does sound better. We like the four Ancients better so please call us by that from now on." the third one said.

"Ok, so I know part of your story, would guys fill me on what really happened?" I asked intriguingly.

The fourth one spoke, "Well it happen a long time ago and we all knew each other. We were the wisest in the land. Every year we would get together and share stories and tall tales. Each having great wisdom and then one year we decided that we should share our wisdom with the world. After that day, we went back to our home towns and people from all round came to ask questions and share the wisdom that we had," he paused. "Then the next year we came back together in our secret spot. We talk about all the questions that people had for us. We decided that we should write down our wisdom on scrolls and pass them out to people who needed them. That is when we decided to split up and do 365 because of the days in calendar year."

The first cut in and said, "Yeah we did so we split them up and each did ninety one each. The year passed once again and we all meet up. We picked a different spot this time and we didn't know we were being followed when we headed out. We got to the new place and we started the meeting. We showed each other the scrolls and then he made his appearance. It was the general warlord for the Emperor. He demanded us to hand over the scrolls in the name of the Emperor."

Then the second one interrupted, "We told him no we can not have this much knowledge for one person. He still demanded the knowledge. We told him no and then he made the choice to fight us. He thought since we were just scholars that we wouldn't know how to fight. We proved him wrong. We fought him and a couple of his warriors that he brought with him. The three of them fought him off while I was doing spells to send out the scrolls. Just as I sent out the last scroll, I looked over and noticed that we started to lose the battle. That is when I decided to do one last spell. I started the incantation, just as the last one of us fell down and a flash of light was gone off." He paused and then went on. "What I was enchanting, one more scroll to trap our souls till the day that we were set free. It worked and the numbers 365 was written. It was also shot out into the deepest parts of the earth. It land in the castle of the vampires and that is why your vampire or the life taker that you linked with had it."

"Wow what a great story, I bet you guys would like to move on to the next world and promise that I'll keep you wisdom safe," I said to them and graceful bow to them.

"Actually we were going to ask you if we could tag along with you. We have been listening to you since we were hand off and it seems like you would be more fun and exciting then going up to heaven and watching the action. So could we join you on your quests and were sure we will be able to help you out?" they asked me.

"I see no problem with that and then I guess either you guys can float around or hop into my body. Which do you prefer?" I asked them.

"How about in the body since we do not know this world, we're just the old ones. We know about your other quest and we do have an answer to find the last sign on the Black zodiac. The answer is you. You're one of the last ultimate's to walk this realm. Each one was destroy during our time on this earth. There are few left but mostly in hiding. Now the thing we don't get is why the last scroll leaded you here and not the place where we were cast into the scroll," the first one said.

"We know why he's here. Here is the spot to finish the Black Zodiac. Stonehenge was formed for many reasons but the main reason is that it was gateway for both Zodiacs's to come forth and become the last piece of the puzzle. The ultimate will come forth here at Stonehenge. The Ancients do know the summoning spell to call forth them," the black one said.

"So I see why you wanted me to get the scrolls and the Zodiac together. I guess I must complete my quest since one is done and the next will be done as well," I replied to the answer that was giving and faced the two Gods.

I stood in the center of the circle and I let one of the Ancients take over my body. He started doing the chant and then the pathways start to light up. Then each person that I was linked with came through each doorway. All twelve then formed a circle around me. Each started to glow and there energy was flowing into me. I felt there powers and was lifted off the ground, my wings came out and then I felt like I was being transformed.

The two spirits said one thing, "Here it comes; the ultimate to help us out." A spiral of black and white light was formed around me. The rest of the group could not see inside the ball that was now formed around my body. The ball landed on the ground and then a voice rang out, "So you're the one that will become the last ultimate," it snorted at me.

"Yes I will become the last ultimate of this realm and I wish for you to join me on my quests," I asked seriously.

"Well I'll join you since I can see inside you and you have a pure heart and good intentions. Just to let you know that I have a lot of power and I'll be able to help you out a lot but I wish not to become on either side. The reason you have one black wing and one white wing is to keep the balance in this realm and I would still like to have that followed," it said.

"I understand," I told it.

"Welcome to this realm Arch Angel Ethan," it said and then the ball vanished. I used my new wings to float down since the ball bounced up just before it vanished. My wings we still the same size and but the color has changed to a metallic black and metallic white. I felt like I had more power and everything else was upgraded within me.

The white and black spirits didn't go back into my body. The only ones that were there when I got back were the four Ancients and the godly spirits. The others return back to where they were when we started the ritual. Then the second Ancient started to talk, "Welcome back, Arch Angel Ethan."

"You guys can still call me Ethan Rush. The whole Arch Angel is way to long to say," I told them with smile. "What about the others?"

"I knew it. You would become the Arch Angel. There has only been one other time an Arch Angel walked in this realm. I found an old book about him. It was his journals. That is how I knew the ritual and spell. It told me that it was a lot of hard work, even the spirit still thought he was not worthy to hold the power and secrets that it held. He finally proved to the ultimate that herself was worthy of its power and secrets. Then the journal just stopped after that," the first one said.

"Well I guess the person that harness this power thought it would be useless to keep it since he got the power or maybe the power and secrets could not be written down do to the fact that I made a vow not to reveal the powers that dwell within," I told them.

"Well either way now we send you on the last task that we need you for. We have a list of names here that we want you to help unlock their hidden powers," they said and then handed me the list. "Oh yeah just to let you know the twelve people that you used as the Zodiac signs had there memories erased so they do not remember you or anything that has happened." Then they vanished back up into the heavens.

"Well I guess my next task has become more important. You guys ready to start and help out," I asked the Ancients.

They just said, "Yep, it is time to start a new. Meet some great and awesome people." Then they all hoped in to my body and opened the list. The first name was Samuel Coher.

CHAPTER TEN

WELL, I DON'T KNOW HOW TO START; THE WORLD CALLS me a hero, others call me their protector. I do not believe that I am a hero or a protector but after what happened that day I guess that is what I became.

My name is Sam, there is nothing out of the ordinary in my appearance; I'm six feet tall with moppy brown hair and blue eyes. I'm not made of muscles and not much of an athlete. Not of the brave-hearted or particularly courageous variety; I'm just an average guy. Not the typical hero type, ya know?

Time has been passing so slowly after those events that happened, guess I should tell you what made me become the person they are calling me.

Getting up early for school was the way it started. Not really knowing my destiny has chosen this fateful day, I arrived at school parking lot. While I was walking to the building, I saw my friend Josh.

He walked over to me and I said, "Hey Josh, how did your night go?"

"It was ok. Woke up at three this morning," he answered with a yawn.

"So you ready for gym? You're doing basketball right?" I asked him.

"Yeah, I am ready. How are you doing in Karate class?" he replied.

"I'm doing great. I should be red belt within the next couple of weeks. I am thinking of entering into a tournament to see how much I have learned," I told him.

We entered the two-story building of Wilcox High. Kids scurrying about in the hallways with lockers opening and slamming shut. As we made our way to my locker, small talk was floating about the crowded hallway.

We finally made it to my locker and I grabbed some books. "I'll see you in the locker room. Later, man." I said as I went running off to my class.

It was English and it was an easy day in there. It flew by, ending with the usual homework assignment. The bell rang, announcing it was time for the next period. I made a quick dash back to my locker to drop off my books and then ran quickly to the locker room. As I was changing my friend Josh came by and started talking to me.

"You're pretty slow at changing," he said.

"Yeah so what's your point?" I retorted at him, smiling.

"Just giving you a hard time, just relax and take all the time you need. I will see you in the gym," he said and patted me on the back.

I was looking forward to this class all week. I was going to learn the fundamentals of using the Bo staff, something I had always interested in learning. The teacher showed us a few swings and paired us up to practice what was just shown. Just as my partner and I were starting I heard a low hissing sound coming from the vents. I looked up to see if I might be able to see what was making that noise, and when my partner asked, "What're you looking at?"

I said without looking down, "I don't know, it's probably just a couple of rats in the vents scurrying about."

"Hey, stop worrying about those rats and let's get back to practicing," he said to me and then poked me with the stick. I looked down at him and then pushed his stick to the side with mine.

We went back to practicing with the staff but I still was wondering what that noise was. I kept hearing it all throughout the period. The teacher called us back and told us we were doing a good job. Then he sent us to go get changed.

Locker room was busy as normal. Other guys chatting about girls, a few joking about some guy's weird hair style and yet in all the noise I seemed to only have one thing on my mind… What the heck was that noise? My curiosity got the better of me.

While changing back into my regular clothes I looked around and asked if anyone heard that hissing noise in the gym. My friend Danny looked up from tying his shoe. Danny was a little shorter then me with slicked black hair, blue eyes and an average build. "Yeah I heard that sound; I thought it was just the heating vent turning on. What did you think it was?" he told me while finishing tiring his shoe.

"I guess it was some rats that got into the heating vents." I replied just as the bell rang.

I grabbed my backpack and bolted to my next class. My next class was on the other side of the campus and on the second floor. I knew I would not have anytime to go use the restroom. Even through I was in a rush to get to the next class, my mind still wondered back to that noise. I opened the door to the hallway and it seemed a little less crowded then it was in the morning.

I made my way to the stair case and ran up the stairs. With only a minute to spare I made it to my classroom of 209. I took my seat and wait for the teacher to start class.

Just as the teacher started his lecture, I remembered that I need to use the restroom. So I decided to ask the teacher if I could go use the restroom. He excused me and I headed down the empty hallway with some haste in my step. While I was walking down the hallway, something caught my eye. I was not quite sure what I saw but it looked like it went up one of the kids shirts. I thought it might just be my imagination since my head was going in every different direction. Then I looked back and noticed a small tail slide out from the back of the kid's shirt.

"Hey," I yelled as I started running towards the kid.

He turned around just before he was going to open the door to the classroom. I noticed it was my good friend Josh.

"Hey, Sam, what's up?" he said to me.

"Oh Josh it's you. Hey I thought I saw something climb up your shirt" I said as I reached him.

"Huh?" What are you talking about?" he seemed a little puzzled.

"Take off your shirt cuz I swear I saw something climb up the back of it." I said again.

"You're crazy; I did not feel anything go up my shirt. I'm late for class, so I will catch you later," he said to me, then opened the door and entered his classroom.

I then went back towards the bathroom. I took a few steps then I heard a whole lot of screaming coming from Josh's classroom. I rushed back to the room and as soon as I opened the door. The scene was horrible. The first thing I notice was Josh's body was only half there. Pieces of my fellow classmates were strewn about everywhere, and the walls were cover with blood and guts. No one was left alive.

CHAPTER ELEVEN

I HEARD A NOISE COMING FROM THE FRONT OF THE classroom and noticed a small green tail slide into the vents. I could not take any more of this scene so I slowly shut the door and took off down the hallway.

As I was running down the hallway, I ran into my friend James. He stood a couple of inches taller then me with short black hair and dark brown eyes.

"Hey, Sam what's wrong? It seems like you seen a ghost or something," he asked me.

I answered him in a low voice, "I just saw the most horrible scene." As I told him what happened his eyes started to widen. I knew the next thing he was going to ask me.

"Please, show me it," he asked with some excitement in his voice. See my friend James loves all that blood and gore. It was no surprise to me that he wanted to go see it. So I took him back down the hallway to the last room.

I slowly opened the door and everything was still there but there was someone standing in the front of the room. It was our teacher Miss Anderson. She seemed to have an eerie calm about her though.

Once she noticed that we were standing in the doorway she asked, "What happened here?"

I answered her as I started walking towards her, "Some type of snake like creature came in on Josh's back and then killed everyone in the room." I noticed the hissing noise again as I was talking to Miss Anderson. It made me stop dead in my tracks and then Miss Anderson came out from behind the desk.

When she moved from behind the desk, the snake like creature had made her into like a finger puppet. From the waist up she looked fine but she was missing her entire bottom half. We both noticed the snake like creature was wearing the top half of her body and was moving along the floor with its tail slithering from side to side.

It lunged at me and I grabbed it before it could do anything. It sent both of us down to the floor. I was holding it off but was not doing a great job of it. That is when James came to my rescue. He picked up one of the broken desk legs that lay about and came running over to where I was on the ground with the creature.

Just before James bashed it, it ripped through the skin of the teacher, I noticed the eyes of the creature had some kind of strange look about them. I could not explain it but they seemed human. Then James came running at the creature and whacked it off me and flying to the side of the room. Then it went crawling back into the vents.

"Hey, you alright?" he asked as he reached down to help me up.

"I been better," I said as I was getting up. I tried to wipe of some of the blood and guts off me but it did not work. We stood in the room for a few more seconds and then we both made a decision. We both assume that the whole school had been laid waste by that creature. So we both wanted to help out the ones that maybe left.

We walked back out the door and the bell rang, I jumped a little. We said our goodbyes and walked off. I made my way back down the staircase and I ran into David. He was shorter then me and had surfer blonde hair. David had a terrify look on his face. He did not say anything to me but just dragged me to where Ms. Rekow was doing her laundry in the cooking class's laundry room. We opened the door and all of a sudden we saw the creature eating her like an orange, peeling the outsides and then devouring her insides. We both stood frozen in our place. It looked over at us and started moving towards us.

I realized that it was coming for us and I reacted just in time by shutting the door on it. I heard it slam into the door. It tried a couple more times to get through then the sounds of it banging against the door stopped.

I looked back and David was no where to be found. He must have taken off after seeing that creature come after us. I could not take this any more. I just went over to one of the corners and sat down in it.

Now the place I was in had very good acoustics since it was a place with a lot of metal. The main stove that was in the room connected to the air vents above them. As I was sitting in the corner, I was listening to the screams echoing through the vents and the hallways. In my mind, I just imaged my fellow classmates getting torn apart by this creature. Then the screams started to fade away.

As I was sitting there, I started to think about what I could do. Well I could just sit here and hide until it was all over or try and help the ones that were still alive. Just then someone busted through the door.

I looked up from my corner and it was James. He looked over at me and came to see what was wrong. He spoke, "It is a blood bath out there. Bodies, blood and guts all over the place, I do not think that this could happen in real life."

I knew that he was enjoying this a little too much. I asked him, "Did you see the creature? Did you try and kill it?"

He answered back, "No I did not see the creature while trying to help my classmates. It looks like most people got out of here safely but still a lot have died."

"Good, now it is time to take care of the creature," I said to him. I did not know where this act of courage came from but I kind of liked it. It must have come from listening to all the screams and I decided to do something about it.

I walked around the kitchen area and went straight for the knives. I knew I need a weapon of some sort to defeat this creature. I grabbed two butcher knives off the racks and then a couple of smaller ones to be used as throwing knives.

I looked back at James and told him, "Hey, I want you to get out of here. I well take care of this creature."

"Are you sure about this?" he asked me with a concerned look on his face.

"Yeah I am sure. I feel like this is my battle with this creature." I told him.

Then he did not say anything but just gave me that look like he was saying good luck and I will see you when you get done. I went outside the room and started walking towards the nearest staircase. I looked back and saw James turn the corner of the closest hallway exit.

CHAPTER TWELVE

I STARTED WALKING UP THE STAIRCASE AND THEN WAS wondering how could I lore it out. Then I realized that it must like a lot of noise. So I got up to the top of the staircase, I saw Jimmy down the hallway.

I yelled at him, "Hey, get the hell out of here."

He looked up at me and then the creature dropped through one of the ceiling titles. The creature whipped its tail and sliced Jimmy in half. The two pieces split and fell to the floor.

To describe this creature brings back the horrible memories that I try to erase everyday. It wasn't the creature that you see on television. It stood about 7 feet. Its scales sticking straight up from its body that looked razor sharp, each scale was about four inches long and about half an inch from one another.

Its head had a human-like quality to it. Its eyes where a very deep ocean blue and it had a big grin full of sharp teeth stained red from the blood of students and teachers it was eating. Its head was shape with a wide top and slop downward to its mouth.

Just as quick as it dropped out of the ceiling, it ate both halves of Jimmy. I looked at the walls which were dripping with blood. I turned back at the creature and saw that it was looking back at me with his eyes glowing red now.

I yelled at creature, “That is enough. I am sick of this shit and I sick of you. Time’s up.”

The creature just shrieked at me. I knew I was ready for what might come. I reached into my pockets and pulled out the small knives. The creature came slithering towards me. I threw each knife at the creature and they just bounced off its body. One of them got stuck in the locker on the side, another just fell to the floor and another went breaking through the glass on one of the doors to a classroom.

Before I knew it the creature was just hovering above me. I looked up and two giant drops of slime dropped onto my face. Then I thought that since the knives did not work on the outside maybe I could cut him up from the inside but how to get in there without getting rip to shreds.

I did not notice his tail and it slammed me into the lockers. I felt his scales start to cut into me. He unpinned me and I went falling to the floor. I stood up and noticed that he made a nice gash on my ribcage. I knew what I need to do. Just as I slowly got back to where the creature was waiting for me, I just started using the two bigger knives on it body. It did not like that.

It turned around and just opened it mouth wide. I felt its warm breath run down my body, then the teeth started to engulf me and I jumped down its throat. James had just come up the staircase and saw the creature swallow me whole.

James did not like that sight and made some really loud noises. The creature turned around and saw James. It started to shimmer towards James. Faster and faster it was moving towards him.

It just stopped dead in its tracks and then it just started getting cuts on its skin. Then a knife cut straight through where its stomach would be. The creature started to fall over on its side. Just as the creature hit the floor the weirdest thing happened. It started to dissolve.

After a few moments, James noticed that there was a lifeless body in the middle of the puddle of creature guts. It left a nice puddle of green sludge on the floor.

The lifeless body was cover in the green sludge. James ran over to the lifeless body and realized it was me. He started to shake me once he reached my body. He slapped me a couple of times and was just about to leave me for dead when I started coughing up the green sludge that was inside of my lungs.

Lying there coughing out the stuff, James gave me a big hug. Then he let go and let me fall back down to the ground again.

I asked him, "What happened? All I remember that the creature ate me and then waking up to you in my face."

James told me what happened from his point of view and then I slowly remember something. I remember that while I was inside the creature it had human like qualities. I told this to James and he had a shocked look on his face.

We both heard sirens pulling up into the parking lot. "Hey, can we get out of here. I really do not want to deal with the police right now," I said to James as we went down the staircase.

As we walked out the back entrance, the police came in through the front. I was leaning on James since my stomach still hurt a little from the cut that I got. We where going back to my house since I lived about six minutes away.

"Why did you not want to face them, you're a hero?" James said to me while walking.

"I can't face them, I killed a classmate not a beast," I replied.

James replied to me, "You did kill a beast that was rampaging through the school and killing everything in its path. Plus if you did not kill it, I would have been on the list of dead people."

I said back to him, "No, it was human because I remember the inside of the creature had a heart beating and organs just like me and you. So I killed a fellow classmate."

James stopped in his tracks and grabbed me. He looked in my eyes and told me, "You're still a hero and thousands of people would want to thank you for what you did."

I did not answer but just thought to myself why did it have human organs yet the outside looked so different from me. That went though my head the entire time we were walking home.

The only thing I was happy about was the fact that it was Friday. At least I would not have to go back to school even through it would not be opened up for a while after what happened. I was ready to rest all weekend.

We got to my door and then I knew I did not want to face my parents. So I turned around and told James, "You should go home. I am sure word of this has gotten to your parents as well as mine. Go tell them you're alright and I will do the same. I will talk you later."

James said, "Ok, I will go and I will speak to you later."

He left the little patio area that we have in front of the house and inserted my key into the front door. Lucky for me nobody was home yet. I was so beat I just went down the hallway into my bedroom and fell down onto my bed. As soon as my head hit the pillow, I was passed out. That night I had the strangest dream, which kept me up most of the night.

The dream started out with me waking up and getting dressed. I walked outside of my house to get the newspaper and all my friends and family were out there. Thousands of flashes went off as I walked down the driveway. Then all these TV's appeared and were showing the incident. It showed how it happened down to the very last detail. I fell thinking I would land on the ground but it changed in this green bowl filled with red spots all over the place. The teachers and students that died were reaching out to grab for something, maybe me. I started to run away, but my feet were planted to the ground. I stopped trying to run and as I did I turned into a tree and back to a human. I tried saying something, but no words came out. Then these giant red eyes were following me every where I went.

I woke up with a thud and was covered in sweat. I looked over at the clock and it was just past midnight but I knew I was not going to get back to sleep tonight after that dream.

That is when I decided to go for a walk. I got dress and bundled up for the cold night air. I opened the door and I started towards the front yard. Just as I was walking down the street, a cop car and some news reporters pulled up.

I stop dead in my tracks and waited to see what was going too happened. The cops were the first to approach me.

"Son, are you Sam?" they asked me.

"Yeah, that's me," I said a little shyly.

"We just have a few questions for you about what happened at your school today. We got some word that you were the one that took down some creature that was tearing up the school," they said to me.

I looked around and saw my parents and some of the neighbors starting to come out of their houses. "Well I guess you want the whole story so why not come inside."

The news reporters and the cops both came into the house and we all sat down in the living room. I retold them the story from what I knew and after that everyone went home. I fell asleep after I was done.

CHAPTER THIRTEEN

I WOKE UP THE NEXT MORNING AND WAS GETTING READY to go to work. I had a few moments before I needed to leave for work. So I decided to watch some TV. I turned on the TV to watch some shows, but the news was on. I listened to it as I was getting ready. It was talking about how gas prices were slowly going down. Then it had the story about the school. It was done very well, I thought to myself.

I got lost in the story about this and lost track of time. So I turned off my T.V. and left the house. I walked up to my Black Ford Ranger and took off.

I got to work and knew something was up. My coworkers treated me like a king. Even strangers and management were treating me that way.

I asked, "What's going on?"

My friend Chris said, "We all saw this morning's news. You saved everyone at the school from that creature."

I had a blank look on my face. I thought, "Wow. I'm a hero to this little city." The rest of the morning, nobody got in my face or anything. I could have done whatever I wanted and they wouldn't have said a word. I didn't change but the still gave me my space.

I took my break with Chris. I drove us to McDonald's for lunch. As we walked to the front door, something caught my eye, the newspaper. The headlines said "Local Boy Becomes National Hero."

"Hey, Chris, do you have any change I can borrow to buy a newspaper?" I asked him.

He passed me some change, and I bought one. We got our lunches and sat down. I started to read the article but time was running out for our lunch. So, Chris and I went back to work. When we got back to work, I finished the article. It told mostly about what details I gave them last night and from what they saw at the school. They got most then facts but I did leave out the part about the creature having human insides.

As time pasted, two o'clock rolled around and I clocked out. Driving back to my house, I decided to go to James's house. I really did not feel like going home. I took some of the back streets to get there.

I parked my car and walked up to his front door. I knocked on the door and he answered it.

James answered, "What you doing here? I thought you were going to call me."

"Well I just thought I drop by and hang out with my friend. Plus I did not want to go home just yet. Is it cool if I chill with you for a bit?" I asked him and gave him my best puppy dog eyes.

He just shook his head and let me in. I walked over to his phone and thought I give my parents a call to let them know what's up.

The phone rang twice before my dad picked it up. "Hello," he said.

"Hey dad, it's me Sam. Just letting you know that I am hanging out with James. Oh yeah do you think it would be ok if I spent the night here as well?" I asked him.

"Sure, that sounds fine to me," he answered and then hung up the phone.

James overhearing the call walked in and asked, "So you spending the night huh?"

"Yeah if that is ok with you, I just don't want my parents asking a million questions about what happened yesterday." I said to him.

"Sure you can spend the night I just have to clear it with my parents. What're you going to wear since you do not have a change of clothes," he said to me while picking up the phone.

He started dialing before I could answer him. He walked into another room and then came back a few moments later. "Yeah it is cool with my parents if you spend the night and as for your clothes you can borrow some of mine if you wanted to."

"Thanks," I told him then sat down on his bed. He put the phone back on the charger and then sat down next to me.

"You still think about yesterday and the fact that the creature had human guts and not creature guts, aren't you?" he said while looking at the ground.

"Yeah, I just can not get it out of my mind," I told him then his phone rang.

"Hello," he answered the phone.

It was his girlfriend. "Yeah that sounds like fun, do you mind if Sam tags along with us?" he paused. "Great we will be over there in a few minutes."

He hung up the phone and then hit me on the side of the leg. "Hey come on, we are going to hang out with my girlfriend and get your mind off of what happened yesterday," he said to me extending his hand to get me off his bed. I took his hand and we were on our way.

CHAPTER FOURTEEN

WE GOT OUTSIDE AND HOPPED INTO HIS EAGLE TALON. IT was nice car. It was silver with black interior. As we were backing out of the drive way I saw a couple of cars behind us. I did not think too much about them till we turn from Benton to Lawrence Expressway and they start to follow us.

"Hey, James I think we are being followed," I told James and then he looked up into his rear view mirror. He just nodded and then stepped on the gas. We lost most of them as we made some yellow lights but still had some following us on onto freeway. James started weaving in and out of traffic.

I turned around to see if there was anyone still following us. I did not see anyone behind us but just when we were about to get on to 87 which had a two-way on ramp one going south and one going north, one was still with us. I told James about the one that was still following us.

James thought fast and put his left blinker on. At the last moment served to the right which was the way we need to go. The car behind us went left because he was not quick enough to make the turn.

I looked back one more time to make sure nobody was following us and it seemed like the coast was clear. I sat back down in my seat just as we got to our off ramp. About another couple of minutes on the road and we pulled up to James's girlfriends house.

We pulled up into her driver way and got out of the car. As we were walking up, I noticed there was a note on the door. James went running up to the door and rip the note off. He read the note: *We have kidnapped your girlfriend, James. We will give her back if you bring Sam to the top of the Pinnacles.*

We just stared at each other for a spilt second and I noticed that James had burning rage in his eyes. "We must go save her; we just got to save her," he said to me with his fist clenched shut.

I put my hand on his shoulder and just told him, "Ok let's go get her."

He looked up at me and he did not need to say anything. I knew that he was grateful and then we both walked back to his car. We hopped in and got ready for the long trip ahead of us.

Pretty much I just sat there in dead silence staring out the car window. Finally near the end our driving, I broke the silence, "If I go, you will never see or hear from me again," I paused. "Just kidding," as James punched me in the arm and that is when I really start to doubt myself so I just hugged my knees with my head in between them.

James shook me but I didn't answer. He tried again and I looked over at him. I knew that he would do anything for her. I guess that is all that matters when you're in love with someone. I knew he loved her with all his heart and would go to the ends of the earth just to save her. Then I made my decision and spoke to him. "I will do it; I want you to come to the top of the mountains with me so you can take her home safely."

"Ok. I will never forget this. I owe you big time and give you balls for doing this for me," he told me and we laughed.

Without another word we reached the now closed gated entrance to the mountains. We parked the car on the side of the road and then we start our climb up to the top. On the way up to the top, I started thinking about why people would go to such great lengths just to get their way.

We finally reach the top, I looked down at my watch and it read 11:55. Just as we got to the rest bench in the middle of the area, a quick beam of light hit the peak like a bolt of lighting coming out of the sky. When the blinding light faded away, a man dressed in all black was standing where the light was.

CHAPTER FIFTEEN

He spoke to us, "I see you have made it safe and sound. Now that we finally have a chance to meet face to face, I would like to congratulate that person who destroyed the creature that was destroying our land, lifestyle, friends and family. To show our thanks we will make you one of the five protectors of this realm."

Before we could even speak he just moved his hand in a circular motion and I fell to my hands and knees. Just as James got up to help me, the man and I vanished into thin air. James yelled, "Where's my girlfriend and my friend?" then he fell to his knees and started to cry.

As for me I was in the same spot that I was but wasn't frozen. We both arrived but everything looked different. I saw James crying his eyes out. Then the man spoke, "Follow me and I will tell you everything." I went over to him and he started speaking again. "Welcome to the realm underneath the one you live in. We have been watching you since you were born. Some how when you were born you were special, we got this feeling with you but did not know why until you destroyed that creature. See this is the realm that holds different societies together and you will also notice that there is barley any humans around."

I looked around and did notice that there were more wildlife and nature. I looked down into the valley and noticed that there was less buildings and lights.

"The reason why there are fewer humans is that in this realm they are animals, flowers, trees nature, oceans, etc.... Only a few become humans like your friends, this realm has no limits as well. Anything can go on here, so be carefully what you say or do." he paused and looked around where we were. "Now you will be sent back to your realm but your eyes will see both realms from now on."

Instantly I was back to where I was. James was still crying and I looked down at him. He then realized that I was back. He looked up at me and then got up and hugged me. Then I heard in my head as James was hugging me "You will find his girlfriend close by but only you can save her from the other realm."

Just as the voice faded from my head, my left eye was seeing the other realm and my right eye was seeing James's realm.

Just then James let me go and asked all worried, "So where is my girlfriend? Why has she not come back yet?"

I answered while looking around, "She is here somewhere. I must find her and bring her back for you. Come with me." I start walking away from the spot that we were at. I saw footprints in the other realm and nothing in this realm. I followed the footsteps and ran right into a tree.

"Ouch," I said while rubbing my forehead.

James asked me, "What happened?"

"I found her," was all I said. Then I used my left eye to see the tree and I jump on to it. I climb up the tree and she was hanging over one of the branches like a lifeless doll.

James on the other hand just saw me grabbing on to thin air. It looked like I was hugging the air and climbing up onto nothing. His mouth just dropped wide open.

I reached her and then put her over my shoulder. I remembered what the man in black said to me. "Anything can happen in this realm." So I imaged that there was a pool underneath me and I jumped. We both landed in the pool and I swam both of us to the side of the pool.

Just as I climb out of the pool, the voice came back. It said, "To bring here back all you have to do is wake her up and so you do not have double vision you must concentrate on the realm you would like to see."

So I started to think of how to wake her up. They only thing I could remember was fairy tales when the prince would kiss the princess and then the princess would wake up. So I called James over to where we were.

"So I want you to kiss right here and to believe in the power of love," I said to him and point to the ground.

He slowly dropped to his knees and I knew he felt strange that I was having him kiss thin air but it was the only thing I could think of at the time. He bent over and he kissed the air near the ground and she started to reappear back in this realm.

Once he saw that she was reappearing, he put more passion into his kiss. After about a minute of kissing she was fully back in this realm and she slowly opened he ocean blue eyes. I looked into her eyes and it felt like I was able to see the whole world through her eyes.

I took a step back and said under my breath, "So love is as strong as friendship. I wonder how powerful it can really get."

After she regained full conciseness, we started to head back down the hill. James asked me as we walked back down the hill, "How did you know where she was at?"

"I'll tell you later on. Can I drive back and borrow your car when we get back? I have some things I need to figure out and plus I figured that you would want to make sure she is alright." James just shook his head and then reached into his pocket. He pulled out his keys and handed them to me.

About an hour later we finally reach the bottom of the mountain and hopped in the car. The ride home was very quiet since James and his girlfriend were both passed out. It was cute that James and his girlfriend fell asleep in each others arms.

As I was driving, I started to think to myself about everything that just happened. Then a thought popped into my head, I start wondering if you are really dead in this realm but not in the other realm would someone like me be able to save you. It made me think that I might be able to help others by saving them in the other realm to save them in this realm.

We got back to her house around three in the morning and I slowly shook both of them awake. We all got out of the car and then James asked me, "So where you going?"

"I really do not know. I would not worry about me to much you guys should get some sleep, I should be back a little bit later to pick you up. Oh and thanks for letting me use your car." I said to him.

"No problem, that's what friends are for," he said to me then turned and walked over to his girlfriend who was waiting for him by the door. They entered the house and I took off.

CHAPTER SIXTEEN

I WENT DOWN THE STREET TO THE LITTLE PARK THAT WAS there. I got out of the car and I wanted to try out my powers. The first thing I want to see if I was able to switch views from one realm to the other. I concentrated on the other realm. It was really hard to switch views but after a few moments I was able to see the other realm with both eyes.

It really surprised me to see how different this realm was compare to the other one. Everything in this realm was such smaller which made the nature of this realm stand out. The best way to describe how this other realm looks is to think of Lake Tahoe from an aerial view. You have some buildings sticking out from forest covering but nature covering the rest.

I looked down at my watch and noticed the time. I looked over in the distance and saw the sun was rising over the horizon. I concentrated and went back to look at the old realm. Then I hopped into the car and drove back to his girlfriend's house. I got back to the house and it seem like they were waiting up for me. They opened the door for me and I quickly went in.

About half an hour after I got back, James came up to me and said, "Hey I think it is time for us to go. Let me go kiss her goodnight."

He left me sitting in the living room and then came back after a couple of minutes. He nodded towards me and we both headed out the door. As we were walking to his car he asked me again, "So how did you know where she was?"

I answered him this time, "Well I can see this world in different ways then you see it. It is more nature like and has fewer buildings. It seems a lot smaller then this one. There are not a lot of people either, just that people from here become plants and animals and other nature stuff."

I looked over at him and he just gave me a strange look like yeah right. Then he just spoke to me, "Let's just go home."

We hopped into his car and drove back to his place. When we got back to his place and pulled up the driveway the sun has just finished rising over the horizon. We got out of his car and I bid him farewell and as I was leaving he yell to me, "Thought you were going to spend the night?"

"I did. See it is already the next morning. Plus I want to see what this other realm is really about. You can come if you want," I said back at him with a smile on my face.

"Nah, I think I am going to bed. Hey call me when you get to wherever you're going," he said and then went inside.

"I will," I yelled back and then head to my car. I hopped in and then drove around town thinking of who would be up at this time. It hit me that my friend Tony might be up at this hour. I drove over to his house which was not to far from James's house. I parked the car then walked up to his door.

I knocked on the door and he opened it. When he opened the door, I was looking into both worlds. It was an odd site to see both at the same time. In my left eye I saw Tony as a baby bear and in my right eye as a human.

I made a guess that your how you act and feel in one realm determines what you are in another. The reason that tony was a bear in the other realm was that he had a caring side to him yet also was strong when need to be.

"Hey what you doing here?" he asked me curiously.

"I was driving around and could not sleep so I thought I pop in and see what you were up to?" I replied.

"Come in, we can hang out here if you want," he said and then move so I could enter his house. He shut the door behind me. "So I heard the news that you saved the school from that creature thing."

"I guess," I said in a low voice. "I just want to get it behind me and more forward."

"Ok. Do you want to play video games?" he asked me trying to change the subject.

"Sure, that sounds like fun," I said.

We went into his bedroom and he turned the TV on and popped in one of his newest football games that he just got. We played for a little while when he started to get tired. Before he went to bed he told me, "I could hang out here while he slept."

"Thanks, do you mind if I crash on your couch?" I asked him as I turned off the TV.

"Nah, go ahead. Blankets on in the closet in the hallway," he said then he covered himself up with his own blanket.

I shut the door behind me then went to the hallway closet and grabbed a blanket. Then from there I headed towards the couch in the living room. As I lay down, I was out like a light.

I woke up a couple of hours later and checked if he was up. He was still asleep so I decided to leave his house. As I was leaving, Tony's house I thought that I should go home and change. I hopped into my car and drove home.

Five minutes later, I got home and headed inside. My parents were still asleep and I head straight to my room. I grabbed some clothes and changed out of my work clothes that I was still in. It felt nice to be in some fresh clothes. I changed into a pair of cargo shorts and green day shirt.

I still felt restless and I decide to go for a walk. I walked around for a little bit and was enjoying the fresh air and sunshine on my skin and face. I was walking for a little while and my feet took me to my friends Anthony's house.

I got to his front door and knock. He answered the door and looked at me like I was crazy to be at his house this early in the morning. He did not say anything he just let me in and we both walked into his house.

He finally spoke, "What the hell you doing here so early?"

"Could not sleep; want to go shoot some hoops in the park?" I asked him.

"Sure sounds like fun," he said then he started to get dressed. As soon as he got ready we were out his front door. We walked down to the park near his house.

We got to the local park where it had two basketball courts and picnic tables off to the left of the courts and a small grassy area behind them. Anthony brought his basketball and we started to play some on-on-one. He beat me but I was not the greatest at basketball and he played all his life.

We stopped after the second game that we played to take a break in the grassy area. Then he asked me, "So I read yesterday in the paper that you're somewhat of a hero. Is it true that you saved the school from that beast?"

"Yeah, it's true. I did save the school from the beast but there were so many people who died before I killed it. I just wish I could go back to the way things were," I said to him

He put his arm around my shoulder and spoke, "Don't think about it that way. You saved a lot more people and that is how you should think about it."

"Thanks man, I never thought about it that way," I said to him as I was getting up to head back to his place. We said our goodbyes and then I went back home. When I got home, I was feeling a little tried so I went to my room and crashed out.

CHAPTER SEVENTEEN

WEEKS PASTED AND EVERYTHING DID GO BACK TO normal. The school re-opened and looked just like it did before the creature attacked. Then it started to happen, everyone started to treat me a little different. They treated me like I was on some kind of pedestal.

First period was English and the teacher asked us to write about how we felt and thought about what happened the other day. I finished in a flash and started talking to my friends until the bell rang.

I went off to the locker rooms to get ready for P.E. While I was changing all the guys were thanking me for a job well done. I got out of the locker rooms and the teacher wouldn't let me do anything. He was worried that the creature might come back, so he just told me to take it easy.

I was glad that my next class was marketing. We studied ads, but my teacher found a way to incorporate my heroism. I started to get tried of getting the attention of the entire school. I wished everything would just go back to normal, but I knew it wouldn't.

Well next was my cooking class and that flew by quickly because the café was open, and nobody had a chance to thank me. The bell rang like normal, but some of us stayed behind to finish cleaning up. I had to run to my U.S. history class.

I knew the teacher would switch topics to current events for just a little bit because of what happen. I just stared out the window, and spaced out through the entire class.

All day was about me, and I didn't want it to be. To tell you the truth, I hated the attention that every one was giving me. I came back from my day dreaming just as the bell rang. As I was walking to my locker I noticed that in a couple weeks that it was the junior/senior prom.

People started asking me if I was going and I started getting that strange feeling again that something was up. Even the principal came up to me and asked if I was going. I knew he want me there just incase a creature would attack. I did not answer him.

A lot of people asked me to be there dates but I really did not want to go with anyone. A week past and my friend Jennie asked me to go with her just as friends. I finally broke down and said yes. She was all excited and she went running off to tell everyone.

After that day, I walked home and still hoped that things would finally return to normal. When I got home, I open the door to my house and my parents shower me with gifts. They seem to come from all the parents and students that I saved that day. I just left them there without even opening a single one.

I went to the bathroom and stripped off all my clothes, hopped into the shower. Quickly dried off and got dressed. Some how my parents found out that I was going to the prom without me even telling them.

As soon as I got dress they grabbed me and off to the tux place we went. We got there and they measured me from head to toe. It was a nice tux's. It was pure black on the outside and a silver vest on the inside. We paid for the tux and then went back home. I was ready for prom to come.

The next couple of days flew by pretty fast. Everything was still about my heroism but I just rolled it all off my shoulders. Then a day before prom everything seemed finally went back to normal. I was so thankful that everything went back to the way it was.

Then it was prom night. During the day everyone was gossiping about how it was going to be one of the best nights of their lives. Around six o'clock I got ready in my tux and then head over to Jennie's house.

I pulled up to her driveway and got out of my mom's car that I borrowed for the night. I knock on her door and her dad answered it.

"Hello, sir is Jennie ready?" I asked him trying not to be too intimidated.

"She is almost done, please come in," he said.

I waited for her in the living room of house. As I was looking all over the room to see what was up she entered the living room. My mouth dropped at the site of her. She was wearing a white long dress that had a small train on it.

"Do you like it?" she said while twirling around.

"Yeah it looks great. I take it your ready to go," I said to her while I stood up and headed for the doorway. Her dad stopped us and took a couple of pictures before we hopped into my car.

We meet up with some friends for school and had dinner at this very fancy Italian restaurant. The dinner was nice and the place had singing waiters, which just add to the atmosphere that was created to make us feel like we were in Italy.

We got the check and spilt it evenly but I paid for my date. We all said goodbye and we will see you at the hotel.

The hotel was just down the street so the drive there was really short.

As we pulled up into the parking lot we saw a whole bunch of other kids dressed up and walking into the ballroom. We parked and got out of the car.

As we walked towards the hall I had that weird feeling again. I just rubbed it off my shoulders because I just wanted to have a good time.

"Nothing happen," was the words I wish I could say here but shit did happen. Everything was going quite well. We walked up to the entrance of the place, handed the adults our tickets and waited in line to get our picture taken. That took about ten minutes and the pictures turned out great.

I open the door for Jennie and we both held our breaths when we saw the ballroom. They had tables all covered in white, the long banquet table off to the right with food and desserts from end to end. The DJ booth was in the back of the room and right in front of it was a little wooden dance floor.

"Would you like to dance?" I said bowing slightly and extending my hand.

"Why I would love to," she said and took my hand.

We danced to a couple of slow songs and then the DJ changed the beat to some faster songs. We went into a circle of friends and classmates and started dance like it was club.

After about an hour of dancing and goofing off with my friends, I still had that feeling. I walked off the dance floor and went to get some punch. Jennie followed me and then just as I was pouring our drinks and blue dragon dropped through the ceiling of the place and landed on the dance floor with a loud crunch.

My first thoughts were to get everyone out safely but everyone went into a panic. So I just grabbed Jennie and dragged her out of the room. I ran back and just started grabbing people off the floor. The screaming and roar of the dragon were ringing in my ears.

The dragon was feeding off the bodies it crushed when it crashed through the floor. I ran in one more time and most of the people finally got the idea to run for the doors instead of running around like a chicken with its head cut off.

Then I stopped and stared at the dragon. Then I had the thought that James was there. Then right behind me I heard a voice say, "I am."

I turned around and there was James. Just as I turned around James had that look on his face like watch out. I did not see it coming but soon I had the dragon's tail sideswipe me and knocked me across the room. I landed on a table as it broke my fall.

I got up, little dazed from the hit. I picked up one of the wooden legs from the table that I just landed on and started to use it as a Bo staff. While fighting the dragon, I hit the skin of the dragon and my table leg snapped in two. I looked at the two broken pieces that now had some sharp ends to them.

Then I thought since I was not able to whack it, I might as well stab it with these wooden shards. I jab one in the tail and that got the dragons attention. It turned and looked at me with the most clear green emerald eyes. Then it just whacked me with the tail again. I went flying but this time it gave me a better aim and I threw the other wooden shard like a throwing knife.

The shard made a loud whistling sound as it went flying through the air. It hit the dragon's chest where its heart would be. The dragon shrieked as I hit the wall of the ballroom. I fell to the ground and the dragon then shot a fireball at me.

I just dodge the fireball and roll out into the hallway. James was standing there. I looked up at him and said, "Guess it was not long enough."

I was laid out on the floor and saw that James had gone to one of the rooms of the hotel and was holding a sword. I figured each room of the hotel was theme differently. James saw that the dragon was coming to attack again.

He just hurled the sword like spear. This time he hit the wooden shard that was sticking out of the dragon and it spilt into piece and went further into the dragon. The dragon gave out one more shriek and then fell to the floor. The ground shook when it hit the ground.

I got up and said, "Thanks."

"Well now we are even," he said with a smile.

Just as we started walking out we had the cops and news vans swarm the entire hotel. The news crews saw that James and I we walking out of the entranceway. They rushed over to us and started asking us a million different questions but just then a cop noticed that I was limping and rushed over to us.

The cop said, "We need to get this kid to the ambulance."

"I am fine really," I told the cop but then the cop just rushed me and was taking me to where they were making a make shift-examining room. The medics checked me out and bandage me up.

James took care of the reports since this time he was the hero and not me. I got the ok from the medics that I was able to go and then I went looking for Jennie.

I was not able to find her, so I looked one more time. Then I saw one of the friends I left her with when I went to fight the creature. I walked over to there and asked, "Hey Kerrie, do you know where Jennie is?"

"Yeah, she left as soon as she found out that you're all right," she told me.

"Thanks. Are you alright?" I asked her.

"Yeah, I been through worse and you know that," she said to me with a smile on her face. She lightly tapped me on the arm and then walked off to head home herself.

That is when I decide I should head home myself. I am sure my parents are worrying about me. As I was driving home, I started thinking about how long these battles would keep coming. Will I always be there to fight them? Just some many questions that keep running through my head, I did not even know if I wanted them answers.

It seem that the ride home took forever even through it was only about ten minutes. The only questions that really came up more then once was why did they pick me to be the protector of this world's realms?

I got home and changed out of my tux. My parents were asleep so I dodge that bullet. I tried to fall asleep but could not. Since I was not able to sleep, I started calling my friends. Just as I start dialing the first number the man in black popped into my room.

He spoke, "You now know what you will be getting into if you decide to become the protector. I will be coming back in about a week or so to get your final decision. There will be one year of training for this responsibility if you do decide to become one."

Just as quick as he came in, he left just as fast. I was left there sitting to think about if I really want to become the protector. That night I did not sleep a wink but I did make up my mind on what I wanted to do.

Sunday blew by with my parents asking a million questions and just sleeping the day away. Monday at school was that start of finals week and the time I need to tell the man in black my answer.

One night I was up studying for my final when he entered my room. He asked, "Well did you make your decision? You know what you will be getting into if you decided to continue with you destiny."

I answered, "Yes, I will become the protector of this world's realms."

"Great, you will not regret that decision. At the end of this week have everything packed and ready to go. Also say goodbye to this world. I will be back on Saturday to pick you up." Then he vanished again.

I thought to myself, that I needed to learn how he did that. The next day came around and I told my friends some bullshit lie about winning a trip to see the world for one entire year.

That night I went to work and put my resonation and said farewell to them as well. Soon Friday was upon me and I waited to tell my parents about that fake trip I won. I told them and they fought it but then they finally accepted it.

I shed some tears since my mom started crying as well. After that goodbye I just went into my room and waited for Saturday to come. I fell asleep and then around five in the morning there was flash of light that woke me up.

"You ready?" he asked.

"Yeah, so where are we going?" I asked him.

"Some place where humans will never reach," he said. Then he grabbed my hand and led me out the door. "Hold on."

Then we took off.

CHAPTER EIGHTEEN

SOMEDAY PEOPLE WILL SEE WHAT LIFE IS WORTH AND still do nothing about it. What you know in life might just be a bunch of bullshit or it can be the real truth. No matter how hard one person looks at a simple line, you could not tell it has a great story behind it. You might walk that thin line of love or the thin line of hate, but the journey that you walk upon will make that line's life so interesting.

"Beep, Beep, Beep," sounded the alarm clock. The sun slowly peeking through the cracks in my blinds as I hear the chirping of birds with their lovely songs they sing. My hand swung over and slammed onto the alarm clock. Turning it off with a thud and kicking the blanket of my body. Laying there in my white boxers thinking to myself why do I have to go to school today? It is such beautiful day outside and I will be stuck inside a hot and sweaty classroom all day.

I got up and walk across the room to hop in the shower. As I walked past my mirror, I notice that I was getting a little buffer. I am five feet eight, with wavy black hair, and emerald eyes that shine when the sunlight hits them.

I laughed at myself because I never flex in the mirror and it just looks funny. I made it to the shower and while I was showering I heard the door shut and a car start up. I knew it was mom leaving for work since she is always leaving before me.

I got out of the shower, grabbed some plaid boxers shorts, khakis shorts, and some shirt. I hopped down stairs to see a note written on the white board in the hallway. It read: *Here is some money for dinner and for you to go hang out with your friend Ethan.* I took the money off the board and picked up the phone. I decided to call Ethan and see what is going on tonight.

"Hello, is Ethan there?" I asked.

"Yeah it is me," he said in a low voice.

"What are you doing tonight? I am thinking about throwing a bonfire on the beach and wondering if you can get a permit from your boss."

He said back to me, "I got work from three to eight and then I am off but sure I can see if I can get a permit so you can have a bonfire on the beach tonight."

"Cool. Do you need a lift to school, man?" I asked as I was grabbing the keys for my car.

"That would be great. When you coming over?" he replied.

"In about ten minutes so I'll see ya then," I said and hung up the phone. I grabbed some breakfast as I was running out the door.

I hopped into my Black Jeep Wrangler and back out of the driveway. I started driving over to his house. I live in Santa Cruz, California so pretty much everyday was nice and sunny. I still wish I did not have to go to school today.

I turn the corner and saw him standing outside waiting for me. I pull into his driveway and he came running towards the car. He threw his stuff into the back seat and hoped into the passenger side of the car.

I said while looking up at the sky, "Hey, I wish we didn't have to go to school. It is such a beautiful day out."

"Yeah I know but school is almost out and then we will have all summer to party," he told me with some excitement in his voice.

I backed out of his driveway and started driving to our school. I notice Ethan was in a daze like state, so I just turned the radio up to kill the silence but all I could find was people talking about their problems or news.

We went for a while and then Ethan spoke up, "Hey did you see that girl? She was so hot and cute. She had black long hair and legs to die for."

"Why didn't you tell me to slow down? I would like to see the ass that you wanted," I said while hitting him in the arm and laughing a little.

As we pulled into the student parking lot I asked Ethan, "Hey, keep an eye out for a parking spot that is somewhat close to the school.

"Ok. There is one right next that blue truck," he pointed out. I parked the car and grabbed my stuff from the back seat, as did Ethan. We got out and then we heard the bell ring. "Shit, that was the bell for class to start first period and we're going to be late."

"Yeah, but it is easy for me to sneak in to my first period. Besides I do nothing in my first period anyway," I told him with big fat grin on my face.

We were walking towards the doors and I heard Ethan's drop his books. I turned around to see the site, and then yelled back to him, "See ya next period."

As I walked down the hallway to my classroom, I see students running through the hallway to get to their classes and lockers. To bad I did not miss a thing because my first period is to T/A for Mr. Katz.

I got to my room about two minutes after the tardy bell rang and started taking roll call for him. Then the teacher gave me some papers to grade. I got done with all the tasks that were given to me by the teacher.

That is when I notice that it was only half way though the period, so I just started to mess around on the teacher's computer. I hit up some my emails and video game updates while surfing the web. After doing that, the rest of the period flew by and the bell rang for the next class.

I went off to my locker to grab my history book and a pack of playing cards because I knew that I had a sub that day and we were just going to be watching a movie. So I thought since Ethan and I are in that class together we could play some games to pass the time. I closed my locker and headed to class.

The bell rang as I just stepped through the door. I was waiting for Ethan, so we could start playing cards. Then finally he walked in and I waved him down to get his sorry ass over here. He took the sit next to me and I busted out the cards, just as the movie started.

"Hey, you know what?" he said excited.

"No what?" I responded.

"I saw that girl again. The one walking down the street, she was going in the main office building as I was running to my class this morning. So what is the name of the game?" he said as he noticed me still shuffling the cards in front of him.

"The name of the game is poker. You should ask her out the next time you see her." I said with a big fat grin on my face.

The movie was playing and I passed the deck to Ethan so he could deal the cards. We played for few rounds and Ethan lost every hand we played. After a few hands of losing, he got up and walked out of the classroom to go use the restroom. He left me all alone, so I had nothing to do but sit and watch the movie. I was starting to fall asleep when the lights turned on. The movie was over and I saw Ethan walk back into the room.

He came back in and sat down in his seat with a big fat grin on his face. I asked him," What is with the ear to ear grin?"

"Remember that girl I was telling you about, well she gave me her number and wants me to call her after school. I helped her find her class and told her I might show her around town sometime," he told me still with the grin on his face.

"Sweet, I wish I could go to the bathroom and meet a girl," I said with a laugh. Just then the bell rang and Ethan and I started walking to our next class.

Our next class was Gym. We entered the lockers and started to change.

Ethan started to change when I asked, "So you going to let her play with your tool tonight?"

"No, I leave that up to you," he replied and grabbed his crotch. We both laughed and finished changing. After we both finished changing, we went into the main gym.

After the teacher took roll call he told us that we were playing some basketball and it was going to be my team vs. Ethan's team. It was a very close game. By the time the class was over both of us were out of breath.

I looked over and noticed the coach was watching the game very closely. It seemed he was look at who was really good so he could recruit people for next year's basketball team.

I took one more shot and then the coach blew the whistle and we had to end the game in a tie. We put the balls on the rack and started heading into the locker room. As we were walking in everyone could not stop talking about the game that was just played. We got to our lockers and started to change back into our normal clothes.

"That was a great game," Ethan said while taking off his shirt.

"Yeah it was. I wish it went a little longer. I would have totally made that point in the end," I said while I let my pants dropped to the floor. I grabbed my towel to wipe of the sweat that was still on my face.

Some of the others guys were joking around when I snapped a towel at Ethan's back. I got Ethan to laugh a little because I missed him. We finished getting dressed and went over to the coke machines.

"Hey, Ethan can I borrow a buck so I can get a soda?" I begged him.

"Sure, no problem," he said as he reach into his pocket and pulled out his wallet and give me a buck. He handed it to me and I went to the machine. I got a mountain dew and then went outside as the bell rang for next period. "See ya at lunch," he shouted as we both went towards our next class.

"Yeah see ya at lunch," I yelled back.

The next couple of periods flew by and then the bell rang for lunch and I went to the normal spot underneath the big oak tree in the center of the quad where we all normal meet up for lunch. As I got closer to the tree I yelled, "Hey guys, what's up?"

"Nothing really, why do you ask?" they yelled back.

"Just wondering what you guys were doing tonight? I was going to throw a bonfire tonight and was going to invite everyone. It starts around seven and you can leave whenever you want to. Hope to see you guys there." I said and walked off. I really did not have time to stop and talk too much because then I saw Ethan. He was sitting with his normal crowd over by the water fountain off to the right of the oak tree and I walked towards him.

"Hey guys, so did Ethan ask you who is coming to the bonfire tonight?" I said while sitting down next to Ethan.

"We will be going," they all said at the same time.

"Hey Josh, want to go get some food before lunch period ends?" he asked.

"Sure, let's go get some food. I'm starving." I said. We got up and head to the line. I took us about five minutes of waiting in line before we got to the front. I got a burrito and soda and he got Togo's sandwich and Mountain Dew. Then we just headed back to the spot.

Just as we got back, the bell rang for class. We totally just shoveled the food we got down our throats and then we all said are goodbyes.

I told Ethan, "Hey meet me at the Jeep after school if you need a ride."

He nodded his head and walked off to his next class.

The end of the day flew by. I had computer applications and science as my last two class of the day. Nothing really much to say besides I fell asleep in science class and woke up about five minutes before the bell rang to let us go home. It rang and I rushed out of class to my locker.

As I went to my locker, I saw my girlfriend standing there waiting for me. Her name is Sarah. She has to be the most beautiful girl I have even laid eyes. With her long brown hair that reaches past her shoulders, greens eyes that shine like mine, and the same height to boot.

"Hey cutie," she said followed by a kiss on the lips as I reached my locker.

"Hey so what you doing tonight, I was going to throw a bonfire tonight for who ever wanted to come, so you coming right, babe?" I asked as I opened my locker and searched through it for a book.

"I would not miss it for the world. I know you throw the best bonfires in the county of Santa Cruz," she said.

"Ok, babe I will see you there," I said and we kissed goodbye. I watched her walk away for a spilt second and then I off towards my car when I saw a nice BMW M3 pass by and I thought to myself that I wish I had that car. I saw Ethan waiting for me and he was leaning against my car. I got to my car and unlocked the doors for him. We jumped in and drove off.

CHAPTER NINETEEN

We drove out of the student parking lot and as we were driving down the street I asked Ethan, "So are you going to call her when you get home?"

"Hell yeah I am!" he shouted at me.

"So are you going to call me when you get done with that phone call or just leave me hanging?" I said while we waited at a light.

"Yeah I guess I will," Ethan said with a little down tone in his voice.

"Cool," I replied. So the rest of the trip to his house, we talk about the normal stuff like how the rest of our classes went and joked around. We got to his house and I pulled up his driveway. "So I will talk to you later."

"Yeah and thanks for the ride," he said with a nod and walked to his door. I backed out of his driveway and turned on the radio. Nothing really was good on the radio and then a few minutes later I got to my house and went inside.

Just as I entered my house, the phone rang. I ran to the charger and picked up. "Hello," I answered a little out of breath.

"Hey, is this Josh?" the voice on the other end said.

"Yeah, who is this?" I replied.

"It is me Erik, so I hear that you're throwing a bonfire tonight," he asked me.

"Yeah I am. So I take it you want to come," I said and thought that the word travels fast throughout my school.

"Well, it is not just me that is asking but about half the football team and some of cheerleaders as well. So is it cool for us to come?" he asked.

"Sure. It starts around seven and it ends whenever you want to leave," I told him.

"Cool. Thanks I well tell the others," he said and hung up the phone and so did I. Just as I was putting the phone down it rang again. "Hello," I answered as I picked it up again.

"Hey it's me Ethan," he replied. "So yeah when is the bonfire starting again?"

"It starts around seven till whenever you feel like leaving. Speaking of the bonfire, do you think I can stop by your work to get the permit early?" I asked.

"Sure but I will only be there for about an hour than I have a date with that girl I meet today. By the way her name is Heather so we do not have to call her that girl. I will be going over to her house," Ethan said with some excitement in his voice.

"Will you be coming back after your date? By the way, what did you talk about?" I asked curiously.

"Of course I will be coming back to the bonfire after my date. I would never miss one of your parties. I have good feeling this is going to be one hell of a party," he paused. "So yeah, I called her up and she thanked me for helping her out at school today. Then she asked what I was doing tonight. I told her that I have work then I was going to a bonfire. After that she asked me if I would like to come over after work to her house instead of going to the bonfire. I said sure that would be fine and then I told her I would see her around nine tonight."

"That sounds really awesome. Hey would you need a ride to work and you should totally invite her to the bonfire, if your not to busy," I said to him.

"No thanks, I will walk to work today and I will ask her when I see her tonight. Well I got to go get ready so I will see you when you come by to pick up permit for the bonfire. Later," he said and we both hung up the phone.

Just then my stomach growl as I put the phone back on the charger. I walked into the kitchen and grabbed a pizza from the freezer. I popped it into the oven and was just sitting there waiting for it to finish when I decided to call my girlfriend.

"Hello, is Sarah there?" I asked.

"Hey, Josh what's up?" she answered.

"Nothing much, I was wondering if you would like to go to the Boardwalk with me?" I asked as I heard the oven timer go off. I walked over to the oven and pulled out the pizza as I wait for her answer.

"Sure, when you coming over to pick me up?" she asked as I sliced the pizza up.

"Whenever I finish eating my pizza, then I will be over to your house," I told her.

Then the both of us said, "I love you."

"Ok I will be waiting for you, babe," she said and hung up the phone.

I sat down at the table and finished the pizza. I walked out to my car and started it up. On my way to my girlfriend's house I started to notice the small things in life and just took my time for some odd reason. It seemed a lot clearer today. The sky was a light blue and not a single cloud in the sky. Some of the birds were chirping and it felt like something was in the air.

I reached her house and honked the horn. I got out of the car and leaned against it. She came running out of her house and gave me a big hug and kiss. "How are you doing, honey?" I asked.

"I am doing fine now that you're here," she giggled.

"That is good to hear. So you ready to go to the Boardwalk?" I asked as I started to enter my car.

"Yeah, but can my brother come along with us? Then we can drop him off before the party starts," she asked and giving me her best puppy dog eyes.

"How could I say no to those big sad puppy dog eyes? Sure he can come along with us. It does not seem like a hassle," I said while she gave me a kiss.

She whistled for him to come and hurry up. He came running out the door and we all hopped into the car. "So here is the plan. First we go visit Ethan to get the permit. Then we hang out till about five. Drop off your brother and then go to the store to get the food, drinks, and anything else we need. Sounds like a plan?"

"Yeah sounds good to me but can we pick some of my friends up after we drop my brother off?" she asked shyly.

"Sure, they can help with the shopping and dragging things down to the beach," I said then turned back to Sarah's brother. "So Kyle, how have you been?"

"I have been doing ok. So I got this new video game Metal Gear Solid 2. Have you played it yet?" he said as his eyes lit up hoping that I had.

"No but I heard it was pretty cool," I replied. "You think I could play it with you sometime."

"Sure I am stuck in this one area but maybe you would be able to help me. Since I know you're really good at these types of games," he said.

"Sounds like fun," I said and we were off to the boardwalk.

So we got to the Boardwalk and we all headed towards Ethan's booth that he works at. He works at one the gaming booths down on at the end of the Boardwalk near the shopping stores. As we were walking down there I asked Sarah, "Hey would you like to go on some of the rides or just play around in the arcade?"

"I guess the rides would be fun," she told me and grabbed my hand.

We walk over to his booth. "Hey Ethan," I said as I walked up to him.

"Hey Josh, Sarah and Kyle, what'd you bring the whole gang for?" he said with laugh in his voice.

"I thought we could all hang out before the party. So who did I ask to get the permit for tonight?" I asked him.

"Ok. Let me go ask my manager for you. You guys just wait here and chill," he told us. So he went into the backroom and I heard him talking to his manager, as I picked up the toy rifle and took aim at the back of the booth.

Sarah asked me, "Is he coming to the party?"

I told her, "Yeah, but he is leaving the party early to go on a date with this new girl in town and maybe come back with her later on in the evening."

"Cool," she answered just as he came back from the back of the booth.

"It is all set. I will bring you the permit when I see you at that party tonight. Is that cool?" he asked.

"Yeah, so did you bring a change of clothes for whatever comes up tonight?" I said to him and gave him a sly smile.

"Yeah I did. So I will see you guys a little later. Have fun hanging out," he said to us as we started walking down the pier.

We headed towards the ticket booth and brought some tickets for the rides. We went on the water log ride first to cool down a little since it was pretty hot out here. Sarah and I went on the Big Dipper and Kyle went on the Wipeout. It was about four-thirty when we got off the ride and I told Kyle and Sarah, "That it is time go."

So we headed back to the car and went back to my girlfriend's house. We got back to my girlfriend's house and they both hopped out of me car. She let her brother into the house and she went in to make a few phone calls to tell her friends that we were on the way to pick them up.

She returned with a bounce in her step and smile on her face. She got in the car. "Let's go," she said while buckling up.

"Where to first," I asked while backing out of the driveway. She told me the directions to the houses and we picked up two of her really good friends. As we headed to the grocery store the girls were chatting up a storm. I tuned them out as we arrived at the store. I parked the car and jumped out so I did not have to listen to the mindless chatter anymore.

As we entered the store, I assigned each person to search for one item that was needed so that we would be able to get out of here a lot faster. Still to this day, I have never been so quick in a grocery store. It took us about fifteen minutes to get everything we needed and met back up in line to pay.

We loaded up the Jeep and then jetted over to the beach. We reached the beach about five thirty and we unload and started setting up.

I had Sarah's friends go set up the food area and Sarah and I were getting the fire pit ready. The wood was pile higher then any basketball player can reach. The food would have been gone on for miles without anything doubling if we did not run out of table space. We had every type of soda know to man sitting in the ice buckets at both ends of the table.

We just finished before seven and we started seeing people walking over to us. I noticed the first group was Erik and his friends walking over to us.

"I am going to go get Ethan and I will be right back, sweetheart." I said as I started walking to the steps that lead up to the Boardwalk.

"Ok, I will see you in a little bit," she yelled back to me.

"Oh yeah, tell Erik to start the fire," I yelled back at her.

"Sure, honey," she yelled in a sweet tone.

I walked up the steps and headed towards Ethan's booth. Nobody was in the booth when I got there. Suddenly a hand from behind grabbed my shoulder. I quickly turn around and saw Ethan standing right behind me.

"Hey," I said little out of breath. "What are you doing out here? You're supposed to be working till eight or so I thought."

"Yeah but my boss let me have the rest of the night off. It was slow and he said to go enjoy yourself at the party with your friends," he paused. "So where is the nearest restroom so I can go change?"

"How should I know you're the one that works here? Shouldn't you know the answer to that question," I said with a little laugh. I followed him to the nearest bathroom and told him, "I will be down at the party, so hurry your ass up."

"Yeah, I'll be there as soon as I change into some better clothes," he yelled from inside the restroom. I saw some of our friends walking by and I sent some them to go mess with him while he was changing.

CHAPTER TWENTY

As I reached the steps and the fire was blazing into the dark night sky. Seeing people moving around like a feast of plenty was going on and thanking the person who did this for them. Slowly walking closer, I heard the music for the stereo blasting out tunes like there was no tomorrow.

As I entered where people could make me out, a big roar of clapping came rushing in my direction. Thousands of hands wanting to thank me and congratulate me on the best bonfire of the season, as the sea of hands and smiling faces started to fade one person stood out. I walked over to her and planted a big huge kiss on her lips. She gave me a hug and whispered in my ear, "You're the best boyfriend I will ever have. Thank you. I love you so much."

I whispered back, "I love you too. Thank you for helping me out so much. You my reason for doing these types of things, you're my inspiration."

As we finished the hug, I started walking around to see who came. Erik and his football buddies, most of the cheerleading staff, skaters, emo, geeks and half the school came out. It looked like everyone was enjoying themselves. I made my way back to the food table to grab a bottle of water from the ice bucket. I looked up and saw in the distance that Ethan was walking towards the party. I went out to meet him.

"Did you like your surprise that I left you?" I laughed.

"Yeah, it was really funny. Them scaring the crap out of me and all," he paused to punch me in the arm. "So here is the permit and do not lose it. I am heading out in a while and I will see you before I leave." He handed me the permit and walk off in a different direction. It was about eight when one of my friends wanted to make a toast.

Then I saw Ethan stand up on the table and started to speak, "To my friend Josh, without you, this party would have never happened. You have been a great friend to all of us and will be one in the future. Best wishes in everything to you and your girlfriend. Hope you guys never break up." A big cheer rose from the crowd.

Everyone started chanting "Speech, Speech, Speech."

"Ok, Ok." I said and got up next to Ethan on the table. "Well I could not have done this with out Ethan, my best friend, and Sarah, my girlfriend. Babe, come on up here?" I paused and wait for her to join Ethan and me on the table. "I thank you Sarah for being there for so many years and being my girlfriend. Ethan you're the one who has kept me out of trouble over the years and if not for you guys I end up in jail. My hope for all you guys is so great and I am still waiting for someone to knock me off my throne." Laughter filled the still night air. "Well thanks to my friends and my girlfriend to help me out to make me who I am today," I finished and then an up roar of whistles and clapping disturbed the calm murky night.

When I got down from the tabletop, Sarah and Ethan hugged me. Ethan told me, "Hey it is time for me to go meet Heather, I'll see you guy's later." Then off he went walking towards the steps.

After all that was said and done, we turned the music back up and went back to dancing around the fire. I looked around and noticed the firewood pile was getting low so I went to my car to pick up some more firewood.

As I was walking I notice something shimmering on the parking lot ground. I walked over to it and picked it up. It was like a pendant hanging off a nice silver chain. I thought to myself that this might be a great necklace for my girlfriend, so I picked it up and put it in my pocket.

I got to my car and started unloading the firewood. As soon as I grabbed the firewood from my car, a hand grabbed me from behind. I turned around and nobody was there. I finished gathering the wood and did not think twice about the hand that grabbed my shoulder. I ran back to the beach and add more wood to the pile near the fire.

Just then Erik came running up to me and said, "Dude, I owe you big time for throwing this kick ass party. There are so many fine chicks here."

"Yeah I know. So how many did you ask out or dance with so far?" I asked with a curiosity look on my face.

"Well… none yet but the night is still young and plenty of me to go around," he said followed by a shallow laugh.

"Well wait right here," I told him. I walked around in search for the new girl Erik will fall in love with. I saw her sitting on the bench next to the fire. I slowly walked over to her and sat down next to her.

"Hey I am Josh. What's your name?" I asked in a low clam voice.

"My name is Ginette. You're the one throwing the party, right?" she said.

"Yeah but see that guy over there," I paused to point at Erik. "He really likes you a lot and he is afraid of getting rejected and wanted to ask you to dance. So I am asking for him. Would you like to dance with him?"

"I would love to dance with him," she responded

"So go over there and tell him that," I said while pushed her up off her seat and in his direction. I saw her in the distance a few moments later and they both started to move around the fire. They reached where I was now standing and Erik gave me a nod with his head as a thank you.

I nodded back. Just then my girlfriend walked up behind me. She kissed me on the check and came around in front of me. She sat right next to me and said, "That is really kind of you to do that for Erik. You never really think of yourself do you?"

"I hardly ever think of myself. I try to help out where I can." I told her with a smile.

She said with a tear rolling down her cheek, "I do not know what I would do if you left me." She got up and gave me a big long kiss on the lips. Then she started walking towards the table to see if it needed to be restocked to get her mind off what just went on.

I went over there and gave her a hug and whispered in her ear, "Thank you and I love you so much."

Just then Ethan came back from his date. I looked at the time and it was a little past eleven. "Man you were gone for a very long time. What did you to do?" I said give him a little nudge with my elbow.

"Yeah, I'll tell you everything in details as soon as I get something to drink," he told me and walked over to the end of the table and grabbed a bottle of water from the tub. He took a drink and started walking back towards us. Then he started to tell his story. We hung onto his every word and then once he was finished we went back to partying.

CHAPTER TWENTY-ONE

Time flew by and the fire never died out. Most of the guest stayed till two in the morning and after two the party started to dwindle down to seven people. Ethan, Sarah, John, Justin, Mike, Cathy and me just sat around the fire and told stories about each other.

"Hey how about we play truth or dare?" Justin yells out.

"Sure," we replied back to him.

"Since you suggested it, you get to go first, Truth or Dare?" I asked Justin.

"Truth," he answered with a smirk.

"What is your darkest fear?" I asked him.

"My darkest fear is that I am afraid of heights. I can not go on tall buildings at all," he told us with a little fear in the tone of his voice.

"Truth or Dare," my girlfriend asked me.

"Dare," I said to her.

"I dare you to go swimming in your boxers," she told me.

"Ok, but I will want someone to come with me on this dare. Is that ok?" I asked the group.

"Sure, but who will be the one that goes with you is my choice," she said devilishly. I love it when she talks like that. It turns me on.

"Truth or dare," Ethan asked Sarah.

"Truth," she answered him.

"Who was the first person you had sex with?" Ethan asked.

"It was Josh. He asked me so politely when it was our first time and I just could not say no to those green eyes," she told everyone with a sly grin.

"Truth or Dare," John asked Ethan

"Dare," he replied.

Sarah spoke up. "Ethan is going with Josh on a midnight swim in their boxers."

"Ok," Ethan said while standing up. Then Ethan and I started stripping down to our boxers and started to walk towards the ocean. Everyone was cheering and watching with excitement.

"Yo, Ethan let's stay together in the water. I do not want to get lost or something," I said.

"Yeah that sounds like a smart idea," he replied.

So we hit the water and just stood there so we could get use to the coldness. Everyone ran down to the tide line to watch us as we took our nice cold swim.

"Go further," everyone yelled.

"Ok, ok," we yelled back.

We walked in further and the bottoms of our boxers were getting splashed by the waves. I looked over and Ethan was shivering. Then I realized that I was too.

"On three we both dive into the water so we really do not freeze to death," I said.

"Ok. One, two, three," he said. We both dived in and splashed out of the water like dolphins jumping for fish, both of us freezing our ass off when all of a sudden a giant wave came up behind us.

"Watch out," the group yelled.

Ethan and I turned around but it was too late. The current pulled us under the water. I tried to get out of the current but no luck. Our bodies floated back to the shore. John, Justin and Cathy ran over to Ethan. Sarah and Mike ran over to me. I was ok but start to cough up some water when Sarah and Mike reached me.

"Guys come over here," the other half yelled.

I got up and ran over to where Ethan's body laid. I told someone to go call 911 while I started CPR on him. I keep telling him to hold on. Even though I think I was just saying that for myself more then him.

John said, "That he was going to meet the paramedics and show them here."

I keep on doing CPR till John came back with the paramedics. I did not know how long I was doing it. They joined in with the compressions and told me that I could stop and they would take over. They roll Ethan onto the stretcher and put one of those oxygen masks on him. They rushed him back to the ambulance and we follow them there.

One of the paramedics asked, "Who is going to ride with us?"

I told them, "I would go." They loaded him into the ambulance and I hopped in back with one of the paramedics. On the way to the hospital, I told them the whole story.

After I told them what happened the paramedic say, "So that is why you guys are in your boxers."

"Yep," I said.

"We should check you out as well," the paramedic said to me as he was getting ready to check me out.

"I will be fine; I just want Ethan to be alright. Do you think he is going to fine?" I said as a tear rolled down my cheek.

"I think he will be fine and be alright," he said to reassure me. Then I just reached out and grabbed Ethan's hand and put my head down.

We arrived at the hospital and they rushed him in. I went into the waiting room when a nurse asked me to fill out some paperwork. I finished the paper work and handed it back to the nurse. A couple minutes later, Sarah arrived with our clothes and just sat down next to me.

"Hope he will be alright," I said as I started to cry.

"He will be fine. He knows how to fight. He will find his way back. Come on we need to go home," she said while rubbing my back.

"No, I want to stay with him till he wakes up." I told her then looked down at the ground.

"Ok," she said. Gave me a kiss on the top of my head and left since she needed to get home. The doctor came out and saw me sitting there.

"Are you a friend of Ethan Rush?" he asked me while looking through his papers on the clipboard.

"Yeah, he's my friend. Is he going to be alright?" I said looking up at the doctor.

"Well he had a lot of water in his lungs and has loss conciseness but we did stabilize him. If he makes it through the night he will just be fine," the doctor said to me and patting me on the back. "If you want to see him if is in room 209."

The doctor left me and then I went off to his room. I opened the door and there he was lying on the bed with a couple of tubes coming out of him and into the machines around his bed. I took a sit next to his bed and just started talking to him like he could hear me.

"I know you're strong but here is a little more strength to help you out," I said and then grabbed his hand. I did not let go of his hand and just sat there, listened to the heart machine beep. All of a sudden the heart machine started to flat line. The doctors rushed in and pulled me out of the room.

About an hour later the doctors came out and told me the news that he did not make it. They told me to go home and get some rest. So I decide to walk home since I had no car there. It was better if I did not drive anyways. As I was walking home a car drove by and a shot was fired.

CHAPTER TWENTY-TWO

I awoke in a cold sweat. It's been a year since that accident and I am still dreaming about it. I really do not know why I 'm dreaming about that day. I looked over at my clock and it read three in the morning. I knew I would not be able to go back to sleep. So I threw the covers off my bed and start thinking while lying there.

My family moved to Santa Clara after that night. I am still with Sarah and we been going out for about four years now. I made some new friends but I still missed Ethan. I visit his grave to pay my respects on that day.

As I was just lying in the dark; I decide to start my day. I went off to the bathroom and took a shower. It was a nice, long hot shower to clam my nerves and just release any thoughts that I might have. I got out and dried off.

I looked in the mirror and said to me, "Today will be a good day for you." Then got dressed in some shorts and a shirt and looked over at the time. It read four thirty and I still had about another two hours till I need to get to school. So I just sat and watched T.V. It rolled around to six-thirty, when I grabbed my stuff and headed out the door. I hoped in to my car and took off.

I went driving down the street when I got a phone call. "Hello," I answered.

"Hey, is this Josh?" the voice asked me.

"Hello, Sarah?" I asked the voice.

"How did you know? I was going to surprise you," she told me.

"Your voice gave you away. It is so sweet. How are you doing, sweetheart?" I asked.

"I am doing just fine. How did you sleep? I slept pretty well," she said.

"I had that dream again. The day Ethan died. I woke up at three and did not go back to sleep." I told her with a yawn.

"Sorry to hear that. Hope you have a better day. Well I got to go. I will call you later. Bye, sweetheart," she said.

"Bye, I love you," I said back and hung up the phone. I arrived at school and saw my friend Sam.

I parked my car and Sam came walking towards me.

"Hey Josh, how did your night go?" he asked.

"It was ok. Woke up at three this morning," I answered and then rubbed my eyes.

"So you ready for gym? You're doing basketball right?" he asked.

"Yeah, I am ready. How are you doing in Karate class?" I replied.

"I'm doing great. I should be red belt within the next couple of weeks. I am thinking of entering into a tournament to see how much I have learned," he said excitedly.

We walked to his locker and he grabbed some books then said, "I will see you in the locker room. Later, man." Sam walked off and I started to head towards my locker. I got stopped by the massive crowds in the hallway.

Some of my friends asked me, "If I was ready for basketball game tonight?"

I told them, "I was ready and I will do my best."

Finally, I got to my locker knowing that I had less then five minutes before I needed to get to my first class. So I grabbed my stuff out of my locker and merged back into the crowd. I got outside the hallway and into the quad. Then made my way to the locker room on the other side, since I did not have a first period I just waited outside the locker room for second period to start.

You could say I was a popular and almost everyone knew me. I truly did not try to become popular, it just seem to happen. I still throw the best parties around, everyone wanting my advice on things and I help them out to the best I can.

Well anyway second period started and I got changed and met Sam at his locker. He was still changing and I said, "Hey, your pretty slow at changing," followed with a small laugh.

"Yeah so what's your point?" he said while continuing to get dressed.

"Just giving you a hard time, just relax and take all the time you need. I will see you in the gym," I said and patted him on the back.

I entered the gym and it was quiet and empty. I was the first one in there and noticed the basketballs were in the corner of the gym. I grabbed one and started to shoot around. People started to come in and joined me in a little game before class started and then the teacher came out.

"Put that ball away," he told us. One of the students went and put the ball away, while the rest of us lined up for roll call. Roll was taking and the teacher put us in teams. I saw Sam was practicing over on the side of the gym which distracted me by the movement of the Bo staff that he was using and then out of nowhere the ball hit me in the side of the head.

Chris came running up and said," Hey you all right? Sorry I did not mean to hit you in the head. I did not know you were not paying attention."

"It is ok. Let's just keep playing," I said to Chris. The game went on. I heard a low hissing noise coming from the vents but I thought nothing of it. Time was running out and the game ended up in a tie. The score was 42 to 42.

The teacher called us in and told us to go hit the showers. I slowly walked into the locker room and heard that low hissing noise again. As I entered the noise filled locker room, I walked passed Sam's locker and he was already gone. I got in there and almost everyone was gone. I started to change and the bell rang. So quickly I threw my shorts and shirt on and ran to my next class.

I got stopped by some of my friends and we talked till the tardy bell rang. We said are goodbyes and walked off. Then just when I was walking into my class Sam came running up to me.

"Hey," I heard him yelling at me.

"Hey Sam, what's up?" I said back to him.

"Oh Josh it's you. Hey I thought I saw something climb up your shirt" he said to me. Now I thought that was a little weird cause if he saw something but I did not feel anything crawl up my shirt.

"Huh? What are you talking about?" I said to him with a puzzled look on my face.

"Take off your shirt cuz I swear I saw something climb up the back of it," he said.

"You're crazy; I did not feel anything go up my shirt. I'm late for class, so I will catch you later," I said as I opened the door to my classroom.

Sam walked off and then as I was just standing there I felt my chest start to get tighter. Then I lift up my shirt and a green tail was wrapped around my body. That is when I took my shirt off completely.

I just stood there and felt the creature get tighter and tighter. Now everyone's eyes were on me. Everyone one in the class started standing up and scared half to death. I saw all my friends just staring at the creature. I looked down to see it was just an over grown snake. It had green scaly skin.

The teacher phoned the office and nobody picked up. He tried again. No answer. The teacher asked one of the students to go downstairs to the office and see why nobody was answering.

"Ok I will go," Chris said. He went out the back door so he would not make me move.

"Everyone in the office is dead," he yelled as he entered the room.

Chris entered through the front door and forgot that I was standing there. He yelled it again and the creature moved its head and was looking at Chris. It lunged towards Chris and bit his head off. The rest of Chris dropped to the floor like a sack of potatoes.

The creature did a quick hiss, and then it tightened its hold on me. I heard my bones starting to crack. I heard screams and my body splattered all over the place, everything covered in red and little tan pieces as well. Everything from my waist down was still standing there.

CHAPTER TWENTY-THREE

As I floated above the classroom, I saw the snake creature start to devour everyone in the class. Hearing each scream in horror and then seeing each one get eaten by the creature. The screams dying down and then the room went dead silence.

The creature went up into the vent and I saw Sam run into the room. As I floated up there I looked outside the window. I saw all the spirits floating up into the sky. I looked down and saw some of the spirits go straight through the ground as well.

I guess heaven and hell does exist but who makes the decision which way we go? Up or down? I thought. Just then a beam of light from above and below shined on me.

It was like they were probing my essences. It went on for like three minutes. Then the light from below disappeared and I felt the light from above starting to pull me up into the sky.

As I was going through the roof I saw the creature one last time. It looked up at me and had a big fat grin on its face. Floating up into the sky, looking at everyone else going faster and then me I finally reached my destination. It looked like a vast and endless place. It goes on as far as the eye can see.

The place was all lit up; nothing was dark and spooky about this place. It felt like I was standing on glass. I look down and there was nothing underneath me. I started walking in the direction that I was facing.

Not knowing if I was going the right way. There was not a single soul around. I felt that I was heading the right way though. Finally I saw something in the distance and started running towards the object. Then it just popped up in front of me.

It was pale white gate with circles above the gate that had an inscription on it. The inscription read: *Those who stand at the gates of heaven shall be judged by their soul, heart and mind.*

As soon as I read the last word the world went black. A voice spoke, "Now for the test to see if you mind and soul has the eight most powerful things in the world."

All of sudden I was in my bedroom; there were two people in my bed having sex. I walked towards the bed and I knew the woman. The woman was my girlfriend and I wanted to find out who the man was.

The man stood up and turned towards me. It was me. I did not know what to do. All eight feelings were rushing through my heart; I felt love, hate, sad, happy, peaceful, friendship, laughter, and loneliness. I guess I had to guess what my soul was thinking.

I choose happiness. The reason I choose that was because I was happy for my girlfriend that she moved on but the strange thing was it was with me that she moved on with.

The voice came back, "You passed." Then my self-image grabbed a weapon and was coming towards me. A weapon appeared in my hand and I guess they wanted me to kill myself.

I dropped the weapon and braced myself for the blow. My self-image raised the metal bat and then vanished.

The voice came back, "Congrats. You passed all the tests. You now have to find the light. Soon the light will be in darkness where everything is born. Darkness is in every heart but will the light over power it?"

The voice stopped and I was left in darkness. I just sat down and started to think about what life would be like without my friends, lovers and family. It made me fell lonely. Then I realize that I had to move on and stop thinking of what everyone else will do.

The voice, "You will not find it that way."

Well I guess I will look inside me to find the light. While I was searching I found that I really did appreciate what friends I had. They played a big role when I was alive.

I closed my eyes and saw my heart slowly fading into darkness. That is the key, my heart. My heart is the light born into darkness and stays in the darkness till brought back into the light. But how do we bring the heart out of the darkness.

The voice answered, "Its peace you want. Peace of mind, piece of a heart, piece of the light. The light will come once the peace is reached."

"What piece is missing? I got happiness, friendship, love, hate, laughter, loneliness and sadness. What is missing?" I yelled.

I closed my eyes again and saw each piece of my dark heart shatter except one. Then my heart was within my reach but I could not grab it with a piece of darkness still there. What is that darkness? It was the final piece of my heart. Not piece but peace. Peace. Peaceful, I need to find my peacefulness. Where do I look?

The voice returned, "You'll find the piece of your heart but do you know how to get peace?"

"What will peace achieve? No one can achieve peace. At least not by themselves, I can not yet reach my peace without my friends, family, and enemies. So why ask for peace when no one will get it?" I stated to the darkness.

"Close your eyes," the voice command.

I closed my eyes and the black piece of my heart that was there just shattered and the light passed through. I opened my eyes and the gate was back. A figure was on the other side. The gates opened and I walked in.

The figure was moving towards me and then I saw who it was. It was my friend Ethan. "Hey Ethan, what are you doing here?" I asked him.

"I am now the guardian of the gates. What happened? Your not suppose to die till you're an old man. Well let me see what the big guy wants with you. Stay right here," he said.

A flash of light and he was gone. I looked around and some of my high school friends where here. I ran up to say hi but I ran right in an invisible wall. I guess straight is the alone way to go. All of sudden the light went out on all sides. Ethan popped back in front of me.

"What happened?" I asked.

"You passed the entire test. Congrats. You're going back to earth," Ethan said.

"What do you mean?" I asked with a little concern in my voice.

"It is nothing bad. You are now a guardian angel trainer. Plus you do not have to worry about dying ever again. So hurry up, you will not remember what you saw here in heaven but you will remember me and what I said. I will check up on you shortly. Bye-bye," he said and tapped me on the forehead.

Then the floor dropped down from underneath me and I fell into darkness.

While falling down into the darkness, I heard Ethan's voice said, "Remember to live life with the eight most powerful things in the universe."

CHAPTER TWENTY-FOUR

WITH A SOLID THUD, I WAS ON THE GROUND OF THE classroom with blood all over my body. I laid there for the next couple of minutes trying to get my bearings; my cell phone began to ring. "Hello," I answered it though I was still little woozy from the trip.

"Hi Josh, this is Sarah," she said happily.

I was so happy to hear her voice. "I am so happy to hear you. I guess you heard the news," I said to her.

"Yeah, are you alright?" she asked.

"I guess so but I need to get home. So can I call you later?" I asked.

"Yeah you can. I just wanted to know if you were one of those that didn't die. Now that I know you are safe, I can feel less worried. I love you babe. Bye," she told me.

"I love you too, sweetheart. Talk to you later," I said and hung up the phone. I walked out the back hallway. Still dripping with blood and half naked, I went out the closet door to me. I walked through the parking lot, jumped in my car and left.

Soon I was at my house and luckily nobody was home. The first thing was to get rid of the blood on me and my clothes. After that I just went downstairs and plopped down on the couch.

As I was just relaxing, my girlfriend popped into my mind. I decided to go see my girlfriend. On my way over the mountain on highway 17 there was a car wreck. As I went pass it, I saw one of the people involved being put into the ambulance. It looked like some one ran into a rock slide. The car was really smashed and it had slowed down traffic to a crawl.

I finally made it to my girlfriend's house and was greeted with open arms. A big hug and kiss was the first thing that was given to me. We went inside her house and sat down on the couch. After the day I had, all I wanted to do was hold her forever. I did not want to move from that spot. We just started talking about how are days went and before we knew it, we both fell asleep in each others arms.

It was about one in the morning when I woke up and saw Ethan sitting next to me.

"You guys really do make a nice couple. I wish I was still alive to be there. Anyway, are you ready to meet your destiny and face your fate?" he asked in soft voice.

"I guess I am ready for my destiny and fate. So tell me what I am going to do?" I asked.

"Come with me," he said as he reached out his hand.

"Well let me kiss my girlfriend goodbye," I told him as I bent down and kiss her on the forehead.

"You will not be gone for too long. You will be back before she even knows you're gone." Ethan answered.

As soon as I got up, we were transported to an empty room. The walls were all white and it seemed a little to bright to look at. Ethan just walked over to the wall that we were standing by and opened up a wall panel.

"Hey Josh, come over here. I know there is nothing in this room but just come over here," he yelled at me.

"Ok, ok I am coming," I yelled back and shielding my eyes from the brightness of the room.

"This is your training center, so when we send you new guardian angels you will help them train and show them the ropes in here. This little counsel has every test, training, and workout session you will need to complete this task," he paused and pointed to control panel that he opened up. He pulled out a book and handed it to me. "Here is the book of codes for each one of you're trainings.

Then he just tapped me in the middle of the forehead. "Now you just got all the info to do each one yourself."

"Thanks," I said then started walking around the place. I heard Ethan punch in some numbers on the key pad. All of a sudden, Ethan and I were floating in outer space. The walls were covered with small dots that looked like stars and below us was the earth. It looked so peaceful up here. "So where is this place?"

"Well right now we are in outer space hovering over the earth and that is were we are." He paused and smiled at me. "No really it is a place right down the street from your house. So you can bring any one in this building to train with you and we will ask you to train with you're friend Sam when he gets back from his destiny trip. Well that is all I need to tell. Have fun and now back to your girlfriend's house."

"Wait, I have so much to ask you," I said to him.

"Well that will have to wait I will be back soon enough with some trainees. Now that you know I am still alive, I will be able to visit you more often," he paused. "If you need me just call my name I will show up in a flash."

Then a big flash of light blinded me and I was back cuddling with my girlfriend. I fell back to sleep with Sarah in my arms. We both woke up around nine in the morning and started to make some breakfast. Then she went upstairs to change.

Just as she left my eye sight, Ethan popped in. "The big guy said you can have two personal guardian angels and you can pick them. You send them on personal watches that you not able to do yourself or just do not want to do. So pick wisely and tonight you will get your first two guardians angels. Later," he told me and then vanished.

Just as he vanished, Sarah was coming back down the stairs. "So you ready to go?" she asked.

"Yeah," I said and put the bowl into her sink. Then we both hopped in my car and drove back towards my house.

"How did you sleep last night?" I asked her.

"I slept fine and then I remember you telling me about this warehouse you got a couple days ago," she replied.

"Yeah so I get to show you it and all its glory," I said while driving on the freeway. She then turned on the radio and we started talking about what to do this week since my school was closed for about a week after what had happened and her school was on some weird schedule that she only has to go in for one day.

We got down to this small white building which was only about two or three blocks from my house. It was no more then like one story tall but it had no corners and one double door painted forest green. No windows on the outside but little air vents that were barley visible to see.

We walked up to the forest green door and unlocked it. We open the door and it crack like it has not been used in a while. On the inside, there were vents and nothing else on the walls. It still had the white paint that was a bit too bright.

She asked, "So where is all the training equipment?"

"Just close your eyes and you will see everything once you open them," I said. Just then I hit the key pad and entered first training session code. It popped up in front of my eyes. "You can open your eyes."

She opened her eyes and her mouth dropped to the floor. "Where did all this come from?" she asked me after the shock left her.

"Do not question where or why, just enjoy what we got. Close your eyes one more time, I got one thing to show you," I said. She closed her eyes again and I grabbed hold of her hand. I enter another code and the room changed. She opened her eyes and grabbed hold of my hand even tighter then she was holding it when I grabbed her hand. We were standing on top of the old twin towers right at the break of dawn.

"It is so beautiful. How can this be? How much did this cost you?" she started to ask me when I just put my hand over her mouth.

"I told you not to ask why but just enjoy the beauty that is before you," I told her and let go of her mouth.

"Ok," she said back to me. She hugged me and gave me a kiss.

I made it back to the white building that we saw in the beginning. We decide that we had enough surprises and left the building. We headed back to my place.

"I wish some people would see that the world is just not that far from heaven or hell. It is the things we do in life that make it one or the other," I whispered to Sarah as we pulled into my driveway. "Most people know that but forget it from time to time and need to be reminded that life is truly worth it."

After I said that she looked at the time and told me "I think I should be getting home now." So I backed my car out of the driveway and went back to her place. After I dropped her off, I decided I should get some training in and so I went to the training center.

Strangely enough Ethan was waiting by the door with to people next to him. "Hey Ethan, so I guess these are the two angels I will be training this time around," I asked.

"Yeah, I would like you to meet Mrs. X and John Choate," he said and vanished again with out explaining anything else to me.

"Hey guys, I guess we should start training. Are you ready?" I said to them and we all went in with out really talking. Then I opened the green door and then it shut behind us.

CHAPTER TWENTY-FIVE

I GUESS THAT EACH PERSON HAS DARKNESS WITHIN HIM OR her and we are lost among it till we find a way to deal with it. A soul that is lost can be recovered; you just need the right tools to help guide it back to where it belongs.

Each time one dies we lose a piece of ourselves to the world that is unseen and unheard of. What piece we lose is something hard to describe but I know that once we fall we can get it all back. I wonder how many have fallen to the will of others and how many pieces will we get back once we fall for good. It is time to search for those who have fallen souls among the world of the living.

I awoke to the sounds of my brothers watching TV. It was nothing more then I want to watch this channel, no I want to watch this one. The TV sounded like it is about to bust. I slowly stretch my body out and pulled back the covers. I look down my tall slender body. Only wearing my plaid boxers, I got out of bed.

I start to get ready for my day, so off to the bathroom I went. I took a shower and then start brushing my teeth. It has been a while since I looked in a mirror and saw my cold icy blue eyes starring back at me. Now I grabbed the bottle of gel from the cabinet and put some in my hand. I put the gel in my hair and got it ready to spike up my black hair. After getting my hair spiked up, I return to my bedroom. Looking threw my drawers and found my work uniform since I was heading to work in the first place. Throwing it on and heading out the door so I would not be late for work.

It was a normal Saturday for me. I hopped in my car and drove off to work. Driving towards work, I thought to myself that hopefully something interesting would happen today. Finally getting to work, I exited my car and walked to the front door.

On the other side of town, I woke up to the sounds of my boyfriend get up and getting dressed. I spoke to him, "Babe, what are you doing? Get your cute butt back to bed."

"Sorry babe, I got to get to work," he said while pulling up his pants.

"Ok, will I see you later tonight?" I asked.

"Yeah just meet me in Santa Cruz," he told her and kissed her on the forehead. He grabbed his shoes and walked out of the apartment as she threw the covers off her body. She looked like a modern day daisy duke. Wearing only black bra and panties to match, her curves would make any woman jealous in a heartbeat and her hair was spread out among the bed, which looks to be about shoulder length. She stood up at the height of five foot seven then stretched out. She took off her clothes and walked into the bathroom to clean up. After the shower and drying off, she threw a robe on and sat down in her living room to watch some TV.

I entered the building and got greeted friendly from my boss Travis that was working with me.

"Hey John, how was your night?" Travis asked.

"Not to bad just fell asleep and woke up to my brothers fighting over the TV again," I told him.

"Sorry to hear that. Well hopefully work will go by smooth and peacefully. So we got a light day today. Just run those movies over there and we will see what is next to do," he said as he went into the back room.

I walked over to the stack of movies and put them in order. Grabbing a stack of them and ran them up and down the aisle putting each movie away. The day started out pretty slow but I felt like it was moving pretty fast to me. I got done with running the movies within a few moments and walked past the soda fridge and noticed it needed to be restocked.

I went into the back room and started grabbing sodas to restock the fridge. Just then Travis walked into the backroom and said, "It is a real slow day so far, so just take your time. No rush."

"Ok, boss. I am just going to restock the soda fridge and then just help customers that come in," I said in response. I finished stocking the fridge and Travis was not kidding, it really was slow. Not a single customer has came in since we opened, then I just kicked back on the back counter and watches the day slowly pass by.

On the couch flipping through channels and nothing really on, she decides to make something to eat. Looking at the time it was about noon, she walked into the kitchen. Looking through the cabinets and finding nothing, she decided to go grab some lunch at the shopping center down the street.

She got dressed and was getting ready when she noticed that there was a message on the machine. She thought to herself that she would check it after she got back from lunch and picked up her keys then strolled out the door.

It was a nice day outside and she decided to go for a walk. On her walk she did not really pay attention to the scenery because she was lost in her own thoughts. Nothing really important just what is for dinner, when to leave to meet her boyfriend, what movie to get to pass the time, etc.

She reached the shopping center and made up her mind to have some sushi for lunch.

At the same time, I was on my lunch sitting outside when I noticed a girl walking into the sushi house. "Wow, that girl was hot. I wonder what she is doing later tonight," I said to myself. I looked at my watch and notice it was time to get back to work and tossed my trash away.

After lunch she walked around the shopping center and was still thinking on which movie to rent. She stopped in front of Blockbuster and slowly opened the door. I looked up when the door opened and noticed it was the same girl from before. "Wow twice in one day, I think I will try to get her number," I thought.

I walked up to her and asked, "How are you doing today?"

"I am ok. I am having trouble deciding on a movie to rent. I do not know what to get," she said while looking at one of the titles.

"Well my name is John and I would love to help you pick out a movie. Let's see what we have," I said.

We started walking up and down the aisles as I pointed out some of my favorite movies. She seemed distracted and a little spacey but I did not know why. We finished going around the entire store. I went back behind the counter and waited for her to pick her movies. She went back down a couple of aisles and picked out a few movies.

I was just waited for her to finish shopping and while walking through the line, she picked up some popcorn and soda to go with the movies she was renting. I thought this was my chance to get her number while I ringed her up.

I started to ring her up and then asked, "I was wondering if you would like to go out sometime."

"Sure, cutie," she said and grabbed the pin off the counter.

I finished ringing her up and then she wrote down her number on the piece of paper. Then she walked out of the store. Just then Travis walked up behind me and asked, "So did you get her number, Romeo?"

"Yep and I am going to call her tonight just when I get home and change out of my work uniform," I told him with smile across my face. The rest of the day went by really slow and I kept looking at the clock. Finally three o'clock rolled around and I thought, "Only two more hours to go."

She got home and changed into some more fancy clothes. Just when she was about to leave, she remembered that there was a message on the phone. She walked over to the answer machine and pressed play.

Beep. Do not look up today while on the road. Beep. She thought that it was weird message but did not pay to much attention to the warning on the machine. Then she grabbed her keys and off she went to meet her boyfriend in Santa Cruz.

On my break, I noticed that my cell phone had a message on it. Pressing the buttons to retrieve the message and putting it up to my ear it said: *One new message; do not look up on your last break. Press seven if you like to delete it.* I punched seven in and deleted the message not really thinking too much about it. I told Travis, "Hey I am going on break and will be back in a few moments."

She was driving on Highway 17 when she looked up and noticed a small streak of black stretching across the sky and at the same time I looked up and noticed the same thing. Then it vanished and where the black streak was in the sky it turned blue again.

While she was looking up she did not notice a rockslide was happening right in front of her and she smashed into one of the giant boulders that land on to the road. She hit it and she flew through the windshield landing on the road. Two more cars tried to stop but it was too late for them as well. People behind the accident whipped out their cell phones and called 911.

About twenty minutes later the police and ambulance pulled up to the intense horrible scene that made a complete mess of the highway. The cops start to move traffic along the two-way highway as best as they could. Then for some reason she noticed a Jeep pass by the accident scene. As it slowed down to drive by, she noticed that their eyes connected but she did not know how to reach out to him. Then the Jeep sped up as it moved pass the scene.

Back at Blockbuster, I looked up at the black streak and then noticed it vanished in an instance. I thought that was odd but then had to get back from my break. "Yes only two more hours till I am off," I said while entering the store. I didn't notice that the store was completely empty.

I walked into the back office/storage room and Travis was sitting at the desk. "Is there any work from me?" I asked Travis.

"Yeah there is. The studio wall needs to be updated with those posters, grab the ladder and go work on it," he said and went back to his paperwork.

I went and grabbed the ladder from the back, set up the ladder and positioned it so that my back was facing the metal racks that held the movies. I was doing the first frame on the studio wall; I unclipped the plastic that holds the poster in place and makes it shine. I pulled out the poster that was in there before and dropped it down to the floor. Then replaced it with the new one poster board and clipped it back in.

I moved over to the next panel and did not realize that the leg of the ladder was on the poster board that I dropped onto the floor. So while working on the second panel, I move the ladder and the leg slipped on the poster board. The ladder threw me off and I fell onto the movie rack. I got pinned on the rack and couldn't move my body to get off the rack. Travis heard the loud noises and came running out but it was too late for Travis to help.

As soon as Travis got out the office door, the loose piece of plastic came sliding off panel and cut my head straight off. One clean cut straight through my neck. Blood splattered all over the place. My body became like a fountain. My head rolled down the backside of the rack and hit the ground with splat.

I stood right next to my body looking at the clean cut that once held my head. The racks holding my body perfectly in place, I had no voice to yell something to say that I was somewhat alive. I had nothing but sadness and loneliness inside me. I started to walk away, waiting for the next thing to happen. I thought there would be a bright light or flames to carry me away to my next destination but nothing happened.

Back on the mountaintop, she realized that she was dead but she still wanted to make it to her boyfriend. So she starts running down the hill towards the bottom. She was running through cars and just trying to get away from that horrible scene as well. She made it down to the bottom of the mountain and into Santa Cruz. She walked towards the building that her boyfriend was working in.

She entered the building and walked straight into her boyfriend's office. She saw him kissing another woman and walked over to where they were. She raises her hand and slaps both of them but her hand just went through them both. Tears started falling from her face and then she remembered that she meet this new guy name John and thought maybe he would see her or something. It was worth a shot she thought.

I was sitting on the curb outside of work, watching them remove my body and head from my old work place. I thought to myself what now, where do I go, and what am I waiting for. I looked up from where I was sitting and saw the black streak again. I guess I will just sit here and wait till I get picked up from this world. I rested my head in my hands and just started to cry.

She was walking back up the hill again, when she got back to the crash site and they were still clean up the mess. On a stretcher was her body cover in a plastic sheet so none of the passer bys would see the body. She poked her head through the plastic sheet to take a look at her body. As she was staring at her body, she wondered why did this happen to her. Then she remember the message *do not look up while you are driving* echoing through her head. She sat down next to her dead corpse and started pondering.

Ok so I am dead, so why have I not gone to heaven or hell. Why am I still on earth? Or is this earth? I guess I am being punished for all the bad things I've done in my life. So what, do I just wonder around making up for my sins and mistakes by helping others she was pondering.

Just then out of the corner of her eye she saw the black streak in the sky again. She thought it was that streaks fault. She starts cursing it out even though no sound came out of her mouth. Then something else started to happen. She began to float off the ground. She realized that her emotions where causing her to fly so she even got more pissed off and started to go faster up into the air. Then she turned her body to aim for that black streak in the sky.

I was crying my eyes out because I didn't know what to do. I did not realize that I was being lifted off the ground till I heard something fly over my head. I looked up and saw a duck pass my head. Then looked down and realize that I was a good hundred feet in the air. It started to make sense of what was going on and I realized my emotions were controlling my flight.

I looked straight ahead and saw something heading straight towards me. I tried to move out of the way but it slammed right into me. Both of us went falling to earth. I tried flying again but did not work. We hit the ground with a thud and cloud of dust engulfed us.

I got up and started walking through the dust cloud try to find what just hit me. I saw a figure stand up in the cloud and then it started to move. I ran towards it and the closer I got, I notice it was the shadow of a female body. The dust started to settle down and the figure became clear. I noticed it was the girl that I talked to early.

It was like a horrible dream and I wish that was the punch line. I walked up to her and saw that she was covered from head to toe in dust. I reached my hand out to help dust her off and she accepted the help. She looked up at me and noticed that it was me that was helping her.

When she realized that it was me dusting her off, she tried to speak but nothing came out. I thought that it was weird that nobody can see us and we couldn't talk to anyone. I thought that if I met someone that is dead like me that we would be able to talk to each other. Guess not.

I turned around and notice that there was another person just standing there. He was dressed in all black and not saying a word. I did not know if he could see us or not but I got the strange feeling he was here to take us to the next destination. We finish dusting ourselves off and then started walking towards this man in black. I felt a hand on my shoulder.

I turned around and she was pointing up towards the black streak in the sky. Yeah I know that is what caused my death and then I thought that it probably what caused her death too. I pointed to the man in black.

CHAPTER TWENTY-SIX

THE MAN BLACK STARTED WALKING TOWARDS THE TWO OF us and then walked right up to me. He raised his finger and pointed to my throat and then just pushed on it. Then he walked to her and did the same thing. "Speak," the man in black said.

"Hey I got my voice back," I said a little shocked.

"My voice is back as well," she said.

"Well I am glad you guys can talk now. I was waiting for you guys to figure out how to talk but instead you figure out how to fly," the man in black said with a curiously look upon his face.

"Hey what the fuck is going on, why are we not in heaven or hell, who are you?" I asked quickly at the man.

"Yeah I would like some answer and what was with that weird black streak in the sky?" she asked while pointing towards it.

"All will be explain in good time but first we need to get you two out of here," the man said.

"Why? Where are we going?" I asked him.

The man did not answer just grabbed our hands and we went flying off. We landed on the top of the Rockies Mountains. "We will be safe here for now. Ok, so to answer your questions. First I will explain the black streak," he said.

"What is it and why did terrible things happen to us when we looked at it?" she asked puzzled.

"I guess I should tell my name is Rush. I am somewhat of a guardian of the realms. You two are dead if you have not figure that out yet. Now you are John Choate and you are Mrs. X. Now that we know each other, even through we have all meet before. We can move on." he paused. "That black streak in the sky is a destiny streak. I even called you guys and left messages not to look up but I guess you didn't listen to my warning even though I knew you wouldn't listen anyways."

"Ok but what does this destiny streak have to do with us. There must be a thousand people who have noticed the black streak in the sky," I said.

"True but thing with destiny streaks is that each one has an affect only on the people that it needs to affect and this one was not meant for the two of you. It was meant for two others but they dragged you along for the ride to get back at me. I do not want you guys to be affected by this destiny streak but it was going to happen either way," he said to us and looked back.

"Ok so let me get this straight. We are dead; do to that destiny streak in the sky. So what are we suppose to do now?" she said.

"Well you guys are not really dead and you're not really alive. Your bodies are dead. You're in the realm of the wandering spirits or as we call it the fallen realm. See this world is made up of realms upon realms. Each one covered by the next but it is very hard to see then with a limited state of mind. I, the guardian of the realms, am the one that makes sure that the people or things of nature are able to see what they need to see. So the Earth is made up of these realms and each one has watchers and guardians. This realm your in only has guardians. That is why we could not stay were we are at. Those guardians are the ones that decide what to do with what lands here in this realm." he paused. "I needed to reach you before they did, so I would not be chasing you around this realm."

"Ok that makes sense. Well somewhat. I've heard of that theory but nobody could prove it," she said.

"Your right there is no proof, so nobody could actually show that these other realms existed. Now the reason I needed to get you before they got you," he said.

"Hold up," I said looking confused. "You're saying that there are millions of worlds out there and each has different realms and within these "realms" there are people that protect us from getting stuck there or worst, destroy. So why can we not see them or touch them or anything?"

"Good question. Ok, so each realm is made up of different creatures and nature. The guardians and watchers take form as those creatures in the realms. So for the human realm on Earth we take disguise of humans and animals. So to answer the question that you can't see us is false because you can see us but you just do not know it. Usually you see us as something other then humans for example in your realm dogs are mostly guardians and cats are mostly watchers," he paused for a brief moment. "For the second part of that question, is that humans do not see the other realms because they do not believe in these other realms. It is just like the whole Santa Claus effect, when your young people keep up the reality that he is real then you grow up and stop believing in him, so he does not exist. Does that make it a little better to understand?" I spoke to them.

"A little but I think I need time to wrap my pretty little head around this. Please continue with what you were talking about." I said still confused but trying to understand it all.

"Ok, so the reason I needed to get to you before they did was that you two are special cases. That destiny streaks was not meant to be for you two, it was meant for someone else. What happened is, that the streak was being manipulated by the guardians of this realm to bring you here and destroy you," he paused again and was looking off into the distances. "Speaking of that I am going to have to fly real fast because over there about thirty feet from us, they are trying to find you guys," he said and grab are hands again. We flew even faster this time and ended up on the Empire State Building. "The view is great from up here. Sometimes I wish I could just stay here and watch the world."

"Who is after us and why us?" she asked.

"They are the ones working for the person that is trying to get rid of me. You guys are Fallen Angels that I was going to need but didn't tap you till later on but plans have changed and those types of angels are very rare on Earth in general. There are three types of angels. Guardian Angels which protect the ones they are assign to, that includes their trainers, there are Temporary Angels that are people that get tapped from guardian angels to move the world's to meet their destinies and last is Fallen Angels which are the ones that keep the balance of Good and Evil. Fallen Angels do not choose what side to be on but it is more of the Fallen Angels choose for themselves by what they do to help out the Worlds they are on or in," he told us.

"Why are we not on Earth since we are Fallen Angels?" we both asked him.

"Pretty much, that destiny streak was not meant for the two of you and the guardians of this realm pulled you through the streak by killing you in the other realm. Now they want to destroy you. It is my job to pull you through the realms that leaded you back to your realm and help you to become the Fallen Angels that you were meant to be," he told us.

"Ok, so why are we not able to see the people after us and how do we get back to the other realm?" I asked him.

"The reason you do not see them is because you still do not believe in what I am telling you and I understand it is hard to sallow with out seeing it. To get out of this realm is going to be a little harder then just going through the streak again because I bet they are guarding the portal," he told us.

"Is there any place to rest in this realm so we do not have to keep jumping around," she asked.

"Yes one more flight and we will be there but I did not know how much flight time you guys can handle. See people like us just have time spans on our wings but I been around for a long time so my time is really, really long but your guy's time is somewhat around ten to fifteen minutes so that is why we rest then fly," he told us. "You guys think you can be up for one more flight?"

"Well to get away from those things that want to destroy us I am up for anything," she said and looked over at me.

"Yeah me too," I said.

He grabs our hands one more time and we vanish into thin air. Next thing we know is that we appeared in the middle of a forest. I look around and there was nice little cabin in the woods and no people in site or at least from what I could see anyway. We walk into the cabin and it was nicely set up. Made completely of wood and then the furniture was brand new which seemed never to be touched. The kitchen was almost the size of a five star restaurant. We walked up stairs to the rooms and each with a king size bed and closet. One thing I didn't notice was this place had no electronics. It had plugs but the only things plugged were lamps and kitchen appliances.

"Hey Rush, where are we?" I asked

"We are in the forest outside of Lake Tahoe," he said while turning some lamps on.

"Nice place but why no electronics?" she asked.

"They are here but the reason you can not see them is that you think they are not here. Just believe in them. You guys are the ones imaging this place and the furniture that is in here. See this house is just an empty place but when people walk inside and start to think of what they what, it will appear. So I take it you guys are hungry, what do you guys want?" he asked us.

"We can make it. We have hands and legs that work and we have plenty of room to work together in that big kitchen," I said as I walked into the kitchen. We started to make a big sandwich and then X came in and started to make some soup over the stove. Rush was just standing there with a big fat grin on his face. "What is the grin for?"

"Nothing just seeing how you two work well together which means it will be easy for use to get past them," he paused. "Plus I have not seen that in a long time."

"What?" she asked him.

"Teamwork and willingness to help others," he answered with a smirk.

I continued making my sandwich and the soup started to boil. X poured it into the bowl and sat down next to Rush at the table which was next to the kitchen. I finished making my sandwich and sat down next to X when I asked Rush, "Where is your food?"

"My food has been sitting here in front of me the whole time. Remember that this house does what you want it to do but it does thank you for doing things on your own," he says. "It shows that you guys know the true value of life that you should not take things for granite."

We ate in peace and just enjoyed our food. After the food, X and I wondered how we were going to get back to the world we knew. "Hey, guys come into the living room," Rush said.

We get into the living room and it is decked out like an army command base and on the table in the middle was a map and some little figure of the enemy and ones of us. "Ok there are two ways of doing this. The first way is I can open a portal to the other realm, or we can fight/sneak through the one they are guarding."

"Well why didn't you tell us you can make a portal," I stated.

"If you want an easy way to do this thing, then I guess it is the easy way we shall take. Mrs. X do you have any thoughts on this," he said and looked up at her.

"I think we should do it the easy way," she said.

"Ok. We should be able to get back within the next couple of hours but I need to tell you something about being a Fallen Angel in your realm. First off, is that your bodies are basically not able to be use since they are gone. You will get a new body and you get to choose what it looks like but you can't make it the same as the one you had before," he paused.

"Ok that sounds fair. What else?" they asked.

"The second thing is that you will have training and missions to help people out. You will be set up, as you like so whatever you want it is yours but I would not try to be really fancy because you would not enjoy it the way you wish. Last thing you guys will be able to make one wish that I will make come true since you died before your time. Do not tell your wish now think about it and tell me after we get back," he finished and then walked outside

The living room changed back to the way it was when we first entered here. I sat down on the couch and just started to think about everything that I was told and how to start a new life, which can be scary. Who should I start it with, where should I live and if I should try to help out the ones I left behind? I looked over at Mrs. X and she too looked like she was in deep thought.

She was thinking the same things and how to live the life she always wanted. She knew this was a new start and it could take her anywhere she wanted but she started thinking that it seems that when she was with John that she felt safe and secure.

She walked over to me and sat down next to me. She started to speak, "I was thinking. I do not know if this is to bold but I was wondering if you would like to go out once this is all over."

"Yeah that would be great. I was going to call you once I was off work today but I guess that would never happen. So yeah I would love to go out on date with you once we get back to the other realm," I told her and both of them smiled.

"Hey guys come on I am about to open the portal," we heard Rush yelling from the backyard. We came running out to the back yard and saw him standing in the middle of the yard with a design on the ground around him. He was standing in the middle of circle and it had four dragon's head at the points of a compass. He started the chanting and moving within the design. After a few moments have passed I noticed that in the background of where he was dancing that a small little rift was piercing through the air behind him.

I walked into the design with Rush and followed his movements. X was watching both of us with a curious look upon her face. Then she looked behind us and noticed that the rift was getting bigger with each complete set of movements that we did. After she saw that, she walked into the design and followed Rush's movements, the rift started to become stable and was holding.

"Ok guys it is time to cross over into the rift," he paused and looked up to the sky. "Shit they felt the rift and are coming after it to close it up and get you guys." X and I where frozen in place. "Come on guys hurry up and get in the rift."

All I felt was someone pushing me into the rift and I saw the creatures that Rush was telling us about. Each had wings like a demon and teeth sharp and red with stains of blood on them. The bodies of snakes and the worse screeching sound that I would never forget.

Rush final pushed both of us through the portal and it started to close. Just as Rush was going to jump through, one of the creatures grabbed him and pulled him back. I wanted to run out and help him but Mrs. X grabbed on to me and held me back. Just before the rift finally closed, I saw a group of guardians jumping on him and I saw that he was getting torn to shreds. Limbs and clothes and blood went flying all over the place. Then the rift closed and we were in complete darkness.

CHAPTER TWENTY-SEVEN

Mrs. X let go of my shoulder and asked, "Now what do we do?"

"I have no clue. I guess we can start walking around," I said. Then I felt something in my pocket. I reached into my pocket and found something in it. I pulled it out and it was a note from Rush.

It read: *I knew that I would be defending the rift from the guardians so I slipped this into you pocket so you could make it back safe. So you're now in the halls of darkness that connects the realms together. Hopefully you have not moved yet or this might be a little harder then I wrote. Anyway, to get to the correct realm that would be right in front of you, I set up the rift so you just have to walk a straight line. Please listen this time and do not move left or right because if you do then you will either fall into another realm or switch the path that I laid out in front of you.*

Good luck.
Rush

Mrs. X and I stood there and shed a couple of tears. Then I decide that I would take the lead. I grabbed her hand and told her, "Do not let go. I will get us out of here and back to our realm."

"Ok," was all she could say since she was still a little emotional, from everything has happened. She just started walking with me. I notice other realms moving on the side of us as we were walking the straightest path. It was about five minutes and saw a light at the end of the hallway.

As we were walking up I noticed that there was a figure standing next to the lighted portal in front of us. The figure was dressed in pure white. It almost blended into the light that was coming from the realms portal. We walked up to the doorway and started to push it open when the figure spoke, "STOP, You can not pass with out clearance from me the gatekeeper."

I stopped pushing on the door and thought Rush never said anything about a gatekeeper. He moved in front of the doorway and I asked him, "How do we get clearance from you to pass?"

He spoke only two words, "Peacefully combat."

Mrs. X and I just had a confused look on our faces and then we looked back at the person. "What do you mean peacefully combat?" we asked. He did not respond or move.

"Ok, I guess we need to figure out what this means and then we will be able to pass through the gates," X said to me.

"Sounds like a solid plan to me," I said. I sat down on the black pathway and motioned for X to sit next to me. I was thinking about the two words and it was like a riddle. I looked over at X and she was trying really hard to figure this out.

"I think I got it," I told her. I got up from where I was sitting and walked over to him. I told him, "I think I got your answer. It is that there is no such thing as peacefully combat.

No matter how you fight there is always someone else that will throw a fist or say a word or something to make it ugly or not peaceful."

"You are correct and for that answer you guys may pass through the gate. Plus I know you guys would figure it out," then the keeper smiled and moved to the side of the gate.

I walked up to the gate and was trying to push it and then I looked to my right and saw that X was standing right next to me. She was pushing as well and then we got the gate opened and walked on through.

A bright light flashed us and then we were floating above the world. I did not know what we were waiting for but then the man in black was walking towards us. We ran up to the figure and then he removed his hood and it was Rush.

He spoke, "I see you guys made it through without any trouble and you passed the gatekeepers test. So you guys ready to make you new life then I will take you to your first training session. Who wants to go first?"

"Hold on one sec, how did you get out of the guardians grips? We saw you get torn to shreds." I asked him.

"Well that is simple I just cast a spell called mirage tunnel. Basically it made a dummy of me then I go into the ground and pop up somewhere else."

"Ok that sounds to simple but if that is what you did, cool," I told him

Then Mrs. X stepped up and said, "I would like to go first. Well lets go with lifestyles first. I want to have my own house nothing to big just like a two bedroom home and the location would be in the Santa Cruz Mountains where I die but not on the spot but close by. Then I just want a job that I like doing which is helping people. I guess I would like to be a doctor," she paused.

"Just to let you know all the basic needs will be supplied so do not worry about food or money," Rush said.

"Ok, so next would be appearance. I remember you said we could not look anything like how we did when we were alive so I think I want to look like the average person. I wanted to be five eight in height, blond wavy hair, and black eyes with a cold stare that could kill. The body is normal with about c cups for breast and a nice flat ass," she finished.

"Ok, anything else before you head back on earth?" Rush asked her.

"Nope but how will I be able to contract you?" she asked.

"Just fly towards Orion's Belt and I will meet you over there," he said and pointed.

Then in a flash she was shot down like a rocket towards earth. "You're next," he said to me.

"Ok, so I guess I will go with appearance first. Well I like that I was tall and would like to keep that. So I want to be about six one and with dirty blonde hair. My eyes will be a clear and smooth as emeralds. I want to be lean and to have a great tone body. As for down there I wish to be the same size as I was before I died. Now for place to live I want to live in Santana Row in one of the pent houses. I want a roommate as well," I told him.

"Ok, anything else?" he asked me.

"Yeah I want to have job that is able to see how the world works. I guess I like to travel and see the world for all its wonders. I know, how about international business man with all the knowledge to help change how people do business in this realm," I told him with a grin.

"Ok and off you go to your new life," I told him.

I was shot off like a rocket just as X did. It was early the next morning when I awoke to the sound of my cell phone ringing. "Hello," I said still a little sleepy.

"Hey this is your boss and where the hell have you been? I have been blowing up your phone. Well that what happens when you party too much with your friends, anyway that is not the reason I was calling you. I just want to tell you that you need to be in my office first thing Monday morning so we can go over your new schedule. Ciao," he hung up the phone and I was left with my mouth wide open.

I threw the covers off and my body was just how I descried it. I got up in my boxers and started to walk around the house. I notice my roommate was in the kitchen. "Hey what did I tell you about walking around in your boxers?"

"Sorry, Eric it was just a long night. Let me go get some pants on," I said and went back into my room. I threw on some pants and then walked back into the kitchen.

Eric said, "So I got to go but I will see you later for dinner, right?"

"Yeah I will be here for dinner," I said and then he walked out the door. Then I just remember something. I ran back to my cell phone and look through the numbers and most of them where business contracts, then I notice one of my contacts labeled X. I gave it a call and she picked up.

"Hey John," she answered.

"Hey X," I replied back.

"Did you get the message that we need to meet up for lunch today?" she asked.

"No I did not but I am sure it is around here somewhere. So I guess I will see you at lunch then. Goodbye," I said and then hung up the phone.

I just held the phone to my chest and then I finished getting dressed and found the note saying the place and time for lunch. I looked over at the clock and it was almost time to meet up. I grabbed my keys to my car and notice there were a lot more fancy then the one I use to own. I went down to the garage and my jaw dropped when I saw what was parked my parking space. It was nice midnight blue Ferreira. I beep it and got in.

I just pulled into the parking lot of the place where we were meeting for lunch and got out of my car. X was sitting on the outside just basking in the sun. I walked up to her and she took off the sunglasses that she had on and I said, "Hey."

"Hey to you too cutie," she said back with smiled.

Then out of nowhere Rush appeared right behind me and say, "You guys ready to meet your trainer and where most of your training will be held."

"Yeah sure," we both said and then we were gone in a flash. We were hovering over a white building with a green door in front of it. A kid about our age was pulling into the park lot of the building.

We landed in front of the building and Rush said," Josh, this is John Choate and X. Have fun." Then he vanished and we all walked into the building with Josh and the big green doors closing behind us.

CHAPTER TWENTY-EIGHT

I SEE NOW THAT LIFE IS NOT WORTH HIDING WHAT YOU really are. To hide one's self to the world is just a crime and really can hinder the experiences that one might miss out on. Everything in this world is just one great big pot and we are the ingredients that make up the beginning and end. The one thing I could tell you is not worry about the end of your journey but worry about the choices you make along the way. In all aspect of life just live it and have fun.

It was like any other day, I guess. Each person in my household was doing what they normally do at this time. Just to me it felt a little too scripted. I woke up in the morning with a massive hard-on. Thinking back to last night and him, god he was handsome, funny and well, perfect. The best part was that he is my boyfriend and nobody was going to take him away from me. I looked over at the time and saw I had a few extra minutes before I needed to get ready. So I reached down and took care of my hard on and then through the covers off. I got up and head towards the bathroom. While walking down the hallway wearing only my Joe Boxers, when my sister ran past me I asked her, "What is the rush, sis?"

"Just woke up late and need to get to school early today. Got this big project I need to work on," she said while running down the stairs.

"Ok well have fun with that," I said as I walked into the bathroom and shut the door behind me. I strip off my boxers and turned on the water. Making sure it was a not to hot, I hoped in and cleaned up. I dried off and wrap the towel around my waist and reached into the draw and pulled out a bush for my hair. I started to brush my shoulder length brown hair and was still thinking about last night with my boy, which got me hard again. "Damn it," I thought to myself "I do not have time now to get it down." I walked out of the bathroom and quick jetted to my room so nobody would see my towel was tented. Quickly shutting the door, I went over to my drawer and grabbed the first pair of underwear on top. They were a pair of black boxerbriefs.

As soon as they were on me, I walked over to the mirror and took a look at myself. Long thin legs and with a nice swimmers build, not really a jock but I have some really good genes or at least that is what everyone has told me.

I walk over to my closet and threw on some shorts and a short sleeve shirt. While walking down stairs, I saw the door close and then hearing my sister drive out of the driveway with the tires stretching. Turning the corner and seeing my mom in the kitchen, I asked, "Hey mom what is for breakfast?"

"Wow, you're not in a hurry like your sister. Well I guess I can make some eggs or something. I thought you would be in a rush as well," she answered a little shocked.

"Nope, no projects or work so I can take my time this morning," I told her and took a sit at the table.

"So how is your boyfriend?" she asked while making eggs in the frying pan.

"He is doing fine and I will be meeting him at school in a little bit but we did have a great time last night at the movies," I said with a sly grin. She finished making the eggs and sat down with me to talk a little more about how school and life was going. I finished my breakfast and got up and kissed her on the check. "Thanks for the eggs. I love you," I said to her as I started to exit the kitchen.

"Love you too sweetie," she said back to me.

I grabbed my backpack and said bye to my mom. I went out the door to my little beat up car. It was pea green ford pick up truck, hopped in and started her up. It sounded like she was ready to be buried and move on but I love her to death, so I will ride it to the ground before I bury her.

I get down the street when I get a text on my cell phone. It read: *Hey babe, hope you slept well and I'll see you at the spot.* I smiled and replied with a happy smiley face. I got to school and headed towards the spot. The spot was the area right next to theater. It was sort of a little private spot that I found last year while just wondering around school one day. It is good place to hide from the world or just get away from life for a little while. I got there and there was nobody around so I squeeze through the opening. It opened to a little alcove that was between the theater and gym.

I waited a few moments and then saw a shadow moving through the crack and then I heard "Jake, you there?" the voice said.

"Yeah, I am back here." I said back.

The shadow turned into a body and it was my boyfriend. He was average teenager, blond hair, blue eyes, swimmers build. I walked up to him and give him a kiss on the lips and then told him with a smile, "I missed you babe. I had a really fun time last night and would love to do it again."

"I had a good time last night as well. I was thinking that maybe we could do it again tonight if your not to busy?" he said with puppy dog eyes.

"I will have to check but I think it would be cool," I answered him and then kissed him again. We made out for like five minutes when we heard the bell. "Well guess we best be on are way. I do not want to be late again."

"Ok, one last kiss please," he said with same puppy dog eyes and quiver in his voice.

"How could I say no to that face," I kissed him more passionately and gave his crotch a squeeze as well. We squeezed through the passageway and said goodbye and see you at lunch. I was running to get to my class on the second floor of the building. I just made it through the doorway as the tardy bell rang and sat down next to my best friend Sarah.

"You were almost late again," she said while rolling her eyes at me. Then she looked at me and I am just glowing from last events of last night and this morning. "Jeez didn't you two get enough of each other last night? Well I guess if you're in love that does really not matter."

"I guess so but he is just so hot," I answered her with a goofy grin across my face. She has been my best friend since middle school. Sarah has long wavy hair and blue sparklingly eyes. She must be about five seven with a nice body that could just be like your average women that you see on the street. "So what did you do last night?"

"Me, I did nothing but homework and watch TV. Yeah I know so much fun mister I went out on a date with the one that every girl in the school wants. Why are the cute ones always gay?" she said sarcastically.

"I do not know but I guess I am just lucky," I told her while trying to hold my laughter in. The teacher started class and Sarah and I were just listening and passing notes back and forth to each other. The period went pretty quickly and the bell rang for the next period. We got up and walked out of the classroom together.

"Hey so what is going on for tonight?" she asked as we head down the hallway.

"Well I was going out with Eric. Did we have plans or something?" I asked and was hoping that I did not forget because I knew she would hit me if I did.

"Nope just wondering," she answered.

"How about we all go out tonight?" I said quickly.

"You sure, I mean I do not want to intrude on your guy's time," she said with a little worry in her voice.

"You would not be intruding, trust me. I will text him in my next period to make sure it is ok. So see you at lunch then?" I said and started walking towards my classroom.

"Yeah, see you at lunch," she said and walked the other way.

I got to my next class and sat down. Just as class started, I looked out the window and there was a guy dressed in black. He was in the courtyard and was just staring directly at me. I looked down at my desk and looked back up and he was gone. I thought that was weird but shrugged it off. I went back to what I was doing and reached into my pocket and whipped out my phone. I started to text when the teacher walked up to front of the room and started lecturing about some dead person that I thought was really boring.

I text Eric: *Hey babe I was wondering if Sarah could come along with us tonight. She really wants to hang out with the both of us.* I hit send and wait for a respond. Just as I put my phone into my pocket I felt it buzz. I got it out again and read the text. *That does not seem to be a problem, but as long as I can have some alone time with you some time tonight.* I smiled at the thought of what that meant and then text him back: *Sounds good sweetheart, love you and see you at lunch.*

I put the phone back in my pocket and it buzzed again. I pulled it out and it read: *Ok love you too and see you at lunch.* I put it away and tried to pay attention to history class but the teacher was so boring. So I just looked out the window and just started to daydream about what might happen tonight.

I thought about what to do tonight and a list started running through my head: miniature golf, swimming, arcades, just chillen at some ones house and watch a movie or two. I got pulled back to reality by the bell ringing. Quickly grabbing my backpack and walked outside. Good thing that my locker was right next to the class or I would have been late to my next class. As I was dropping off some books at my locker, I heard some people bulling a kid. I turned around and just yelled, "Hey, leave him alone!"

CHAPTER TWENTY-NINE

THEY STOPPED AND LOOKED UP AT ME. THEY STOPPED picking on the kid and walked over to me. One started to speak, "You're that gay kid that helps everyone out. Well why not help me out by getting on your knees." He looked around at his friends. They just laughed and enclosed me in middle of their circle.

"Well I guess I can help with that but I think your buddies and girlfriend would think you're a fag but if that is what you want I will be happy to help you come out of the closet," I told him with smirk. His friends busted up laughing after I said that.

"Shut up," was all he could say and he walked off all pissed off. His friends stayed around me as he walked away alone. "That was so funny," one of the guys said while lightly punching my arm. Then the guys around me walked away as well and I saw the kid that they were bulling after everyone had left.

I walked up to him and said, "Hey my name is Jake and I would not worry about them again. If they try anything they will have to answer to me," and extended my hand to shake his.

He did not say anything; just walked over to me and gave me a hug. Then I felt his head on my shoulder and that my shirt was getting a little wet. I looked down since he was a little shorter then me and saw some tears rolling down his face. He looked up at me and said, "Thank you and my name is Alex."

"Well it is nice to meet you Alex and if you need anything, I'm here to listen or lean a hand," I said then without saying a word he just let go and started walking off. I didn't notice Eric behind me and he touched my shoulder. I jump a mile and turned around in mid air. Then I noticed who it was "What the fuck? You scared the shit out of me."

"That was very nice of you to stick up for him. That is why I like you and why I don't want to let you go," he said with a grin on his face. He gave me a quick kiss then walked off to his class like nothing happened.

I ran to my class and did not make the tardy bell but the teacher was running late as well so no harm done. Since the teacher was running late he just threw on a movie and the class had to write a short paper on what we learned from that movie once it was finished. I really don't understand why teachers teach things that have not relevance to life sometimes.

Anyway the bell rang and I move on to my last class before lunch. It dragged even though the topic was pretty cool. The topic the teacher was talking about was Death in different cultures and how culture deals with death. As the teacher showed some slides and picture of this man dress in all black appeared on the screen, it looked a lot the kid I saw in the courtyard earlier in the day.

It did peak my interest but it was not exactly what I was hoping it would be. I took some notes and learned that death is not really anything to be scared of as long as you have no regrets when you die. The bell rang and I was happy since I was about to fall asleep. I went to my locker and dropped off my books and just as I shut my locker Sarah and Eric were there on both sides of me.

"Hey guys what up?" I said to both of them a little sheepishly.

"Not much. How were you classes?" Eric said.

"They were ok. We learned about death in my culture class." I told them. Then we all went walking outside to the benches under the tree and just started joking around when I notice Alex sitting by himself next to end of the building. I asked Eric and Sarah, "How about we go keep him company?" then pointed over to where Alex was.

"Sounds like a good plan. You're so sweet and thoughtful" Sarah said and faked kissed me.

"Yeah let's go before lunch is over," my boy said. So we got up and walked over to him and asked, "So anyone sitting here and would you like some company?"

He answered, "No but I would love some company."

With that said we all sat down and started making conversation with him. We chatted about school and other things nothing really to important. Then the bell rang and I kiss my boy goodbye and said, "I will see you both by my truck after school right?"

"We will be there," both said at the same time.

Then we all went our separate ways. I looked back and notice that Alex was following me. "Do you have gym now?" I asked him. He just nodded is head and continued walking behind me. "Now I know I have a cute ass but how about walking with me not behind me."

After I said that he sped up and started to walk with me. We talked through the doors to the lockers and he went to his locker and I went to mine. I changed quickly and went outside to the numbers were we took roll call.

I sat on the numbers when I looked up and saw that kid in black again. This time he was pointing to me and I started to get up and walk towards him and he just vanished. Again I thought it was weird but did not think too much about it.

The coach came out and said we were going to do some black top street hockey. After he brought out the equipment and we picked teams and I got stuck with most of the jocks and the one that I embarrassed in the hallway early.

Basically the game went on and every time I had the ball he would run over and body checked me. I did not fall down because I knew it was coming so the last time before the period was up I got the ball and I saw him running towards me. So I stopped and he went flying past me and into the fence that I was next to. He hit the fence and bounced back. He lost his balance and was falling down when I caught him with my foot underneath the back of his neck.

I tossed him back upon his feet and asked him, "Do you have a problem with me or is it in your nature to just pick on people that you do not understand?"

He did not answer and just walked away all pissed off again. The coach blew the whistle for us to go change and get ready for the next class. I walked into the locker room and notice that my locker was broken into. My lock that I had on there was cut and then my door was hanging on one hinge.

CHAPTER THIRTY

I WALKED UP TO IT AND THE WEIRD THING WAS THAT MY clothes were stolen but replaced with a completely new outfit. I put it on and it fit just perfect. It was a white jean shorts with a white v-neck shirt. It also came with a white pull over hoodie.

I walked outside the locker room and everyone notice my new outfit. Thinking it was just a little bit to showy but everyone thought it fit me just perfect. I went into my next class and just sat and listened to the teacher talk about how Shakespeare was a great writer and still is to this day. The bell rang and I was so happy to hear that sound.

I got up and walked to my locker. Grabbing what I needed out of my locker and then shutting it, then walked out to my car. I saw Sarah and Eric talking and leaning on my car as I walked towards them. They saw me walking up in my new white outfit.

"Wow that outfit is so you. When did you have time to change outfits babe," Eric said and then kissed me.

"It does look nice on you," Sarah said.

"Thanks I guess. It was weird, my locker in gym class was broken into and they stole my clothes but left these one in its place. I guess it was like a gift from heaven," I pause. "So we ready to head out and have fun?"

"I had been waiting for this all day sexy," Eric said.

"Me too, I have not hung out with the both of you guys in a long time," she said as she hoped into the old truck. Eric follow suit and I walked around to the other side and opened my door. I threw my stuff in the back seat with Sarah and hoped in. I started it up and we drove out of the parking lot.

"What is the plan, guys?" I asked driving down the street.

"Well, I think both of us are hungry and I am sure you could use a small bit to eat," Sarah said.

"Sounds good to me," I said.

We headed to Denny's down the street from the school. We sat down in a booth next to one of the windows. The waitress came and we placed our order. We started talking about the events that happened to us today. I told them about me seeing this kid dressed in all black and how the kid that was bullying Alex started bullying me in gym class and how I embarrassed him again.

Eric told us what happened to him at school and nothing much happened to Sarah. Yet the strange thing was that my boyfriend also saw the kid in black during his day at school. Sarah just gave us a confused look and then the waitress came back with our food. We thanked the waitress and just dug in like we have not been feed in days.

After eating we just sat around for a couple of hours and talk about everything and anything. Sarah looked down at her watch and noticed it was about seven thirty and she needed to be home by eight. "Hey guys, I need to go home," she said to us.

"Ok, let's pay the bill and get you home, darling," I told her. We got up and went to pay the bill. As we were walking to the car, Eric pulled me aside and said, "We are going to be alone for a little while after, right?"

"Hell yeah sexy," I said and kissed him on the lips when Sarah came back to see it.

"Hey guys, it is my ass if I do not get home on time. Plus you can do that after you drop me off," she said and grabbed both of us by the arm and dragged us towards the car.

"Sorry just do not get much time with him Sarah," Eric said as we all piled into the truck.

I floored it to get her home on time. We pulled up her driveway with ten minutes to spare. She bounced out of the car and then looked back in through the window. "See right on time darling," I paused and she gave me that look that I am going to kill you but in a fun way. "So, we will see you tomorrow at school?"

"Yeah and you boys don't get into to much trouble tonight," she said to us while getting out of the car.

"We would not even think about," we said with two big fat grins on our faces. We watched her go into the house and then we drove off. He started messing around with me while I was driving. He leaned over and started nibbling on my ear and a rub my inner thigh.

"Babe, I am trying to drive here, you do not want me to crash the car do you," I said to him seriously.

"No but I think your so cute when you try to be serious. I can not wait till you stop the car and I can have you all to myself," he said and sat back down in his seat.

I just smiled at that thought and pulled in the parking lot of the school since I know it is always empty late at night and nobody really drives by it. I looked at my watch and it was about eight thirty and turned off the engine. Then Eric leaned in and started to kiss me. I kissed him back and we were lost in thought and did not even notice the other car that pulled up to the spot right behind us.

CHAPTER THIRTY-ONE

WE WERE MAKING OUT WHEN A BAT CAME SMASHING through the window. Glass shattered inside and outside the car. A hand grabbing me and almost pulling me out through the window, I tried to open the door and hit the person grabbing me but it didn't work. I got pulled out of the car through the window and Eric was trying to get out and help but someone was leaning on his door.

I was being dragged across the parking lot. My back getting all torn up by the rough pavement, he dropped me about ten feet from my car and started to kick me. First one landed in my stomach and I grabbed his foot and use it as way to unbalance him. He tried to kick me off but instead he went down to the ground with me. I got up and so did he. I punch the attacker in the face and it felt like he had a mask on so when I tried to punch him again I missed and grab his mask instead. It came off.

It was the same guy from early today, the one from hockey and bullying Alex. Just as I pulled his mask off a third guy came up behind me and slammed the baseball bat across the middle of my back.

Losing my balance, I fell back on the ground. Eric then realized that nobody was guarding my side of the door. He crawled over the seat and got out my door. When he got out of the car he saw me get hit with the baseball bat. He went running to me but the guy with the baseball bat took one swing and hit Eric square in the guts. Eric fell down to his knees and was gasping for air.

I saw that and it just got me even more pissed. I went into a flying rage. I got up from the ground and tackled the guy with the baseball bat and knock it out of his hands. I was punching the guy on the ground when I felt four hands on my shoulders pull me back and holding me down on the ground. They let go of me and then the guy from earlier just started punching me all over my face and body, while the other one was kicking me. I was trying to protect myself but I was not able to cover my body. That's when the third guy got off the ground and grabbed his bat. He walked over and took one swing and landed square on the side of my head.

I was not moving after that hit. The three of them noticed that I was not moving and got scared. They ran over to their car and hopped in. They took off in a heartbeat. My head fell to the side and the last image that I saw was my boyfriend finally getting up and running over to me. I felt him on the side of me crying and weeping.

It seemed I was alive but was not able to move a single bone in my body. I felt everything that was happening to me. He pick up my body and started carrying, my now lifeless body. Blood dripping leaving a trail from where I laid to my truck, he opened the door and put me in there truck. "Babe, just hold on ok. Just hold on," I heard him saying to me as he got in the drivers seat. The truck started up and off to the closest hospital.

We got to the ER room and it was packed. Eric was carrying my body into the hospital and the nurse saw the blood dripping from my body and she came running up to him. She asked him, "What the hell happened? Here put him on the gurney." He put me on the gurney and the nurse rushed me into the Operation Room.

Eric sat down in the waiting area and then the nurse came up to him and asked, "So what happened? Can you fill these forms out and can we get a number to contact his parents?"

"Sure. He got gay bashed and I was there trying to help him but I got whacked as well but I am fine. The number to call is 555-4357. I will fill this out and give them back to you," he said a little teary eyed.

"Thanks," said the nurse and she walked off. The nurse called his mom and she came rushing down. When she got to ER she saw Eric sitting with his head in his hands. She walked over to him and tapped him on his shoulder. He looked up with tears in his eyes. He wiped them away and said, "Hey, I guess you heard the news. Sorry."

"What is the news? What happened?" she asked. So Eric filled her in on what happened that night. "Oh so you tried to help but also got beaten up. At least you tried and that is what counts now it is up to the doctors to finish him up."

She sat down next to him and just hugged her son's lover. The nurse came back and asked for the forms back. Eric handed her the forms and she walked away again without updating the family about me.

They laid me on the gurney and rushed me into the operating room. Over the PA system I heard "Paging Dr. Rush, Paging Dr. Rush." About a few minutes later a man dressed in black scrubs walked into the OR and was washing his hands.

"What do we got here?" he asked.

"Well looks like an old fashion beating, has been hit to the head with a wooden bat, been kick in the ribs, and used as a punching bag. Have liaisons on his up torso and arms. Has internal bleeding and does not seem to be responsive," the nurse finished saying and start to cut open my new white shirt which was now stained red.

The doctor was now just bending next to me. He whispered in my ear, "It is time for you to meet your destiny. It will be ok but this is going to hurt."

What the doctor did next was reached into the bag that he brought with him. He brought out a strange looking device that was like a long tube with a scalpel knife at the end. He made his first cut into the chest right below the rib cage. The knife went straight through my skin. I screamed but nothing came out.

The tube went into my body and then the tube stop a little before my stomach. He reached into the bag and turn on a switch. It started make some funny noises and then I felt a suction pulling at my coconscious. It felt like my soul was fighting to stay alive in this body but was being pull out of the body.

Soon I was standing over my body and Dr. Rush was the only one who noticed. The doctor told the nurses, "I got what I came for and now you can try to save him."

The nurses had a very confusing look on their faces and then Dr. Rush vanished with me and the real doctor came into the room. The cut were my soul was sucked out of had been healed. The doctors tried everything to get me back to life but after a few hours they declared me to bruised and the blow to my head with the bat was the thing that killed me.

The doctors came out and went to deliver the news to Eric and my mom. They both just broke down and started crying. I knew deep down that Eric was heart broken and my mom world was shattered. They got some consoling from the doctor and then both of them left and went back to my house.

Dr. Rush let me watch that scene and then after it was all over he popped back in. "Hey I know it is hard to lose everything but it is time to become part of destiny," he said to me with a sounding echo behind him.

I did not response back; I just did not know what to say. I fell to my knees and just started to weep. The Doctor sat right next to me rubbing my shoulder. I opened my mouth and asked with some angry in my voice, "Why me? Why now? You just came into my life and took everything away from me. Why should I trust the man that did not even give me a fighting chance?"

"Well for starters it was your time and I see you got my gift. I can grantee that you will see Eric again and everything should be fine at that time. You have been picked to become the person that you where suppose to be. Any more questions?" he answered seriously.

"Who are you? I have been seeing you all day and now you appear in front of me," I asked him with my fist starting to ball up.

"Well I am Ethan Rush and today I was warning you about him but I guess I need to work on my warnings, thing is I can not talk to you about your future but can warn people what is going to happen. Each time I appeared I was telling you to watch out. The last time I appeared you where making out with your boyfriend," Ethan said to me.

"Ok, I am dead and you want me to become something great. I don't think being dead will help me become great," I said to him and let go of the anger inside me.

"You really didn't want to do this I can send you back. How about this I'll show you what your destiny is and then you can decide if you want to or not." Ethan said.

"That does sound fair. If I decide not to, would you bring me back to life when I was in the OR," I asked him.

"Yep and you would not remember anything I told you. Your life will be just the way you left it. I do warn you that this is your one chance to become apart of destiny's fated plan and change the lives of everyone you meet," Ethan told me with smile on his face.

"Deal," I told Ethan. As soon as the words left my mouth we were in a place of complete darkness. Nothing could be seen for miles in any direction. I looked down and my clothes we all lit up. I looked over and saw Ethan's black outfit was also lit up.

"Welcome to the hallway of realms. A place where everything is connected, see each planet has different realms on it and we have gate keepers to help control the flow of who comes in and out of each realm. The one that was in charge of this realm just was promote to a different realm to be its keeper," he paused. "Before I get into more detail do you have any questions?"

"So far I understand what you are saying. For some reason it feels like I have been here before. Every time I dream it seemed like I was walking these halls to find something," I told Ethan.

"See destiny was just telling you that there might be something here that you are searching for or it just means you where meant to be here. Either way, I believe you were drawn here," he paused. "In these realms on Earth there are eight of them. What I want from you is to watch over these realms and make sure that the chaos and peace remain in balance of the other realms. That is all, minus the fine details," Ethan told me while walking down the lit path under our feet.

"Still, why me?" I asked curiously.

We stopped where we were and he turned towards me. "I choose you because you're the only one I saw fit for the job. You have great compassion for others, able to think on your feet, and know when enough is enough. Like when you were getting beaten up by those guys, first you were protecting yourself but when you saw Eric get hit you stopped thinking about yourself and just wanted to help him. That what makes you perfect for this job; that you think about others before you think about yourself," Ethan said to me and touched me on the shoulder.

"That is a very true but I do not know if I am ready for my destiny," I said.

"To be honest I truly do not think any one is really ready for their destiny but the funny thing about destiny is that when it does hit, everyone steps up to meet it and shines like nothing you ever seen," he answered back.

"Can I think about this?" I asked.

"Sure I will give you one day to think it over. Meet me tomorrow on the roof of the hospital and I will be waiting there at eleven o'clock at night," he told me and then we both vanished. I landed in my house and I was in spirit form.

I saw my mom and Eric sitting at the table. Neither of them were talking just sort of lost in their thoughts, so I just floated right next to them. I tried touching Eric and I went straight through him. I have seen movies with ghosts in them but I did not think it was really how they were.

Eric started to talk, "I should have been able to help him out more. I wish I tried harder. Bet he's in a better place and still thinking of others."

Mom spoke up, "Don't blame yourself. You did the best you could and that is all that is asked of you at least in my eyes. You didn't run and hide or worse joined in. So stop beating yourself up, the person you should be blaming is that jerk from school. He only did this because he didn't understand my boy or he is just scared little faggot. He was just jealous because he had to work for his glory and my son was just a natural at it. Do you want to spend the night in his room and feel free to take anything you want," she said to Eric.

"Thanks, I don't know if I want anything but I would love to sleep in his room one last time," Eric said and then went up to change into his PJ. I followed him up and watched him stripped down to his boxers and hop into my bed. As soon as his head hit the pillow he was out like a light.

CHAPTER THIRTY-TWO

I thought to myself that maybe I could enter his dreams like in the movies. "Well here goes nothing," I said and jumped into his body and you know what, it worked. I was in his dream. He was dreaming of the event that just happened. After he got hit, I got next to him and tapped him on the shoulder.

He turned around and was ready to punch me but he saw it was me standing behind him. He hugged me and then started to cry. Under the tears I heard him say, "I miss you so much. I don't want you to go. Please tell me this was all just a bad dream."

"Babe, I miss you too and I would love to tell you it was just a dream but it is not. I need to talk to you about something," I said to him seriously.

"What is it?" he asked me while trying to hold back his tears.

"Well I have been given this destiny task to become something great and help everyone out but if I take it I will get to see you again some time in the future. If I don't take it then I'll be able to come back to you and live again. I really don't know what to do babe?" I told him as a tear rolled down my cheek. The scene of me getting beat up changed to just a black room with a spot light on us.

"Well I want to be with you too but then again helping people out has always been something you want to do. I want to be with you but if you say that we will see each again, I can wait. Plus you'll probably be able to watch me from where you are going. I say do the destiny thing and we will meet again. I will be waiting for you my love," he said then kissed me.

"That does make sense. I'll get to see you again and then we will be able to be with each other at that time from what the man in black said," I told him.

"You met the man in black and he told you this. I bet the man in black is a really cool guy. I see that you outfit is all white except instead of a hoodie it is now a white trench coat. I'll miss you and always love you babe. See you later in life," he said and kissed me and woke up in a cold sweat. A couple of tears rolled down his cheek.

He was not able to go back to sleep so he went to go take a shower and get ready for school. I was just floating around inside my house and knew I was not going to waste my time that I had left before my choice. I decided to make my attacker pay big time for the shit he did to me and for the pain he put my friends and family through.

The sun rose up and I was just waiting in front of the guy's house. When he stepped outside, I saw my chance to control him. As he was walking to his car, I was waiting in the car and he got into his car and sat on me. I merge with him and then the fun began.

Just as he was pulling his car into the parking lot, Ethan appeared in front of me. He asked, "What are you doing?"

"I'm getting a little payback for him killing me. Is there something wrong with that?" I snapped back at him.

"No, there is nothing wrong with that but I warn you that Hate is a powerful thing and I hope it is out of your system when you take the role of gate keeper," he told me.

I told him, "This well get it out of my system and I take it you know my answer is yes I'll become the gate keeper. So let me have some fun with this guy and then I'll be ok."

"Have fun and meet me at the spot tonight," he said and vanished. I hoped back into his body and the first thing he did was go to his locker. He started taking books out of his locker and then turned around. For some odd reason, Alex was standing right behind him.

"What do you want faggot?" he said nastily.

"Just to say I think you hot and I want to ask you out," Alex said.

Just before he said something I took control of his voice and said "Sure I'll go out with you but first I need to say something to everyone. Hey guys, I need to say something. I'm gay and I don't care what people think about me and I want to apologize to everyone that I hurt. Now Alex lets go to the bathroom so I can service you."

I made him grab Alex's hand and they both walk off to the closest bathroom. They enter the bathroom and Alex was now completely overwhelm and was just standing there in disbelief. I started taking completed control of the guy and push him in the handicap stall and locked the door behind us. I got down on my knees and reached out and undid his jeans. They fell to the floor and pulled his shirt over his head. Leaving him in just a pair of red boxerbriefs, he finally came back from his disbelief and just in time too. I was reaching up to pull down his underwear and he pushed my hand away. "I thought this is what you wanted, sexy," I said.

"No, this is not what I want. I wanted something more then just sex. So I think you should better leave, I don't want to go out with you," he told me.

I got up off my knees and left the bathroom. I stepped out of the guy's body and walked back into the bathroom to listen to Alex. Alex started talking, "I thought that would be great then I realized that sex is not everything. I am going to start living like Jake. By the way where is he today? Oh well I am going to change and tell him the next time I see him."

I just thought to myself, good for him. I knew he would do that so I just didn't want to push him too far to fast but I know he will be a great person someday. I didn't see Eric at school and I was hoping he would see that. Since I couldn't find him at school, I went over to his house.

I found him in his room just sitting on the bed holding the stuff dog that I got him last year for his birthday. I looked up and asked, "Could I just say goodbye to him. It is just that I did not get a chance to do it last night in his dream because he woke up too fast."

"Sure. I will allow it," Ethan told me. I started to reappear in his room.

"Hey babe, it is really me this time, I came back to say goodbye. If you want I can stay for a little while," I said while walking over to him.

"Is that really you, Jake? Was that dream real or was it just my head playing tricks on me?" he asked softly.

"It was real," I said and I sat down next to him and hugged him. I took his head and put it up against my chest and started rubbing his head. "It was real, babe. I want your blessings before I make any final decisions. So I guess, I got this great destiny but I want to be with you. I love you and never want to be apart but the man in black said we will see each other again down the road but I do not know how long that might be. So what do you think I should do?"

"Well I know you and I know you will make the right decision. I think you should go for it like I said in the dream. I can wait for you and bet you will be popping in from time to time to see how I am doing. Since it seems that you will become this powerful figure that watches over the world, I just know you will be great," he said and then leans over to kiss me.

I kiss him back and did not let go of him for a good two hours. We just cuddled and remained in each others arms. I looked over at the time and it was not even noon yet. "Hey babe do you want to go do something or do you want to stay like this till I have to go?" I asked him.

"I just want to stay like this till you go," he told me. So we just cuddled for the next couple of hours. Time past so slowly and I was thankful for it. This memory will last with me till we meet again. I got up about an hour before eleven.

"Do you want to come with me?" I asked.

"I don't think I would be able to see you leave for a second time. I will walk you to the door and say see you later, sexy," he said. So we got up and he walked me to the door. "Well babe, I will see you later sexy."

"I will see you later, my sexy boyfriend," I said to him and faded through the doorway. As I was walking to the hospital, I started thinking about how this was the greatest day of my life. I could have not pictured it any better.

I made it to the hospital roof just at the strike of eleven. Sure enough Ethan was standing there, dressed as a doctor all in black.

"So what is your answer my friend?" he asked me even though he knew already.

"Yes, I will do it and thanks for the awesome day," I said to him and smiled.

He just smiled at me and walked up to me. We started to walk towards the end of the building and both took one step off the edge. We vanished into thin air.

CHAPTER THIRTY-THREE

EVERYTHING HAS A POINT. EVEN US HUMAN BEINGS, I didn't know that at that the time of my awaking but it seemed more important now then it did back then. If you don't believe in destiny, that's fine by me but here, is some proof that everything happens for a reason.

It all started on Friday night, Anthony, Ty and I were going to the Limelight club in downtown Mountain View. I was getting ready to go clubbing when I pause to look in the mirror. I was your average teenager, blond hair, blue eyes, swimmers build, and a little shorter then most people. I went to my closet and threw on a nice silk blue shirt and some black jeans, kissed my parents good night and told them, "I'm going to be home late."

"Ok son. We'll leave a light on for you," they said as I walked outside. The weather was a little bit cold but nothing to major to bother anyone. Just cold enough to make a small shiver, I got to my car and started it up.

I started to drive over to Anthony's house to pick him and Tony up for the night. I got to his house and he opened the door with a big smile across his face. He's a little taller them me with black spiky hair and deep green eyes.

"You guys ready yet?" I asked him while making my way to his room.

"Yeah almost ready, let me just call Ty to tell him we're on our way," he told me while picking up his phone.

"Let's go, he is ready," he told me.

"Ok," I said as I got up off his bed.

He told his parents that he was going and we hopped into my car and drove down the street to Ty's house. Ty was waiting on the street curb as we drove up to his house. Just a little bit taller then Anthony, black spiky hair and dark blue eyes that you could stare at for hours and he stood up as we pulled in front of him.

"Hey guys, ready for a wild and crazy night," he said as he jumped into the car.

Anthony said excitedly, "Hell ya we are ready." Off we went towards the club. While in the car, we chatted about everything and anything on the way to the club. We got there and found parking about a block away from the club. We got out and grab some small stuff to take with us to the club.

"Hey guys, is Tony going to meet up with us?" I asked while walking.

"I think so," Ty answered.

"Yeah he is. He should already be inside," add Anthony.

We got to the door of the club and the first bouncer checked our Id's. Then a second bouncer padded us down to make sure we didn't have any weapons or anything, paid the fee and went into the club. It was packed. It was an old theater before it was transformed into a night club, so the space was not that big. It had two rooms. The first room had a bar and coat check that had two doors leading into the next room which had the dance floor and another bar.

In the dance room there were stairs that went up to a small second floor balcony. On the second floor there were a few couches and sitting space so you can make-out or just sit and watch the dance floor below.

I spotted Tony dancing with a few girls and I point him out to the others. We made our way over to him and we said, "Hello."

"What took you guys so long? I have been here for at least an hour," he said over the loud music.

Ty replied, "Sorry got caught up with parents doing chores for them or I wouldn't be able to go out tonight."

"I see. I know how that goes. So Eric did your parents leave already for the weekend?" Tony asked.

"Yeah they left about the same time I went to pick these guys up," I answered.

"Cool. Would it be alright if I crashed at your place tonight?" they all asked me at once.

"I see no problem with that. Why are we talking when we can be dancing and trying to get with new people?" I said to them and walked off to another part of the dance floor to dance.

The night went on and we were dancing through it all. It was about eleven when I went to the side of the club for a little rest. I found a sit and noticed Ty dancing with a girl and so was Anthony. I was looking around for Tony when I decided to get a better view of the dance floor. So going up the stairs, that is where I found Tony making-out with one of the girls that he was dancing with when we came in.

I just smiled at him and then went back downstairs and became a wallflower. I knew that these guys would be at this for another couple of hours, so I went outside to get a breath of air.

As I went outside, the bouncer stopped me and said, "No in and outs."

"Ok," I said back to him and just continued to walk past him. I walk out to the street and since the club was near a train station and I decided to start walking towards it. As I started walking, my mind started thinking about some really weird images. The images started battling one another. Even stranger was that each image was a piece of my body. Well I got lost in my thought and bet if I wasn't lost in my thought I would have noticed it.

Down the street before I started walking, a gentleman was getting in his car and just had a fight with his girlfriend a few minutes before that. In a rage, he started to drive off. Still pissed off he didn't notice the kid walking out into the street at the time.

All I heard was a screeching tires and the smell of brake dust. I got hit by the truck and went flying about five feet into the air. I landed on the sidewalk with a thud and the last thing I remember was the guy rushing out of his truck and starting to go in a panic state.

He picked me up and put me in the back of his truck and drove to the nearest hospital. Luckily it was just up the street from the nightclub. Still in a panic, he rushed through the doors with me in his arms and yelled, "I need help, I just hit this kid with my truck and I think he is still alive. I need help."

The nurse ran up to him with a stretcher and quickly told him, "Lay him down here and we'll take care of him." Then you see a doctor dressed in all black come through the double doors. He walked up to where I laid and just signaled the nurse to follow him. The nurse followed him back through the double doors and vanished once the doors to the emergency room swung closed.

The man waited and waited for hours till the nurse came back through the double doors. The nurse saw that the man was still waiting there and walked over to him. She tapped him on the shoulder and told him, "He'll be fine."

"That is great news can I go sit with him till he wakes up," he asked her with some tears rolling down his cheek.

Back at the club, it was midnight and Tony, Ty, and Anthony went looking for me. They didn't find me on the dance floor or up on the second floor so Ty went outside and walked to where the car was parked while the others still searched inside the club.

Ty got there and my car was still parked there. Ty called Tony and Anthony up on his cell. "His car is still here," he told Anthony.

"Well he has to be here some where. Can you go walking around outside just in case he might have gone for some fresh air?" Anthony asked.

"Sure, I'll go check around out here and did you check the bathrooms in there?" Ty asked back.

"Nope but we'll go check them and he is not picking up his phone since we tried it twice," he said and hung up the phone.

They all searched a little while more and then it started to get a little late. Since they were not able to find me and needed to get home, they thought it would be cool if they hitched a ride with Tony since he drove and they would call me in the morning to find out what happened.

Back at the hospital, the gentleman called his girlfriend to say he was sorry and tell her what happened. He said that he would be here till morning if I didn't wake up sooner. I was laying there and my cell phone rang.

The gentleman decided to answer it, "Hello."

"Hello is Eric there?" the voice asked curiously.

"Eric who?" the man asked back.

"Who is this?" the voice asked the man.

"My name is Dante. Eric must be the name of the kid I hit with my truck. Who am I talking to?" Dante asked.

"I am James. One of his best friends, which hospital is he at?" James said with a little worry in his voice.

"He is at the El Camino Hospital. Are you coming?" Dante stated.

"Yeah, I am. Are you going to be there when I get there?" James asked.

"I'll wait for you," Dante said.

They both hung up the phone and just before dawn broke; James reached the hospital and asked one of the nurses at the front desk, "Where is Eric Shawl?"

The nurse looked up at him and then back down at her charts. She replied, "He is in room 209."

James thanked the nurse and ran off to room. It was located on the second floor of the hospital. He opened the door to room 209 and saw his friend lying in bed with tubes all over the place. He ran over to the bedside and then noticed Dante seating in the corner. "You must be Dante. Thanks for helping him and not running away like everyone else would do," James said to Dante thankfully.

"You welcome. Can you do me a favor, when he wakes up have him call me," Dante reaches inside his pocket and pulls out a business card. He hands him a business card. Then he collects his jacket off the chair and walks out the door. James puts the card on the side table and kneeled down towards Eric's body that lied before him. He grabbed Eric's hand and started to cry a little bit.

Eric's phone rings again. "Hello," James answered it.

"Hey, is Eric there?" the voice answered.

"He can not make it to the phone. Who is this?" James asked.

"It is his friend, Anthony. We went clubbing last night and I just want to make sure he is alright," Anthony said.

"Well, he is not alright. He got hit by a car and now his life is a little blip on a screen," James said in a teary voice.

"Where is he? I'll be right there," Anthony said as he waits for an answer.

James told him what hospital he is at and the word spread fast and soon his phone was ringing off the hook. It seemed like the entire school was calling him that morning. About a half hour later, Anthony showed up with Ty and Tony in tow.

Anthony walked up to my bedside and says, "What were you doing outside the club and not paying attention. I am sorry that I was not paying any attention to what was going on or I would have been there with you. I wonder what was going on in your head to make you not see the car coming," he said.

"It is not your fault," James said. "Hey, do you guys mind staying with him. I need to go change and grab someone. I'll be back within the hour or so."

"Yeah, we don't mind keeping him company. Go, get some rest and come back we'll be here watching over him," they said and just took a seat around the bed.

James left the room and they all sat in silence around my bed. Each lost in their own thoughts. Each wishing they were there to help me out.

About an hour had passed and James returned with his girlfriend. "Thanks for keeping him company. You guys can go if you like, we'll watch over him now," he told them.

"Yeah we'll go but if there is any changes please call us," they said as each of them left the room.

CHAPTER THIRTY-FOUR

JAMES TOOK A SIT NEXT MY BED AND HUNG HIS HEAD SO NO one can see him cry. He slowly reached up and grabbed my hand. His girlfriend is rubbing his back to comfort him. You heard him in a soft whisper, "Hey friend, I know you're strong and I know you will pull through this. I'll be here for you when you wake up. I'm not going to leave your side till you make it out of this little trip in your life. Just wake up and we can do everything like we use to do."

James and his girlfriend sat in silence when James felt my hand squeeze his. James looked up from the floor and saw that my eyes were open. I started to freak out a little but then I turned my head to the side and saw James sitting there next to me. I started to relax after I saw his face. I tried getting up but was too weak and fell back down onto the bed.

"What happen?" I asked slowly not remembering a thing and looking at my surroundings.

"As far as I know you got hit by a truck and Dante, the one that hit you, brought you here," he said wiping the tears from his eyes. "He left at dawn and told me to tell you to call him when you feeling a little better."

"Ok but where is here?" I asked looking around.

Just as I finished asking him, the nurse came in. "I see you have woken up from your little nap, Eric. So I guess I must start taking you stats," the nurse said. She started to ask the entire normal question routine about name address and insurance. I answered to the best of my knowledge. Then she took my blood pressure and did the flashlight shinning in my eyes check. She wrote down her findings and when she was done, she said, "The doctor will be in shortly."

"That was odd," I said to James and his girlfriend.

"Yeah, she seemed a little less friendly then normal. I thought nurses were here to cheer the patient up not just rush them along their way. Oh well maybe she is having a bad day." James said and paused. "So we are so glad you're awake. I was so sacred and just didn't know what to do without you to keep me out of trouble. What were you thinking to make you not pay attention?"

"I was having a weird daydream about my body parts fight this darkness. It was like my body parts were representing things that are inside all of us. There were eight things. I am starting to remember it now. The eight things were love, friendship, hate, happiness, sadness, laughter, loneliness, and peace. It was the strangest day dream I've had in a long time." I told them while thinking back to it.

"Well you will get better and we will all just be fine," James said.

The day went on and James, his girlfriend and I were just laughing and having a good time while I rested and waited for the doctor. There came a knocking on the door.

"Come in," I said with laugh.

"Hello, my name is Doctor Rush," he said. He was dress in all black scrubs. I thought it was a little out of place for a doctor to be wearing all black in a hospital. "I see you're awake but I thought you would be out for a few more hours. Anyway, the nurse told me that you seem to be doing fine. I see no real need to keep you here so you'll be able to go home tomorrow."

"Thanks doc. I hopefully I get better but just one question. Why are you dressed in all black?" I curiously asked.

"Well I'm not your normal doctor. I'm an on call doctor and this is the color that best suits me. I just wanted to be different then the rest of the hospital, so I really don't belong here. Plus it was the only color left that I didn't need to wash," he said with a smile.

"Oh ok," I said thinking that it made some sort of sense.

"I'll be back in a little bit to check up on you," Dr. Rush said.

"Ok doc. Hope you have a good day," I told him.

He leans in and whispers in my ear, "Time to become awakened." Then he walked out of the room. I still think I have a strange doctor but didn't pay much attention to it. I went back to talking to James and his girlfriend.

About an hour later, I was getting a little tried and asked if they would stay with me for the night. James said he would but his girlfriend had to go home. I said my goodbyes as they left the room. He walked her out to his car and they both got in. He drove her home and they kissed goodbye. I fell fast asleep just after they left.

James came back and walked into my room to notice that I had fallen asleep. He just sat in the room and watched some TV. A couple of hours passed; James started to notice my body start to twitch. He paged for the doctor but his nurse came running in.

My body was now flopping like fish on the bed. It looked like I was fighting and getting the crap kicked out of me. Something on the inside of my body was kicking my butt.

CHAPTER THIRTY-FIVE

THE NURSE RAN OUT THE DOOR TO PAGE DR. RUSH AND to get him in there ASAP. The doctor in black came in with a small pad that was hook up to a television set. He did not talk; he just cut open the gown and placed the pad over my heart. My tossing and turning stopped as soon as he placed the pad on my chest. He hit the power button on the TV and the screen went black for a few moments then turn to a pink back drop. The doctor looked up to James and the nurse and says, "Just watch the screen. It looks like this is going to be interesting."

On the screen, body parts start to appear out of nowhere. Above each of them have a title of one of the eight things that Eric said early. It went as follow: left arm: hate, right arm: friendship, left leg: sadness, right leg: happiness, his soul: love, heart: loneliness, face; laughter. Each was doing its own thing when the darkness came out from the background. The pieces noticed it and got together to talk.

Laughter said with a chuckle, "I think we should just fight it like everything else that we come across."

Sadness said with a sigh, "I do not think so. We will just lose and not win. Each time we fight I just get more depressed."

Happiness smile and told them, "Don't listen to him, he is always like that. I say we try to cheer it up. It seems to be very dark."

Friendship cheerfully asked, "Can we make it our friend?"

Hate said angrily, "We need to get rid of it. It does not belong here."

Love said passionately, "I think that I am falling for it. Guys we better do something about it or I'll just love it to death."

Loneliness said with sorrow in his voice, "Do what you want I don't care."

The darkness started to move towards the group of body parts and the parts broke up and tried something different. As the darkness move around, the ground it touched was turning to black.

First up was friendship. It went up to it and started talking to see if it wanted to be a friend to him and the group. The darkness just ran over it as if it wasn't even there. Then the strangest thing happened. The doctor was not looking on the screen but at Eric. James and the nurse looked at Eric and noticed that Eric's right arm started to vanish into thin air.

James asked franticly, "What's going on?"

The doctor didn't answer. Just looked back at the screen with his eyes starting to narrow if he was ready to see what would happened next. Next up was happiness, it tried to cheer up the darkness like it said and the darkness didn't want to listen and ran it over as well. The gang looked over at his body and his right leg vanished.

Next up was Laughter. It ran up to the darkness, and fought it the only way it knew how. It started to tell jokes at the darkness which was now starting to grow in size after taking down the other two. Laughter said right before he got eaten, "I guess I was not that funny."

Laughter was gone and then Eric's head vanished, then the darkness started to take form of the body parts that it had eaten up. So the right side and a head had formed. It went directly to sadness and just ate it up so fast we didn't even noticed it was gone.

Next Hate made a weapon from the walls, which looked like a sword. The battle between Darkness and Hate was a good one to watch. Every time the sword would hit the Darkness, dark streams would shoot out. When the dark streams would touch the walls and ceiling, it would change the color from pink to black.

While they were battling love came up with the idea that it just needed a great big hug. So it walked up behind the darkness and hugged it. Hate saw that as a chance to get a really good blow to the Darkness. Just as Hate raised his sword, it saw that Love was getting sucked into the darkness and on the outside that Eric's body/soul vanished along with Love on the screen.

All that was left was his heart and his left arm on the screen. Hate was starting to get some really great strikes and got the Darkness backed up into the corner of the area. James started cheering for Hate to kill the Darkness.

The one thing you need to know about darkness is that is doesn't play fair. By the time that darkness was cornered it had covered all but two spots. The two spots were where Hate and Loneliness were. As Hate was going to strike darkness, darkness vanished and appeared behind Hate and took his own hand and stabbed him with his now like sword; then Hate dropped his sword and was devoured by the Darkness.

Now on the bed where Eric once lied were just his heart and the outline of his veins pumping away. The darkness now looked like a twin brother of Eric on the screen. It started to creep up on Loneliness. Loneliness looked up and saw the darkness. Loneliness started to talk, "I guess you think that you have it all but you are missing one thing. That is not me but nothing is completely dark. Their will always be light. James if you can hear this and want to save your friend, just believe in everything he has told you."

Just as the last word left Loneliness's mouth, he was destroyed by the darkness and Eric's heart vanished. The screen went complete black like the pictured died. On the screen it had the little dot of light but everything else was black.

James fell to his knees and started to cry. Then a voice came out of the screen, "Just remember what he told you before he went into his sleep."

Darkness started to speak, "Where did that voice come from? I'll find it and destroy it." The voice sounded a lot like Dr. Rush. The Darkness was thinking because it went quiet and nothing but that small dot of light was on the screen.

The Doctor turned to James and said, "What are you going to do?"

James was silent for a moment and then spoke, "I guess I have nothing to do but believe in the lessons that he taught me."

So James walked over to the bed and got down on his knees, repeating the eight most powerful things. "Loneliness is your heart, love is your soul, the hand you shake with is friendship, the opposite hand is hate, the foot you lead off with is happiness, the opposite is sadness, and the face is laughter," James said.

"I think you're missing one just like the darkness," Dr. Rush told James.

"Is that you, Ethan Rush?" the darkness snarled.

"Yeah that is me. I take it my reputation has traveled over the past years. What are you doing in this kid's body?" Dr. Rush asked.

"I knew you would not leave this kid alone so I'm here to take over this body and use it when I transform. I know I am missing one piece but your friend's friend will never figure it out before I do. "Ha, Ha, Ha," the Darkness said with an evil laugh.

"Well, I'll tell you what if my friend here figures it out before you, I'll have Eric fight you and trap you." Dr. Rush said to the Darkness with grin.

"Well I guess I'll take that bet but what do I get when I win?" Darkness asked all cocky and full of his self.

"You'll get the boy's body as you wish without any restrictions." Dr. Rush said.

"Deal," Darkness told Dr. Rush with eagerness in its voice.

CHAPTER THIRTY-SIX

THE ROOM WENT QUIET AFTER THAT. JAMES WAS LOOKING at Dr. Rush with a confused look on his face. Then went back to thinking what that last piece of the puzzle is. That's it, peace. The last thing that he is missing is peace of mind.

A small flash back to Eric saying Peace which is always hard to find because you will always have something puzzling you or confusing you.

"Peace of mind!" James yells out.

Then a flash of light on the screen appeared and vanished back to the black screen. The Darkness screamed out, "No, how can that kid figure it out before me."

Dr. Rush just smiled and point to screen. James got up off his knees and walked over to the screen.

On the screen it was still black and then we started to see a figure in the darkness. The figure was huge. It looked like a chimera. The head was of a dragon, strong and proud, the body of a lion, courageous, and a tail of a snake, quick and cunning but one thing that stood out was the wings. They were of no animal but of angel. One was white and the other was black. The screen light up with the presence of the new beast on screen. The Darkness was now in the light and the background was black and white so we could see the impressive beast.

Dr. Rush, "So I guess I win. Now meet your doom Anubis, lord of darkness and the underworld. Say hello to Anubis, ES."

ES screeched at Anubis and started to take flight with its angel wings. Anubis dodged the flight tackle and was starting to regain control of the darkness that was still covering some of the area and was trying to making everything dark again so his power would grow. The screen went black again because Anubis was very quick.

Once again you heard laughter but it was not coming from Anubis this time. "I'm free and thanks to my friends and Ethan, I'll trap you Anubis. I guess you have forgotten me old friend. I see your still using your old tricks and it will not work against me," said the voice. Then a flash of light came out of the darken screen and the entire screen was blinding. James and the nurse had to shield their eyes but Ethan just stared at the screen.

Ethan whispered, "Finish him off ES." Then the brightness died down and the screen was all white and Anubis was just standing still in the middle. James looked around and Dr. Rush was no where to be found. James looked back at the screen and Anubis was looking up at ES.

"I guess you like to play games, my old friend. Well this time the game is over and you'll lose. Time to seal you away so you'll never come back," ES said. Then he started chanting and his wings start to glow. Thread like silk shot out of the wings and ensnare Anubis. They started to spin a web around him and then you heard ES chanting again but a different spell this time.

Just as ES finished his chant Anubis was trapped in a round stone coffin, ES grabbed it and flew off the screen to imprison him some where, were nobody would ever find him.

James was wondering what exactly just happened. Then he heard a noise behind him, he turned around and saw that Eric was back lying on his bed. Eric slowly waking up and said, "What happened? I feel like my body just completely died and then was reborn."

James told me what happened word for word. Then the nurse came in and told James, "Visiting hours was over and that I needed my rest."

James said to me, "I'll see you tomorrow and pick you up since you'll be able to go home."

I smiled at him. Then he and the nurse walked out the door. I tried to get some sleep after all that had happened.

In the middle of the night, I had to use the restroom. I got up and went in the bathroom and when I exited the restroom, Dr. Rush was in the room.

I screamed a little then said, "You really need to stop doing that. Knock or something so I would have known somebody is in the room."

"I didn't use the door. I came in through the window and now I'm here to train you a little bit on your new powers."

"What powers? That was all just dream in my head. I don't have wings or a sleeping beast within me," I said to the doc.

"Well the beast is no longer asleep and I need to train you on flight and bringing out your wings and the rest you'll mostly be self trained," Dr. Rush said and then stared out the window.

"I guess I have no choice in the matter do I?" I asked.

"You always have a choice. It's just that your choice to become the Eternal Spirit was pushed upon you when Anubis wanted the powers that you held within. It was fight or die and you chose to fight. That happened when you told

James to find the last piece of the eight. So I'm here to help you fly and control your wings," he said.

"Ok," is all I could say, then Dr. Rush opened the window and grab my hand and we flew out the window. "I don't see your wings. Where are they?" I asked.

"Just look. I can make them invisible and only people like us can see them," he answered. I looked back and saw them and they were huge. We landed in a park that was down the street. I was still wondering why we were in the open area where someone might be able to see us.

"It is time to release your wings. All you got to do is think about it and they'll come out," he told me.

I took off my shirt because I didn't want to rip it or anything. I was thinking to myself wings appear, wings appear. Nothing happened. "What am I doing wrong?" I asked.

"So are you believing in your wings or are you just thinking about your wings?" he answered.

"What is the difference?" I asked with confused look on face.

"Just think about your wings is ok but believing in your wings makes it happen. When one believes in something it will happen as to just think about it makes squat," he said seriously.

"Ok, I'll believe in my wings and not just think about them," I said. I closed my eyes and started to think about my wings and just then I knew they where there. I opened my eyes and still nothing. Then I felt the most horrible pain in my life. It felt like someone taking a wound and ripping it open for the world to see.

On my back, where my shoulder blades where their started getting cut opened and then they split apart, the cut was about ½ inch wide and three inches long. I was hunched over and in so much pain. The wings started to come out.

First the bone and then the bones had blood soaked feathers. It ended and Rush was applauding.

"That was so painful. Why didn't you tell me how painful it is?" I asked with tears rolled down my cheeks.

"If it told you, would you believe me and I need to tell you once a year you will shed you feathers and grow new ones. It is just as painful if not more. Now we need to learn how to control them with just thought and make it like how you use your hands in an instance," he told me and just flapped his wings a couple of times.

I was looking at my wings, my left one was white and my right was black. They just hung there like floppy dog ears. I guessed it just takes focus and more concentration to get these things to go. Then I reached back and grabbed one wing in each hand and start to flap them myself. Yet nothing happened.

Rush was just busted up laughing when I looked over at him. "Well I'll give you an A for trying on your own but I just need to connect your wings to you brain and then you will be able to control them with much ease." He walked over to me and puts out his finger and touches my left wing and draws a line to the middle of my neck. Then he moved over to my right wing and draws a line to connect to the middle of my neck and then draws the rest of the line up to my brain to finish the connection. "Give it a shot," he told me and backed away.

I just start walking and I started to flap my new wings and started to take flight. Rush was beside me and coaching me. "Just go slow at first then we can move faster and faster. How does it feel?" he asked.

"It feels fine and it is like I knew how to do this all the time but didn't have the means," I told him with smile.

"Then it is coming back to you, Eric. That is good to hear you say that so soon, you'll know all your powers and tricks soon enough. Let's head back," he said to me and took a sharp left.

"Ok," I said and followed him. Then we both flew back to the open window of my hospital room. I landed in the room on top of my bed and he stayed outside. "You're not staying?"

"I have to go but I'll be back and if you need me for anything just fly on up. See that star on Orion's belt; just fly in that direction and I'll meet you in the sky over there anytime day or night. It was nice to see you again, Eric. Tell anybody you want to, it is not a secret but just be careful of the people that want the power within," he told me and started to fly off.

"Ok. What am I suppose to do with these powers?" he yelled.

"Whatever you see fit. The choice is yours like you wanted. Have fun, be a kid and enjoy life with the new power. Don't forget about the power of eight and it will always guide you," he yelled back as he flew off into the night.

I started to think after he left, what to do with all this power and how the wings will affect my life from now on. I realized that I was tired and it was not a dream. So I fell asleep about four in the morning and woke up to James shaking my shoulder.

"Is it morning already?" I asked while slowly waking up.

"Yeah it is, sleepyhead, Ready to go home," James asked.

"Yeah let's go," I said. I got dressed and we walked out of the hospital. I asked him, "Want me to fly you home."

"No but if you think you can fly go ahead and try superman," he said jokingly and leaned against his car.

I tossed my shirt at him and brought my wings out. It still hurt a little but not as much as last night. Right before I took off I said, "I'll see you at home."

CHAPTER THIRTY-SEVEN

On one of my quests for the gods, it brought me to Las Vegas. I met two interesting people down there, one that would change the idea of what I am doing and the other to give me the chance to really prove what I had on the inside.

On a humid Saturday morning, in the suburbs of Las Vegas we heard, "Marko, it's time to get up," the voice downstairs yelled at him. Marko kicked the blanket of his warm body. Laying there in his black gym shorts and the waistband of his ck underwear just above them, he start to fall back to sleep.

Knock, Knock, Knock. "I am up, I am up," Marko said to the person on the other side of the door in a groggily voice. Then you heard footsteps slowly going away from the door. Marko got out of bed and walked over to his dresser. Looking at him self in the mirror, we see a reflection of a fit slender man, short black hair, standing about five feet nine inches and deep blue eyes.

He drops his gym shorts and puts on a pair of black tight jeans and a black shirt with some logo on it, then decides to go with a hat today before heading off to work. As he opens the door of his room, he hears the front door closing. He thought to himself, "I wonder why she was in a hurry this morning." Not really giving any more thought to the matter, he slides down the banister of his house and goes into the kitchen.

Grabbing a quick bite to eat and heading out the door. His eyes started hurting from the bright sunlight; he reached into his jean pocket and puts on a pair of dark D & G sunglasses. "It is to bright this morning," he said while walking over to his car.

Across town in the New York New York casino, was the man that had the games down to a T. He just sat down at the nearest poker table that was open. "Hi, nice to meet you … Ethan," he said as he stared at my name badge.

I replied, "Welcome to my table. You ready to play."

"Sure but I think you might want to know my name," he said back with a smile on his face to light up the whole room.

"Sure sir, what is your name?" I asked him with a little puzzlement in my voice.

"The name is Chance and today you will able to play a game but I do warn you that the cards are not in your favor today my friend," he said with devilish grin on his face.

"Well, will see about that," I replied back to him as I started to shuffle the cards. I dealt out the first hand of cards and picked up my hand from the table.

We were playing this new card game called Fate. Played with only one deck, the rules were that each person gets five cards. Then your place the bet; after all bets are in each player simultaneous picks one card and throws it down. Whoever has the highest card gets the pot. It continues for each card three more times. Before the last card is played, you bet on who has the highest hand in the end.

We each bet on the first card, he threw down a king of hearts and I threw the ace of spades. The next card he threw down was the ace of hearts and I threw down the king of spades. "Not bad," I said with the thought that he might have something good.

"You're not bad yourself but still I'll always come out on top," he told me with a cocky voice.

The next card was a tie. We each threw down a queen of the same suite, Mine spade, and his hearts. The second to the last card I threw down the ten of spades and he placed the down the jack of hearts.

"See I told you, the cards were not in your favor," he said while grabbing the pot on the table.

"Well, we still have one card left," I told Chance with a solid face. As I was looking around I noticed that one person stood out of the crowd. He was wearing tight black jeans, black shirt and sunglasses. He walked right pass the table and I felt his energy levels spiking as if they were my own. It seemed to have matched my own energy output. Then he turned the corner and my focus went back to the game.

"So are you going to bet or what?" Chance said to me with a smile like he knew what was going on.

"Oh…yeah, sorry about that, we were betting on the last card. I'll put in half of what I won," I said not really thinking about what I was doing.

"I'm in," Chance said hastily. So we both threw down our cards and mine was the jack of spades and his was the ten of hearts. Basically we both had a royal flush, one of the hardest hands to get in poker. Just when we were about to decide on who gets the winnings, three big security guards and the manager of the hotel came up to us.

"Please come with us," the manager asked nicely. Chance stood up and gave me a wink. Now that I saw Chance he was about maybe six foot and a little muscular in the chest area.

Wearing khaki cargo shorts down to his knees and a Green Day t-shirt, it looked like he could put up a fight.

Just as I was standing up, Chance ducked down from a punch by one of the guards. That pissed him off but it did connect. It landed right on the side of my face. It snapped me out of my daydream. Strangely enough, I was still thinking about that kid that passed by and why his energy levels we equal to mine if not stronger.

That punch sent me to the ground but didn't knock me out. As I was falling, I sweep the legs of the other two guards. Chance went after the manager and noticed that I took two of guards down to the floor with me. He threw a punch and the only guard left standing moved between them.

The guard blocked the punch which made Chance off balance and the guard stepped aside letting Chance fall to the ground. His face just landed in front of the manager's shoes. I, on the other hand, was just getting dog piled by the two that I took down. Knowing that I might as well just go along and see what happens. I let them pile onto me. Chance also knew to just wait till that time was right.

The guards pick both of us up and tried our hands behind our backs. We were dragged through the casino and taken into the kitchen area. We waited for what was next to come. "Well at least I'll not be the only one this time to get caught," Chance told me with a smile.

"Well, to tell you the truth," I snickered. "The company is not bad. When do you want to escape from this place?"

"Well as fast as you can reach in my pocket and grab the dice that are in there." he told me while leaning in my direction. I reached my hand in his pocket and found the dice. I grab them out of his pocket. "Now put then in my hand and I'll roll them."

I dropped them into his hand and he threw them over his shoulder, they clanged on the metal stainless table that was in front of us. We watch as they rolled down the length of the table.

"What are we hoping to get?" I asked as they continued to roll.

"We just don't want snake eyes," he said as the dice came to a stop. The first dice had a one on it and the other had a six facing up. "Hold on." We disappeared from the kitchen and reappeared on one of the towers at Excalibur.

"Wow. So you must have the traveling dice. I have heard so much about them from up above," I said while looking around at where we were

"Yeah got them from a pawn shop down the street, wait how do you know about these dice?" he said a little shocked and almost tripping off the tower that he was walking around.

So I told him my story about how I became to be and the gods and the quests that they send me on. While I was talking to him, my mind was still wondering about that kid in casino. I thought to myself, I must find that kid and speak with him. I finished my story and the sun was just about to set over the horizon, when we both totally noticed a crowd of people gathering around the tower where we were sitting.

"Hey Chance, I think we might want to get down before any more attention is given to us," I said as I stood up.

"Yeah but do you have any ideas on how to get down?" he asked me while looking around for possible ways down without hurting ourselves.

"Well we could use your dice and transport us some where else? I could fly us down but that would just get everyone's attention," I said and just when I finished saying that I noticed that kid again walking through the crowd below us. This time I got a better look at his face and noticed it was almost looked like mine except for the black hair. I shrugged off the feeling and then notice that a fire truck was pulling into the area with its blazing sirens going off.

The fireman cleared the area and put up a ladder that reached us. "Come on down," said the firefighter. I let Chance go down first and I followed in suit. "What were you guys doing up there and how did you get up there?"

We made up some story about betting each other that we couldn't scale the wall and who would make it up to the top first. We got a lectured about how unsafe it was and how stupid we were for doing it. They let us off with a warning this time and told us never to do that again.

The crowd simmered down and the firefighters, cops and ambulance left as soon as they knew we were alright. "So where you staying while you in town?" he asked me.

"Actually, I get the pent house right here. Want to come up and have a few drinks or chill out?" I asked as I started walking towards the entranceway.

"Thanks but I still have a few errands to finish up," he said as he walked away towards the bright lights of Vegas. I left my new friend and started heading up towards my room.

Just as I was walking to the elevator, the bellman stopped me. "You're Ethan, the one that rented out the penthouse right?" he asked nervously.

"Yes," I paused then continued to say "What's up?"

"Well a gentleman by the name of Marko stopped by and want to give you this." he paused and hand me a package with just the words brothers on it. "Well here is the package, so is there anything else I can do for you?"

"No thanks," I said. I reached into my pocket and pulled out a five and handed it to him.

"Thanks, if you need anything I will get it for you. The name is Brent," he turned and walked away. I started to walk away when I heard Brent yelling back at me. "Oh yeah, the strange thing was that your guest looked almost like you."

"Thanks, Brent," I paused then heard a small ticking from the package. I started walking to the elevator and pushed the button. While on the way up to my room, I started recalling the day's events in my head but the only image that was in my head was Marko's face.

Ding went the elevator and doors slowly open, I stepped in and pressed the top floor button. As the elevator was going up, the ticking noise got louder and louder. I decided to open the package that I got from this kid named Marko.

I ripped open the package and it was a small leather pouch tied at the top. I untied the package and reached inside and pulled out a small pocket watch. On the outside was a design of a dragon circling around a yin-yang symbol. I pushed the button to open it and on the inside had an engraving. It seemed pretty new to me and it read: *Two halves become one, then destiny will become.* I didn't put to much thought into it, so I just put the watch into my pocket.

The elevator finally came to the top floor. I walked down the hallway, which was paved in paintings from the Dark Ages era. I reach my door and inserted the key. Pulling open the door and got thrown off my feet.

CHAPTER THIRTY-EIGHT

As I was driving down the strip, I had the feeling like something big was about to happen. It felt like the hand of fate was about to push me in the right direction. Driving passed the New York, New York hotel, I saw a guy that looked like me walking into the building. I decided to check it out since I had some time before I was to be anywhere today.

I parked my car into the back parking lot and walked towards the entranceway. As I was walking on I started to feel a little lightheaded. I sat down on the sidewalk and the feeling went away but I felt warm and cozy on the inside. It seemed like I had found something that was not there before.

I got up and walked inside and started looking around for that guy that looked just like me. I started looking through the casino and then spotted him with my boyfriend Chance. It seemed like they we playing a new card game the casino had put in. Slowly walking over to them, I noticed that they were being watched by the owner of the casino. So I changed my mind and just kept walking past them.

At that time, I noticed that the other guy was watching me, just like I was watching him. For some odd reason it felt like I knew him before. See just to let you know; since I was young I knew I was different. I was able to read people quite well but only recently more weird things have been happening. I have been having dreams about this battle of me and some other person. We were at the brink of destroying each other, and then I would wake up every time. The other odd thing was it seemed like I was angel in my dreams.

I looked down at my watch and notice the time, it was almost noon. I looked back up and saw that my boyfriend and the other person were fighting the owner and other personal of the casino. I turned the corner and went back to my car and drove off to the post office to pick up the package that was sent to me. While opening the package, that man's face appeared again in my mind.

I poured out the contents of the package. A piece of paper fell out and a pocket watch landed in my hand. The pocket watch had a dragon circling a yin-yang symbol and was engraved on the inside. The note fell down to the ground, I bent over and picked it up. As I unfolded the letter, I noticed that the pocket watch was still working.

On the letter was some instruction for me. It read: *Please take this other package to this address and drop it off for him. Wait for him to come in and recite these words. "Destiny, embrace me and unshackle me from these bonds."* I flipped the note over and it had the guys name on it. Just as I finished reading the note, one of the postmen walked up to me and handed me another package with the words *Brother* on it.

Thinking that this was a little weird but must do what it said or I might get into trouble with my higher ups. I made my way to the hotel address and was entering the Excalibur hotel when I noticed a crowd forming outside. I walked over and then looked up. Again it was my boy and his new found friend sitting up on one of the towers of the hotel. So I just ignored it and walked through the crowd. Going through the front doors, I notice that it was not very busy.

"Welcome to the Excalibur, my name is Brent. How can I help you?" he said cheerfully.

"Is there an Ethan Rush? Is he staying in the penthouse suite?" I asked Brent.

"Yeah there is. Is he a friend of yours?" he asked.

I did not answer him back. I just told him, "Please give him this package when he comes in."

Before he could answer, I was already off towards the elevator. I stepped inside and heard the emergency vehicles pulling up outside to get my boy and his friend down for the tower. I pushed the button to go up to the penthouse and when I got to the top floor and maid was cleaning the penthouse suite. It was my chance to get into his room without anyone noticing me or me having to break into the room. The maid finally left after she was done cleaning up.

I made myself comfortable on the king sizes bed and flipped on the tube. Just as the TV got set up and was showing some picture. I heard the door start to unlock. I stood up on the bed and chanted those words. "Destiny, embrace me and unshackle me from these bonds."

Just as the last word came out of my mouth, I was thrown back onto the bed. It was like a shockwave that come out of my body, it shatters most of the windows on that top floor. It stretched throughout the city skyline. Most people thinking it was a bomb or jet, they ducked down and then looked up to the sky. The room I was in had completely been demolished. The roof of the Excalibur was now holy and covered with rubble.

I was now laying on what was once to be a king size bed. I was sprawled out like an s-shape pattern. I screamed from the pain that was coming from my backside. My shoulder blades were ripped open and two skeletons like wings popped out of the wounds that were formed.

I was in so much pain and was arching my back. My hands were trying to rip those things out of my back. The last thing I remember before passing out was slowly walking towards the window.

I woke up lying on my bed thinking it was just a dream, I tried to stand up. The soreness in my shoulder blades came rushing back into me. I screamed out in pain and slowly walked over to the mirror to check them out. My back was a light shade of pink and the slits were still open. I knew touching them would be a bad idea, so I just went back down to my bed and passed out again from all the pain.

Meanwhile, back at the penthouse, I was just awoken by the sound of the hotel door fall off my body. I thought to myself, what the fuck was that? I knew if I stayed any longer I would probably be hauled away. So I took my shirt off and uncased my wings. Flying off and landing on the roof top of the next hotel, so I could at least get my bearings straight.

After a couple of minutes, I realized that must have something to do with Marko, the one who dropped of the package. I wish I knew more about this kid. I tried to follow his energy trail but something or someone was blocking it, so I did the next best thing. I flew up high and noticed a small trail of damage done to some of the other buildings in the area.

I followed the trail of debris to the suburbs of Las Vegas. The strange thing was when I got there the trail ended. "Well I guess I narrowed down my search to this neighborhood," I said to myself.

I flew down and put my wings back into my body, tossed my shirt on and started my search for Marko.

Back at Marko's house, he started to stir in his bed. Marko was standing alone in a field of cattails. Then everything went black.

"Hey Marko," a voice calls out.

"Hello," I replied back and started looking around for that voice.

"How are you feeling? How is your back?" the voice said. Then a hand patted me on the back. Marko fell down to the ground in pain. I screamed out loud but no sound came out this time and soon was on my hands and knees and the voice started speaking again. "So I noticed your in much pain, how if I make a deal with you?" the voice said.

"I would much like that," I said trying holding back the screams.

"You must get rid of this man," the voice paused and a picture of Ethan's face appeared in the darkness. "This man will try and hurt you. He will lie to you."

"I've seen this guy before. He was with my boyfriend," I told the voice.

"Yes he was trying to steal him away from you," the voice said and then a small hole in Marko's chest opened up. The darkness then transferred into the hole and became apart of Marko. The pain in my back was gone and I felt like I was ten times more powerful then I was before.

My wings came out from the slits in my back and they grew in size and shape. They turned into like a metallic black. Just then I awoke from my sleep and was hovering over my bed with my wings spreading around my room. The voice came back and spoke, "You have all the powers of darkness and knowledge to use it at will."

With that said, I put my wings back into my body and fell back down to sleep. The next morning, I got dressed really fast and went to test out my new found powers. I noticed that I was a lot stronger and faster at everything I did.

Down the street, I was looking around then heard some noise coming from the house I was next too. I peeked over the fence and there he was. The guy I was searching for. He did not seem to notice me but I kept watching and saw that he was using the hidden powers of darkness that I've seen before.

I thought to myself, how he obtain the power of darkness unless someone else is you using him. Just as I finished my thought, a gust of strong wind pushed me down and Marko was hovering over me.

"Marko, it is nice to meet you," I said extending my hand.

"Like wise," he said as he hovered back down to the ground and shook my hand. "So I guess I know why you're here. You're here to tell me that I was wrong and must give up all my power."

I looked at him with a blank face. "Not really. I just wanted to ask a few questions. It was more about this pocket watch that you delivered to me." I took the pocket watch out of my pocket and showed it to him. "See I was hoping you could tell me more about this mysterious item."

"To be honest, I really don't know much about this item. I was sent one as well." Marko reached into his pocket and pulled his out. Then the voice came back into Marko's head.

"What are you doing?" the darkness asked hastily.

"He does not seem like a bad guy. Why do I need to battle with him?" Marko replied to the voice.

"Fine if you will not fight him, I'll just take over your body and destroy him myself," the voice said.

Inside Marko's mind were two things: himself and the darkness. They went at it. Each time they would clash sparks of light and darkness would fly every where. Then darkness started to play unfair. He summoned up some fiends behind Marko and they all jumped him at once. Each one grabbing a leg or arm, they started dragging him away to the far reaches of his mind.

"Help me," Marko yelled as he vanished into the darkness of his own mind.

I heard that plead and didn't understand it. "So Marko, I was wondering what you were doing just then."

"Just practicing the ways of darkness, why do you ask?" he said.

"Just wondering, I have only seen that skill done once before but I destroyed him a long time ago," I said to him then paused and noticed something in his eyes. They changed color from the clam ice blue to pitch black darkness.

I knew then that I was dealing with the same darkness from before. "Well it was nice to meet you but I really must be going." I told him and turned around.

I just started walking away without uncasing my wings. I casted a shield behind me, just in case the darkness was going to try and hit me while my back was turned. Nothing happened at this point and time. So I took off and went to Chance's place since my penthouse was completely demolished.

I knocked on his door and said through door "Hey, is any one home?" The door slowly opened and noticed the house was trashed. "Hello, it is me Ethan. I need to talk to Chance."

No answer was returned. I knew better to go inside, so I left that scene and took out my cell phone. I figured I could use some back up and started to dial my friend Josh's number.

It rang twice and then went to voicemail. *You know the drill and hopefully I'll get back to you. Beep.* "Hey it is me, Ethan. I think I'm going to need your help down here in Vegas. The darkness returned and has grown more powerful. Meet me at the spot. Later Days," I said to the machine and hung up the phone.

I just started wondering about Marko and replayed the conversation we had. It seemed that he was a good guy but half way through he was taken over by the darkness. Then I decided to help free him from the darkness since I knew he didn't want that.

I went back to the Excalibur and there was Brent waiting for me. "Hello, Brent, what news do you have for me?" I asked hoping that he at least had some good news for me.

"Well we have moved your room to King Arthur's Suite and you got another message from Marko." he told me. He handed me a piece of paper and the key to my new room. He walked away after that.

I unfolded the note and started to read it. *I know your secret. I would like to meet up with you, on the roof of your hotel tonight.* I shoved the note into my pocket and went towards the elevator. Pushing the button impatiently, the doors opened and I rushed in. Quickly getting to my new suite and just fell down onto the bed and passing out from all the events that have been going on.

I woke up about an hour before the meeting time and got dress in some normal street clothes, a pair of tight skinny jeans and a black green day t-shirt. I went to the stairs since I figured that the elevator was out after yesterday.

CHAPTER THIRTY-NINE

I GOT TO THE ROOF AND THE DEBRIS WAS STILL SCATTERED about. Pieces of air conditioners, broken pieces of wood, feathers from the beds, it was like a war zone. I noticed a figure standing on the other side of the roof. He was balancing on the edge of metal beam that was sticking over the edge of the hotel.

"Hello," I said into the wind. It seemed like the wind was howling and was blowing everything about. The figured turned around and I noticed it was Marko but it still had the darkness in his eyes.

"You made it," he said as he walked down the beam and jump a little to get back onto the rooftop. "Well I know your little secret about those watches. To bad you will not know the truth for I am here to kill you," Marko said while walking towards me.

I backed up a few feet waiting for him to make his first move. "What do you want, Darkness? I know you're using that kid's body but I also know that Marko has something to do with my destiny. He also got a watch with the same engravings." I said and pulled out the watch to show him.

"Let him go and fight me. I know you're more powerful now but still could not use your dark magic to make a body for yourself, huh?"

That just pissed him off and then he use his telekinesis to send some of the wooden beams that laid about straight for my head. I did dodge them but then I felt one grazed my cheek as it went by. The blood started running down my face. He knew I would not fight him while he was still in that body. He kept advancing towards me.

"What happened? Did I get you? Come on and fight me," he said with chuckle in his voice and did a flying jump kick towards my face. I dodge the kick and grabbed him by the back of his shirt and threw him into the staircase's wall that was still standing up. "That's what I want you to do, beat up an innocent person. So you can feel what I been through?"

"I'll not hurt him. So do your worse to me?" I told him. He came charging in at me and gave me a nice right punch into the gut. That pushed me back a couple of feet but didn't knock me down, then he roundhouse kick to my temple. It sent me flying and skidding across the rooftop. Stopping just short of the edge, my head was hanging of the ledge. I looked down and saw a beautiful site of the strip at night even through I should be really worrying about the person I'm fighting.

Just then I saw the shadow of my enemy over me and rolled sideways just getting missed by his foot. Just then I pulled myself off the ledge and made myself drop down the side of the building.

Marko watched as I dropped. I looked back up as I was falling and Marko's face was in shock. That is what I needed to see because I knew that the Marko that I met early was still in there. Just then I uncased me wings, ripping my shirt to shreds and flew off. Marko followed suit. The darkness within him started shooting dark energy bolts towards me.

After that round house kick I took to the face, I didn't know if I was going to be able to make it to the next building. Marko fire a couple more bolts and I was not able to dodge them. One hit me right between my wings and it sent me falling towards the closest building. It just happened to be Stratosphere hotel.

I landed on the roof and tumble a few times. It sent me flying to the other side of rooftop. He landed on his feet and was charging up for one last attack on me since he saw that I was still down on the ground. He did not speak any words but had the biggest grin on his face. He let go of the energy ball and it came straight towards me.

Just inches away from my face a green energy shield sprung up. The energy ball shattered around the shield and I looked up to see three more familiar faces. It was Josh, Mrs. X and John, my three guardian angels. "Took you guys long enough," I said to them as I got up off the ground.

"Well we just got the message and there still a little slow at flying," Josh said to me while landing with a smile.

"Well, well, well, I did hear something about you making a team for the Gods. I guess I'll just have to kill you all and continue the quest myself." Marko said that and then started his attacks.

He was quick but I know inside of him was the real Marko. I would not let him die with out getting to know the real him. I knew what I had to do. I was going to banish the Darkness for good. I start storing my energy and was moving around the top of the roof setting things up.

Marko was tried of these little distractions, so he was going to take them out. He went after Mrs. X first. She did not get the hang of flight with her wings so she decided that a ground battle would be better for her. She landed and got ready to fight him. She really was no match for him.

The Darkness was able to read people quite well so it used that towards its advantage. The darkness engulfed Mrs. X and the next thing we knew was that Mrs. X was down on the ground. In my mind I knew she was not dead because I was able to feel her energy but it still was not strong. It was more or less starting to fade. At that moment, I knew I had to end this battle before any one else got hurt or destroyed.

Next he went after John. John was a little more powerful and he did land a few hits but still was not able to stop the Darkness. Marko land a nice square punch on John's jaw and it sent him flying towards the center of the building.

I set the last item on the top of the building, ran into the center of the building. I slid underneath John and caught him from crashing into the building. "Sorry I was not able to help out more," he said before passing out.

"You did you best my friend, now rest while I take care of him," I said then I looked up into the sky and saw Josh and Marko battling in the air. I placed John next to me and stood up. Josh saw me and knew I was ready to separate the two. I started the incantation and was just working on not screwing it up. My body went limp but Marko's body was frozen in place.

I guessed it worked because I was in his mind. I was searching the darkness and found the corner that the minions tossed him into. I walked over to him. "Hey Marko," I said and put my hand on his shoulder. I paused to wait for a response. Nothing happened. "Hey Marko, why are you hiding in the corner, I know your stronger then that stupid old darkness. He is using you body like rag doll. He is kicking the crap out of us but still we need your help out there."

"I can not help you. I was sucked into the darkness. It is to powerful," Marko told me in soft whisper and the light around him started to diminish.

"No the darkness went inside you. It can not control what it is not his. You're strong and with your new found angel wings, you will grow even stronger. Spread your wings and unleash the power within. The darkness will not win this or any battle against us," I said and just then the spell broke. I got pulled out of his mind and was tossed back into my body again.

I felt drained but noticed that Marko was too. I didn't know if it worked but then I saw him fall. Josh was down on the ground so I use the rest of my energy and dove off the building after him. I was catching up to him and I grabbed hold of his leg. When I touch him, I felt the darkness was gone from him.

I climbed up his body and turned him around so that when we hit the ground I would take the impact. Just before we slammed into the ground, I casted a shield to protect us, we went about ten feet deep into the ground. Creating a crater about the size of a pitcher's mound and passed out.

I woke up remembering what had happened. Not realizing where I was, I jumped out of bed then fell to the floor. Not really caring for myself I needed to know what happened. The door to the bedroom was flung open. A familiar face greeted me on the other side. It was Josh. He walked in and helped me up onto my feet.

"I thought I heard some noises coming from this room," Josh said to me with a smile. "You take it easy. We don't want your wounds to open up again. It took us a while to patch you up." Then he took me back to the bed and we both sat down.

"Is Marko alright?" was the first thing I blurted out. "Where are we? What happened and why does it feel like I have a giant hole in me?"

"We are in Chance's house. Well after you saved Marko from the fall, you remember the crater that you made with you shield," he said.

"Yeah, somewhat," I replied with some concern in my voice.

"Well the shield did protect you from the fall but not the pipe that went straight through your side. It only impaled you and not Marko. After gaining some of my strength back, I flew down to make sure you guys were alright. I noticed the pipe and broke it off so I could at least move you from the spot. I picked both of you up and flew you back to the roof top," he paused to make sure that I was getting all of this.

"What happened to the Darkness that I got rid of in Marko's body?" I asked with a little pain in my side.

"We do not know. After you did you separation spell, it seem to just have vanished. John woke up and so did Mrs. X. Mrs. X attend to yours and Marko's wounds. Then I picked you up and John picked up Marko. Then Marko's phone rang. John picked it up and it was this guy named Chance. John filled him in and told us to bring you guys to his house to rest," he paused again. "So now we are just waiting for you and him to wake up."

"Is John or Mrs. X still here?" I asked with a tear rolling down my cheek.

"No. I told them to go home and I'll look after you guys. I also told them that I knew you would not die that easy. So they took off and I just been chillen here with Chance. He is a very interesting person. He is also Marko's boyfriend," he told me.

"Can I go see Marko?" I asked and was propping myself up with my elbows.

"Sure." Josh said. He moved over to the side of the bed and took my hand. I used him as crutch as we slowly made are way to the master bedroom. Chance saw that I was up and moving around. He got up from the couch in the living room and walked over to give us a hand.

"Thanks for let me crash here," I said to him.

"Well it is least I can do since you helped me out and saved my boy from his death. Yeah they filled me in on what happened," he said with a smile. He grabbed me from the other side and we all went into the master bedroom which was down the hall from the room I was in.

Marko's body lied still underneath the covers and I did notice that I felt his energy start to rise to be equal with mine again. Chance went over there and sat next to him. I went to the other side of the bed and Josh was at the foot of the bed. I reached for his hand and in it was the sliver pocket watch that was given to us. Chance kissed him and he woke up. Then he looked over at me and a smile appeared on his face.

"Ethan you're awake. Glad to see you," he said with a big fat grin. "How is your wound?"

"It is ok," I said as I coughed a little. "I been better but I'm glad to see you're not hurt."

"I will be fine. So did you ever figure out what these pocket watches are for?" he asked as he held out the one in his hand.

"As a matter of fact, I did get that information while I was reading his mind and helping you find your strength. These watches belong to us once before. When we both were young, we were brothers, twins actually. Yeah I know we don't look a like but that is what info I got from the Darkness before he left you. So whoever sent these watches to us knew we would find each other," I told Marko.

"Well bro, guess this means we are going to be seeing more of each other since I have these new found powers. Ok, if we're not angels and not demons then what are we?" he said to me.

I filled him in on my story and what we really are. I told him, "I still had some other quest to do but I'll be back to catch up with you soon enough. Oh yeah one more thing before I go, these watches are also special in one other way. They tell if the other person is still alive. My watch tells your time and yours tells mine."

"Cool, so I take your off to your next adventure. You're not even fully healed yet," he said as he propped himself up on the headrest.

"No rest for people like us. I'm sure you will be figuring that out soon. Well I'm off and Chance take care of my bro. I'll be back soon," I said and then started to walk out the doorway.

"Ethan, wait," Marko said. I turned around. "Thanks for everything. Hope you have a safe journey."

"You too bro," I said then I walked out the door with Josh at my side.

CHAPTER FORTY

I HAVE HEARD THAT MANY PEOPLE CAN GET LOST IN THE sea of dreams, hopes and foolishness. It takes all different kinds of people to be a leader or even rise to the occasion that is in front of you. I knew that the people I picked to lead were the right people to teach. The other fact is that I heard that human's say that people are greater in numbers. I do believe in that and seen it first hand. How everyone helps the other. Their strengths and weakness cancel each other out and make them the perfect team.

It has been a few months since my stay at the hospital and my brush with destiny. I have been training with my new powers and wings to improve myself. When Dr. Rush appeared and started talking to me.

"Hey Eric, how have you been?" he asked.

"Not to bad. Just training and working on these new tricks. I know you been watching me and you seen that I been helping out the people in need but is there something more that I can be doing to help out this world," I asked him.

"Yeah there is. That is why I've came down, to tell you that you're going to be meeting some other ES and I want you to become their leader," he told me.

"Ok that sounds like fun. When is it going to happen?" I asked all ready and willing.

"I can not give you that info because I'm not allowed too but I can tell you it will happen during some down time and they'll come to you. So don't worry too much about it," he told me then vanished.

He always does that; just pops in and then vanishes without a trace. I wish he would be clearer on what he means but I guess I need to find that out for myself.

I didn't let it bother me and went on with the rest of my errands for the day. I was meeting my new boyfriend, Trevor up in the city. I knew I was going to wait for Jake but doesn't mean I can not have a boyfriend till we meet again. I started driving up to the city and while on my way I noticed the world around me seemed to be moving a little slower then what I was use too.

Was this the sign that I needed to see and meet the team or was that meaning my vision was being changed to fit the new trick I was trying to learn? The trick that I was teaching myself was being able to see inside people's hearts. See what they really are hiding or if they are speaking the truth. My eyesight has become more then just seeing into different realms and what is not there but also seeing what is inside people's hearts.

I reached the city and was just getting to his apartment when I saw him outside. He was standing on the street. I pulled up to him and he entered the car. "Hey Trev, are you ready for our date?" I asked him as I pulled away from the curb.

"Yeah I am. So where we going?" he asked excitedly.

"Well I thought I would surprise you," I told him with sly grin.

As we waited at a red light, I just looked over at him and smiled. He looked back and smiled as well. We finally got this really fancy restaurant. It was at the top of one of the buildings in downtown. As we entered the building, it had a big giant fish tank in the middle of the room and the tables circling around it. The host took us to our table and we sat down. We opened the menus and then I leaned over and whispered to him, "Order anything you want. It is on me tonight."

"Really, are you sure you can afford this?" he asked me.

"Yeah I can, I just got promotion at my job and they moved me into a new home on top of Santana row. They placed me with this really cool guy name John. He is straight and I think he has a girlfriend but I really don't know. I need to take you to the pad so we can make it a little more comfortable," I said as I leaned in kissed him on the check.

"Well, ok then I guess I will have some fun tonight," he said and kissed me back.

The waiter came and we placed our orders. We made some small talk about how our days went and then the food came. We started eating when I noticed that my eyes were acting up again. I looked around the room and noticed that each person had a misty gray shade to them. Sort of like a faint glow about them.

I excused myself and went to the bathroom. As I got there I checked the stalls to see if anyone was in there. Walking over to the sinks, I splashed some water on my face and looked up into mirror. As I looked in the mirror I saw Dante behind me. I turned around and nobody was there. I splashed some more water on my face then Trevor came in.

"Hey, are you alright?" he said while putting his hand on my back.

"Yeah, I am fine. Just got a small headache," I told him.

"Ok, well I'm ready to move on to the next spot whenever you are," he told me and kissed me. He walked out of the bathroom and sat back down. I dried my face and checked myself in the mirror one last time. Exiting the bathroom, I made way back to the table. We finished our dinner and the waiter dropped off the check. I took out my wallet and put down a hundred dollar bill.

As we exited the restaurant, I was thinking why Dante appeared behind me in the bathroom; just then Trevor broke my train of thought. "So where to next?" he asked curiously to were the nights event would end.

I didn't respond to him but alone walked faster to my truck. We hoped back in the truck and started driving up Skyline Boulevard. About halfway up the mountain, we reach a small little turn off point and parked the truck. Both of us got out of the truck and went to cuddle in the bed of the truck. Just watched the night sky pass over our heads, I put my arm around the back of his head and drew him near. I looked over at him and just started to kiss him passionately.

He looked over my shoulder to check the time and it was almost midnight. He broke the kiss and said, "I need to get home, I got an early photo shoot tomorrow."

"Ok," I said coming down from the emotional high. We hopped back into the truck and headed back to his place. We got back to his place in the city and parked the car. We got out and we kissed each other goodnight.

Since his place was on the other side he had to cross the street. Down the street, I noticed a car turning the corner at a very high speed. The cops were following him very closely. I looked over at Trevor and noticed he didn't realize what was going. Trevor finally realized but it was too late. I dove into the street and barely was able to push Trevor out of the way.

I just pushed him to the other side of the street when I slammed into the car's windshield. It smash and I went flying up into the air. Then the car swerved into the light post next to where Trevor was now standing next to. The cops came to sudden stop right where the car had stopped. Trevor came running to where my body had landed in the middle of the street.

I felt fine because I brought out my wings and use it as shield just before impact. While I was in midair, I brought my wings back in so just in cause any one had saw them. I haven't told anyone besides James of my secret, so I had to play along to make sure that my secret was safe for now. I didn't want any one to know who I was till I was ready and able to protect them just in case someone came after them.

I acted like I was hurt and in somewhat pain. Trevor came running over and so did one of the police officers. They called an ambulance and the cop was making sure that I was ok. The cop was checking out where I got hit and he had a curious look on his face. Just then the ambulance arrived at took over before the cop could ask anything. They got me all hooked up and strapped in to the ambulance. Trevor got in since he was the only one there with me at the time. On the ride over to the hospital, since I didn't want to act any more so I tried to sleep but they did not let me sleep, do to the fact that I might have a concussion. Every time I would shut my eyes, I would feel the EMT guy shake me.

They got me to hospital and rushed me into a room, then hooked me up to an IV drip. The doctor on call told me they'll do some X-rays in a few moments. I thought to myself, at least I get to figure out what to tell them about the scars on my shoulder blades. The doctor left and Trevor was crying a little but then noticed he was just happy to make sure I was not hurt to bad or anything.

"Hey," I said to him. He looked up at me and then just wiped away the tear that was rolling down his check. "I'll be just fine and I know you need to get home and get some rest, so go home. I'll be fine." I followed it with a smile.

"No, I want to stay with you and I don't need to go to the photo shoot tomorrow. I'll just call them and re-schedule," he said to me.

"Well, it looks like I'm not going to change your mind so I could use the company. I'll page the nurse to get some blankets and a pillow since I know there is no way we are going to fit on this small bed," I said to him with a smile. "I guess this night was not turning out to be as I planned it. Well at least I had a good time before I saved you."

"Ha, ha, ha," he laughed sarcastically. "It was great and the way you saved me without even thinking about it was amazing."

"Well I was just helping out in anyway I can. You know me always willing to help someone in need. Someone as cute as you will always be first on my list to save," I said and winked at him.

He came over and kissed me on the lips and when he stopped I just looked up into his eyes. In the moonlight, he looked like an angel with his long brown wavy hair flowing over his face. His eyes sparkling with drops of tears flowing from them, his slender body and legs fitting the tight jeans he was wearing.

He sat down in the chair and instantly fell asleep. I joined him in slumber land a few minutes later. I woke up when the nurse was tapping my shoulder.

"It is time for your X-rays," she said.

"Ok, I'm ready," I said to her.

She rolled me out of the room and down the hall. The room was cold and seemed very sterile. She had me get up and lay on this table that was even colder then the temperature of the room. It sent a chill up and down my spine. She pointed the machine at different parts of my body and got back on my bed. She rolled me back to my room and left.

CHAPTER FORTY-ONE

THEN I FEEL ASLEEP AGAIN. I AWOKE TO THE LIGHT OF the sun entering the room. I looked over and saw that Trevor was on the phone talking to someone.

"Cool, so I'll see you here in a few," Trevor said and then hung up the phone.

"Who was that?" I asked while rubbing the sleep from my eyes.

"It seems you had a busy day today. Patty, Stephen, Mike, and Damien all called you while you where asleep. They all seemed to want to hang out but I told them what happened and now they are on their way up here to visit you," he paused. "How are you feeling?"

I look up at him and say, "Well my ribs are sore but beside that I feel fine."

He leaned over and gave me a kiss. The nurse came in and told us, "We need to take a few more X-rays."

"Ok," I said then the nurse just wheeled me back to the X-ray room.

As I was down in X-ray, everyone showed up. They wheeled me back in and I saw everyone with smiling faces.

"Hey guys, how is everything going? Sorry to make you worry but I just didn't want to see that cute boy over there get hurt. So I jump to push him out of the way and then the car hit me. The car smashed into the pole and the cops got him and after that they rushed me here," I told them.

"Well we are glad to see you are doing alright," Patty said. She is the shortest of the group with reddish brown hair that flows in nice soothing waves and brown eyes that have a hint of mystery to them.

"Yeah I didn't know what to think when Trevor told me that you were here," Stephen said. The tallest in the room with straight brown hair, pitch black eyes, and very thin and boney.

"Well I heard that this hospital has some great staff members," Damien said. The second shortest in the room, he had dirty blonde hair that was about shoulder length. His eyes we like the gray mist; it seemed to be like fog covering the ground on an early morning and he always had the hint that something was up.

"Well it seems everyone is alright and you don't look too banged up," Mike said while rolling his eyes. He was the second tallest in the room. Lean but muscular with spiky blonde hair, you could see the passion in his deep blue ocean eyes.

It was strange when I thought about it that each of us in the room was either dating one person or in a relationship. Patty and Stephen, Mike and Damien, and Trevor and I, I thought that was interesting. "Well thanks for coming guys even through you didn't have to drive all the way up here to see me. I think I should be fine and they might release me today if all goes well with the X-rays," I said cheerfully.

"Well we wanted to come up here since you're our friend. We worry about you," Patty said and Stephen shaking his head to agree with her.

"Plus who is going to drive you home after you get out of this hospital. You car is still in front of Trevor's house remember," Mike told us.

"I completely forgot. By the way Trevor could you call my work to tell them that I will not be able to make it in for the next couple of days," I said.

"Already taken care off, I did that while you were sleeping," he told me with a smile.

"Aw… how thoughtful. I guess I would be lost with out you guys. Thanks guys for coming. I would give you guy's hugs but my ribs still hurt a little bit," I told them.

They all laughed and then the nurse came walking in. "Wow, was not expecting this many people to be here. I know one of you spent the night and the rest must have arrived while he was in X-ray. Well we do have the X-rays and the doctor will be coming into discuss the findings with you shortly," she said to us all.

When she said that I thought well my secret will no longer be a secret. Just as I was thinking that my eyes start to twitch like before but this time it was different. I was looking straight at my friends and saw inside them. Each of my friends had a color and a set of wings within them except the nurse. The nurse was the misty shade of gray like the people at the restaurant. Then my eyes went back to normal. I blinked and realized that this was the meeting that Ethan was telling me about.

The nurse left the room and we just chatted a little bit more. About a half an hour later, the doctor came in with the X-rays in hand. "Hello Mr. Shawl, how are we feeling today?" he asked.

"Not to bad, my ribs are a little sore," I told him.

"Well it does look like you have any injuries but we did notice something strange about your back," he paused and put up the X-ray on the light screen. "See these two gashes on you back seem to be just on your shoulder blades. Could you please take off your shirt?"

I did as the doctor asked and then I turned around. The marks were where my wings came out were still there. I wish I had faster healing on my back but I guess it is time to tell the world about me, even though I wish it was later that I had to tell everyone and not now. He touched one of them and I screamed out in pain. I forget that if touched while they are healing hurts like a bitch.

"Sorry about that. You can put your shirt back on," he paused again. "We blew up one of the scratch marks and it looks like there is some extra bone growing inside the wound. We can not explain what that bone is but we would like to do some more test. We are asking you since we can not make you do these tests. We hope you'll let us study you more just incase this pops up within someone else down the road."

"Thanks doc. I'll think about it and get back to you," I said to him with weak grin.

"Ok, we will keep you over night just to make sure that it is nothing serious," he said then left.

CHAPTER FORTY-TWO

I GOT BACK INTO BED AND EVERY ONE WAS STARING AT ME. "Well I guess I need to explain what that is," I said to everyone.

"Ok, I guess we should hear this," said Trevor while looking around the room.

"Remember that accident that I had a couple of months ago. When Dante hit me with his car and drove me to the hospital. Well something was unlocked that day and I think you guys might have it as well. The thing that was unlocked inside me was my ES or Eternal Spirit. The marks on my back are actually where my wings come in and out. That is why I screamed when the doctor touched them. They get sore when the wound is healing itself. I used them to protect myself against the car last night. That is why I have no scratches on me," I told them and then looked down at the floor.

"Well that sounds like a bunch of crap," Mike said forcefully. "I think you hit your head a little too hard on the fall and you making this up. Well I'm glad that you're feeling better but Damien and I need to get going so see you around."

"Well if you believe me or not; I plead you to not get too emotional because I believe you guys have it to. That is the way you unlock you wings and the Eternal Spirit," I told him while he was walking out the door.

We said goodbye to Mike and Damien, then the attention was fully back on me. "I guess you guys want me to show you my wings. Trevor, can you hold my shirt for me," I asked him. I took my shirt off and went over to close the door.

I started to lean forward and let at a small yell that was muffled. Then the bones of the wings started to come out. Then the feathers appeared. They expand to fill one of the walls in the room. Everyone was amazed. Then Stephen asked, "Why are you wings black and white?"

"Well I guess it is how the way my insides are. See the wings are not only the powers that I got when this happened. I have been training since that day, helping people out like a super hero. It is kind of cool not to relay on others to help you out in jam. I have been working on a new power that lets me see into the hearts of people. Before the nurse left, it went off and I saw inside of you guys. You had colored spirits with wings. Yes, even Mike and Damien had them to but they didn't believe me. I hope nothing happens to them," I paused thinking about what might happen. "I guess you are earth, Stephen and you are water, Patty since your colors that I see brighter now are brown and blue. Trevor, you are like grayish mist. Color that is not completely clear but not solid which makes you peace I guess, Mike was red which I guess that makes him fire and Damien was air and he was white which is what I saw."

"That is so cool," Stephen said like a little kid on Christmas morning.

"Yeah I guess I can live with that. The up side is that I'll not need a ride to work everyday. Sweet," Patty said smiling from ear to ear.

"So my boyfriend is a person with wings and I'll have them too. I guess that is very interesting. I would love to get a picture of those wings and my own. How do you unlock them? I guess we are a perfect match for each other then," Trevor said hastily.

Just as Trevor said that a sharp pain came from his back. I noticed that he was leaning forward and then I said, "If you like that shirt, I would take it off."

Just then he took off his shirt and we saw that he had two slits on his shoulder blades and the cuts were open. Then the bones that formed his wings came out of his back and the feathers where a misty gray but had almost a see through quality to them. "Ouch, that really does hurt. So lover, why are they just hanging down and not moving around like yours?" he asked me.

"Well that is simple; I need to connect them to the brain that controls function. Come here and I'll connect them," I said. He walked over and I did the same thing that Ethan did to me. I connected them and they started to move with just his thought. "I know you like your wings but I think you might want to put them away since the nurse is coming."

"Ok. How do you do that?" he asked with puzzled look on his face.

"Well, just concentrate on them and they'll go back in. It's going to hurt and then you will want to put your shirt on to hide those open wounds," I told him.

He focused and they went back inside him. The wounds were still fresh on his back. He quickly put his shirt back on, just then the nurse walked back in. "How is everything going?" she asked.

"It's going good. It seems that you can only have one visitor at a time, doctor's orders," she said then walked out the door.

Stephen and Patty said, "Well, we should go and get some stuff done. We'll see you tomorrow and we can talk more about this ES stuff," they finished saying and then walked out as well.

"Hey babe, how do you feel?" I asked and lightly rubbing his back.

"Well, I feel fine. Just my back is a little sore from the cuts," he told me.

"You do get use to it after awhile. What do you think about all this?" I asked him while getting up to hug him.

"Well to be honest a little scared but I know it is what I am so I guess I'm fine with it. As long as I have you beside me we can face it together and train with the others as well," he said with a smile.

"Ok, well I'm going to lead this group of Eternal Spirits to help out this realm. Well I'm glad it is my friends that are going to be apart of this team," I told him.

Well back down south, Mike and Damien were at the shopping mall. They were walking around and looking at clothes. "I wonder if what Eric said was true babe," Damien asked Mike.

"I think he was just doing it for attention. I don't think that it would be able to grow wings from your back. I think he just cut himself on his back from the car that he got hit by," he replied.

Just as they were walking through the mall he saw a pair of shoes he needed to have. He walked into the store and asked the clerk if they had them in his size. They didn't. It pissed him off but he just turned and walked away. Damien notice he was getting a little pissed off so he asked, "Are you hungry?"

"Yeah that does sound like a good idea. Let's go get some food," he said.

"Cool, so what do you want?" Damien asked and pointed to the food court.

"I don't know. Let's see what sounds good," he said as they walked into the food court of the mall. They circled the food court once not really seeing anything that was pleasant. Then they decided on some pizza. They got their pizza and as they were walking to the table area some little kid went running pass and making Mike spill his drink and pizza all over himself.

That set him off. He was so pissed. He felt like he was going to explode but instead he started to lean forward and screamed out in pain. Just then Damien saw two red marks about the same length as Eric's formed underneath his shirt. Then Mike's shirt rip into shreds and the bones of the wings popped out of his back. The red feathers of passion and fire appeared. Mike was down on his knees and started to cry and then Damien stepped in.

Everyone staring at him; Damien new what to do, he grabbed Mike and told him, "To be calm and collective. Just breath and everything will be alright. Let's get out of here." When they reached their car Damien's wings came out. The white wings that comfort and are always there when need. "Let's go see Eric."

"Ok," Mike said and he was a little cheered up to see his boyfriend having wings as well. Both their wings vanished on the way to the hospital but they didn't forget how it felt.

They got to the room and saw that Trevor and Eric we just cuddling in the small hospital bed watching TV. "Hey guys, what's up?" I asked them cheerfully.

Just as I finished asking that question, I saw that both of them were in tears. I got up off the bed and walked over to them. Gave them big hug and said, "They came out didn't they; I'm so sorry that I wasn't there to help you. Are you guys ok?"

Damien spoke while holding his lover, "I'm fine but Mike here was just torn apart. I don't think he can take any more of this. What are we going to do about this?"

"Well, once I'm out of here I was going to train you guys on this new power and we are supposed to become a team and help the world along with Ethan Rush." I paused. "Ethan Rush is the one that unlocked these and he has them too. I think we should all meet him once I'm out of here."

"I'm sorry for not listening and not believing in you," Mike said with a few tears still in his eyes.

"It's ok. It is hard to sallow I know. I didn't believe it myself at first but I had Ethan to help me out even if I didn't believe in it," I said while hugging him. "It will be alright and trust me I bet most of them didn't even see your wings. What they saw was you ripping off your shirt and screaming in pain. The funny thing about these wings is nobody can see them unless they believe in them."

"What do you mean?" Damien asked curiously.

"I mean that these things are only able to be seen if they believe in the other realms and other beings. So I bet that only about one eighth saw them and thought they were really cool. It gives them hope to believe in something or at least that is what Ethan told me. Anyway I really don't know what I'm leading you guys to help out with but I will do my best to and again I'm sorry that you had to go through the horror of your wings coming out that way," I said to them as I started to feel there pain run through me.

"Why did they vanish?" Mike spoke up and wiping away his tears.

"They vanished because you calmed down and focused on them going back inside you. So tell me how it happened?" I asked. So they told me how it happened. I hung on every word. "I was right. They come out the first time by the emotion that is inside you. You had red wings right Mike?"

"Yeah, how did you know?" he asked.

"Well, before you left I was working on my powers to see inside people's hearts. My vision turned on and I saw inside you guys and each of you had a different color ES and wings. Mike was red, Damien was white, Patty was blue, Stephen was brown, and Trevor was a mist gray," I told them.

"What color is yours?" Damien asked.

"I am half white and half black. One wing is black and one wing is white." I said. "Do you want to see?"

"Hell yeah we want to see them," they both said which lit up there faces.

"Trevor, please hold my shirt and you two go close the door," I told them.

The door was shut and the blinds closed. I bent forward and my wings came out. Mike walked over and touched them. It looked like both of them were shocked at the size and how full they were. I didn't notice the shadow in the window. I brought them back in just as the doctor came into the room.

"Hey, guys it's time for everyone to go home. Visiting time is done," he told us.

"Ok, we got to do what the doctor orders. I'll see you guys tomorrow," I walked over and hugged Damien and Mike. I lean in a kissed Trevor and then whispered in his ear, "Come back at midnight trust me I'll be waiting outside."

"Ok babe," he said then they all left.

"Time to get some rest," the doctor said and left the room.

CHAPTER FORTY-THREE

I WALKED OVER TO THE DOOR AND LISTEN THROUGH IT. The doctor started talking to the nurse outside. "I want this patient to be sedated and moved down to OR room stat," the doctor said.

"Ok, doctor," the nurse said.

They both walked away and I went back into my bed. I must have fallen asleep. When I woke up and noticed two figures over my bed. One was Ethan and the other was Dante. Then I rubbed my eyes and they where gone.

I heard the nurse opening my door. "Mr. Shawl, are you awake?" she whispered.

"Yeah, I'm awake. I could not sleep," I replied.

"Well, I'm going to give you some drugs to knock you out, ok?" she asked.

"No thanks. I'll be asleep soon. Did you need something?" I asked and wondering why she wanted me to be asleep.

"Just doing my rounds, I just make sure everyone on my route is sleeping well," she answered cheerfully.

"Ok, hope you rounds go smoothly. If I need anything I'll buzz you ok?" I told her. She just nodded her head and then left the room. I walked up to the door and heard the doctor and nurse talking again.

"He was still awake. I put the drugs in his IV so he should have been knocked out," she told him.

"Well maybe we should just keep him a few more nights till we can see what is going on with those wings that I saw through the window," the doctor said.

"Ok, I'll get the paperwork ready to see what we can make him stay for," the nurse said.

"That will be a great help," the doctor said then I heard footsteps walking away.

"That is what they want," I said while feeling a little tipsy. "I guess the drugs were starting to kick in. I need to get out of here."

I looked over at the time and it was a minute past midnight and looked out the window. I saw my green truck sitting outside. I took off my shirt and brought out my wings and made my wings cover my entire body. Then I jumped through the window.

It shattered and I'm sure someone heard the noise but I didn't look back, I started flying towards the truck and saw Trevor in the driver seat ready to go. The drugs that they gave me were working; I was having a hard time controlling my wings and landed in the back of my truck and passed out.

I woke up and noticed I was not in the hospital. I looked around and saw that I was in my room. Then saw the door slowly open, Trevor stepped though with a wash cloth and some bandages.

"Hey babe, what's going on?" I asked him with weak grin.

"Well you been out for the past couple of days, John and I have been taking care of you since you broke out of the hospital. You got some cuts from the window you broke through and you had a fever for the last twenty four hours.

The place where your wings come from seemed to not have closed up. So we had to wrap them up so you wouldn't be in pain," he paused and then started to lean in to kiss me. He kissed me then started to talk again. "Besides that nobody is coming after you from the hospital but I gave them your old address since I didn't know the new one. So why did you need to break out?"

"Well, I overheard the nurse and the doctor wanting to operate on me to see the wings that were inside me. I guess when I showed Mike and Damien, they were outside the window and saw the shadow of my wings. They wanted to see them for themselves and do strange things to me," I told him in a low voice.

"I'm sorry babe but glad you're awake now and I think we should have a little fun since your back to normal," Trevor said with a grin.

While we both lay in each others arms he said, "Well the rest of our friends should be coming by and then we can talk about our powers and everything that needs to be said."

"That does sound good but I think we might want to get dressed," I said while looked down our naked bodies.

We got dressed and just as I got my socks on the doorbell rang. John was out with his new girlfriend so we could talk in private even though I figured he too knew what was going on. I got up and went to answer the door. I opened the door and everyone was standing there with a big smile on there faces. We all went into the living room and sat down. The living room was set up with a black leather couch in the middle and it was facing a flat screen TV. I did the hostess thing like get people drinks and food if they wanted and then we started our little meeting.

"Hey guys, it is nice to see you guys have not made any trouble while I was passed out. Trevor filled me on what has been going on for last couple of days and I am sorry to worry you guys like that," I said.

"Hey, it is alright we know that you escaped from the hospital and needed your rest," Patty said with a smile.

"Well thanks. So I guess you guys have millions of questions to ask me. By the way, did anything come about with your little appearance at the mall?" I asked.

"Nope, it seemed like it never happened. I guess someone was looking out for me," Mike told us.

"Well, I guess I should tell you that each of us has a great power within and it was unlocked in the last couple of days. The wings are proof of that. Now each of us has a different talent that is why we have different colored wings. I guess I'll go around the room and tell you you're talents. Mike you are fire. Your wings are red. It shows that you have a lot of passion and spirit. It can be a raging inferno but it can also be clam at times. Next is Damien you are air/wind. Your wings are white. It shows that you can adapt quickly to anything that is thrown your way. Larger things that come up you can maneuver fast and efficiently through them," I paused and took a drink of water. "Stephen you're earth. Your wings are brown with a hint of green. It shows that you always are solid but can change instantly to the fact that you have the wisdom within. Your playground is that old and wise world. Patty you're water. Your wings are ocean blue. Able to go with the flow and always changing to fit the conditions you're in. Powerful, forceful, gentle, and kind are your qualities."

"What about me?" Trevor said anxiously.

"For you it is the misty gray see through wings. It is the power of peace. You always have a clear mind that helps each other out. Even through you are not sure that you are helping, it does give others the peace that they are looking for and last is mine. I got two wings; one black and one white. It represents the light and darkness in people. It is basically the balance of life and the battles within us all," I finished saying.

CHAPTER FORTY-FOUR

Just as I finished talking, a flash of light and Ethan was standing next to me. I said, "I was wondering when you would show up. Everybody, this is Ethan, the one that unlocked my hidden powers and taught me. What's up?"

"Nothing much, I just thought I would pop in and see how everything is going. That was great way of introducing everyone and their powers. May I take over to finish why your guys were chosen?" he asked sincerely.

"Be my guest," I said and sat down next to Trevor on the couch.

"Like my friend said, my name is Ethan. Just think of me as a person that watches over the worlds and makes sure everything goes the way it is suppose to. Anyway, the reason you guys were picked was that each one of you was able to unleash your wings with the power of a true emotion. So I want all of you to come up to the roof and we will test you skills out," he finished and vanished again.

We all went up to the roof and waited for Ethan to reappear. All of a sudden six black portals appeared in front of us and sucked each of us in. Each of us had to face the final test to get out of the portals to keep our wings.

During my test, I just sat down on the so call "ground" which was just darkness and started to mediate. While I was mediating, I started to focus in on my friends. Patty was the first person that I saw in my mediated state. I was watching her. She started to get a little freaked out but then she just stopped and waited for the scene to change. It started changing to different random places. She bent down and her wings came out. She screamed since it was the first time that her wings came out. She was watching the images flash by and then realized that none of them was what she wanted. She then started to focus her powers and water started to fill the realm that she was trapped in. The realm got filled faster and then she saw the light where the images were coming from. She swam for the little light and then the realm burst and she fell back into darkness.

My mine was clear again and then the next figure came into view. It was Damien. He was being attacked but he could not see what was hitting him. His wings came out a pearly white. He still didn't see what was hitting him from all different directions.

"This is nuts," I heard him say. Then he thought that if he is wind he can control it. He started to make a whirlwind around his body. It was working and the small needles that were flying at him were now seen. He then changed the wind around him to fire back the needles from where they came from. Just as he did that, one needle flew passed him nicking his cheek and flew to the other side of the realm. It hit the side and popped the realm. Darkness filled my thoughts again.

A person started walking into my vision. It was Mike. His wings were already out. I was wondering what was up. I tried looking around the scene but I couldn't see anything. Then a bright light flared up and three ice poles where around him. In each of the ice poles was something he really had a passion for. I noticed that one was Damien, one was his music, and last one was shoes. I thought to myself which one would he pick.

He started to sit down on the ice and think. As he was thinking his wings were starting to become really flames. He noticed the heat from his wings and then knew what to do. He started to fly around a circle and to create a fire spin. It got bigger and bigger. It started melting the ices poles and then he grabbed the items inside as he flew by them. Just as he grabbed the last item, his flamed wings died out and he vanished into the darkness.

Back in the darkness, another figure came into view. It was Stephen. He was on solid ground. He was the only one besides Patty that has not called upon his wings. The scene changed quickly. Boulders of all shape and sizes came crashing down around him and I believe some crashed into him. The boulders enclosed him and he vanished from my sight. I was watching the boulders and noticed the ground was shaking. Then I noticed the ground was dug up and he popped out of the ground right next to the pile of boulders. He turned his wings into a drill and dug a hole to avoid the crashing of rocks. Just as he landed the darkness consumed him as well.

The only person left was Trevor. I tried focusing on him and I couldn't find him. The darkness was completely surrounding him and me. I was making sure that everyone else was doing alright when I forgot that I was also being tested. Then a hand from the darkness reached out and grabbed my foot. I looked down and noticed whose hand it was. It was Trevor's hand. He pulled me through the darkness and then we both end up next to each other. "Hey babe, I see you figure out one of your powers," I said with a smile.

"Yeah I guess I did. All I did was focus on you and then my hand went through the darkness and I felt something. I pulled it through the darkness and then you appeared," he said with a smile as well.

"Yeah it is a nifty trick with a hat or bag. Anyway I guess this is a test for the both of us since you dragged me here but then again you already passed. You brought me out of my thoughts and made me realize that I was in trouble. So I'll see you on the other side then," I said. As soon I finished that he vanished into the darkness.

"Hey Ethan, nice trial so I guess that means I need to become the leader," I said into the darkness.

He popped out of the darkness and started to speak, "Well, Eric you did pass your test. I kept you in here so I can talk to you for a few more moments."

"Ok, so what do you need to talk to me about," I asked and gave him a puzzled look.

"Well, I just want to say that you did pick the best team and I've seen it coming. You will be a great leader and this team will be the best. Let's go get the rest of the team. Oh yeah by the way Jake says hi and he is doing just fine. The day is coming when you two will reunite," he said then we both fell backwards into the darkness.

Back on the roof top, all six portals opened up Patty was flushed out, Stephen was throw out with a whole bunch of dust, a cone of fire with Mike in the center burst through, Trevor floated down, Damien was forced out with a gust of wind and a few needles. I was just mediating down till I hit the ground.

"Well it looks like you guys passed the first test of your powers and now the last test of your powers," Ethan said.

"Eric, I need you to come up here," he paused. I walked up to him and he was standing on the ledge. "I want you guys to come over here as well."

Everyone walked over to the ledge and then wait for Ethan to do something or say something. Just as we were waiting Ethan grabbed me and we both went falling over the edge. The building grew to be as tall as the Empire State Building and it was clear so you could see all the way down. As we were falling I asked Ethan, "Do you trust me?"

He just winked and then I knew my answer. The team watched from up above and then we were a couple of feet above the ground when I grabbed him and expanded my wings. We flew back up to them and Ethan said, "That is the final test: trust. It is the most important part of anybody's character in a team, can you trust each other." Just as he said that I grabbed Mike and Ethan grabbed Damien. Neither of them screamed.

Just a few feet before we hit the ground, each of them grabbed us and pulled us up. Then we did that with everyone else. After we finished the first round everyone was grabbing everyone while Ethan and I we standing on the top of the roof top.

"Well, see you later my friend, "Ethan said and then vanished off again.

As I waited for them to return I looked up to the sky and said, "I'll see you later honey," and then they all returned.

"So you guys ready for the trip of a life time?" I asked them. Then we all just fell backwards over the ledge and vanished into the sky.

CHAPTER FORTY-FIVE

Just as we were flying up into the heavens we noticed the gods were ready for us. Each of us seemed to have been pair up with one god or another creature. As I was looking back, I noticed my team was being picked off one by one to fight in a different area of the heavens. Soon I was the only one left and knew who my challenger was. As I flew up towards them I started thinking how it all started.

About a week ago, I just finished gathering the last name on the list. As I was flying back home, I got summoned by the gods. "Well I guess there is no rest when you're the son of Gods," I said out loud.

I went up into the clouds and saw the black and white spirits waiting for me. "Hey guys, what's up?" I asked.

"We got some bad news for you Ethan," they started to tell me. "Well a few days ago when you were out collecting people. Something happened."

Flashback a few days ago: *We see the resting place of were Eric threw Anubis. It landed by a lake in South America. It was just sitting there when someone was walking by it. The dark figure then started to chant in old tongue. As I was watching the scene, I noticed the seal that he was trapped in was cracking. The dark figure then took out a small tool that looked like a soul catcher. It was one and then the figure pushed it into the crack that was formed on the seal that lay next to lake. The tool started to glow and the seal turned into ash. Then the dark figure took off.*

"So who was the one that set Anubis free and why are you telling me this?" I asked them.

"Well after Anubis was set free, we received this," they told me and handed me a note. It read: *Hey guys in heaven, I bet you know I'm free and more powerful then the last time. I want to challenge that star of yours, Ethan Rush the one that sent me to the hell that I was in.*

Anubis.

"Ok, so what's up? I'll battle him and win. What else do you guys have for me?" I asked waiting for the next piece of news.

"We just wanted you to be careful. That is all we needed tell you, I guess also keep an eye on everyone that is important to you. He might go after them just to get into your head," they told me.

"Ok, so I guess that I'll be careful and on the look out for any one from his gang that might be lurking around," I said then took off to go home.

As I was flying down, I started thinking I should round everyone up and tell them what is going on. I went flying around grabbing everyone that was from the list since I knew he would attack them or try to.

We met up at John and Eric's pad. It was the biggest meeting place out of everyone's house besides the training faculty. Eric, John, Mrs. X, and Trevor were already there. Mike and Damien were the next to show up and after them Patty and Stephen flew threw the window. "Show off," Mike muttered under his breathe.

Then there was a knock on the door. Eric got up and answered it. "Who is it?" he asked.

"It is Josh. I'm here about the meeting," he said through the door.

"Ok," Eric said and then opened the door.

Just as Josh walked through the door Mrs. X noticed him. "Hey honey, how have you been? It has almost been a year since we trained with you," she said and hugged him.

"I've been doing ok. You know just training and helping out the ones that need it. What's up with you?" he asked.

"Well John and I have been going out and just doing the quests that have been given to us. John would love to see you, come this way," she told him and then dragged him into the living room. The space had a couch in the middle of the room and flat screen TV in front of it hanging on the wall. Most was just empty space that has not been filled out yet. A couple of lamps posts were in the corners of the room to make the light just perfect for the room. The walls had a hint of pink to them but mostly looked white.

There was one more knock on the door. This time John came over and answered it. "Who is it?" he asked.

"It is Dante, Ethan summoned me to come here and join the party," Dante said roughly. John looked out the peephole and there was a tall thin man dress in red and black button down shirt and black slacks.

John opened the door and let him in and then Eric noticed out the corner of his eye and walked over to them. "Hey Dante, I didn't know you knew Ethan. I guess he choose you to be apart of his team. Well welcome and have a good time." Eric said to Dante but still a little cautious as really why he was there.

John shut the door and was wondering when Ethan would be here. The note that Ethan wrote to them said to get ready for a party and he had some big news. He walked away from the door and they all started to enjoy the party.

About an hour into the party everyone started to wonder where Ethan was. Just then the double doors that lead to the balcony few open. Everyone looked and notice two figures standing there. One was dressed in all white from head to toe and the other was dressed in all black from head to toe.

They step onto the balcony and slowly walked in together. I pulled my hood off and everyone had a smile on their face. John asked, "Who is this person next to you if you the one in black?"

"This is Jake," I said and then he removed his hood.

Just as I said that Eric's eyes went wide. Eric seemed happy since him and Trevor broke up about a week ago. Trevor told him that he meet someone else that he fancied. Trevor didn't say who but it was a mutual feeling because for some reason Eric knew it was about time Jake would be coming back.

Eric held back and waited to go rush Jake and Jake did the same because they both knew that I had more important news to tell them before they could talk.

"Well I'm glad you guys could make it. Hope I didn't make you guys missed anything important or pulled you away from anything. I called you guys here to tell you something that will involve all of you. A couple of days ago someone broke the seal that Eric put Anubis in and now he is going to come after me. Now I'm telling you this because he might go after you guys. I wanted you guys to be on guard and to let me know if anything happens to any of you. Eric and I fought him once when I was unlocking his powers. Eric, I want you to be very careful because he knows you better then anyone else," I paused and looked around the room. "So do you guys have any questions so far?"

Mike asked first, "You're talking about the Egyptian God Anubis lord of the underworld?"

"Yes, he is also the ruler of Darkness but we also have the son of the gods down there to help us out. Dante, the man standing behind, is the son of the underworld god. By the way Dante your dad says hi and you should go visit him," I told them.

"Thanks and tell him that I don't follow orders from him," Dante replied to me. That made us both smile.

"So what do we do now?" asked Jake.

"Well, I got a plan to help him come out since I know he'll not do this alone. He has gotten more powerful but so have I. He thinks I'm still weak as I was before. So I have a task for each of you. Jake you will be the one to keep him in this realm. John and Mrs. X, I want you guys to keep an eye on any fallen angels that might talk about switching sides," I paused and threw them some locator devices that showed every fallen angel in this realm. "Next I want Eric and his team to just keep an eye out for anything abnormal. Josh, I'm going to ask you to train these guys for me and I'm going to ask an old friend to help me find where he is hiding. So everyone ready or does anyone have more questions?" I asked and reach for some water.

Everyone was looking around but nobody had any questions. Then Dante spoke up, "What about me?"

"Oh yeah your going to help me with the darkness. Since you are son of darkness, you're coming with me to ask my old friend where he is hiding," I said. "Well, ok that is what I needed but we shall party for a little bit before we go out on our quests."

CHAPTER FORTY-SIX

I TURNED THE MUSIC BACK ON AND THE PARTY CONTINUED like nothing was happening. Jake left to find Eric so they could talk and then I just started mingling; Eric went to his room and wait to see if Jake would come.

There was a knock on the door. "Come in," Eric said.

Jake entered the room and then shut the door behind him. They didn't say anything; they just went up to each other and hugged. They finally broke the hug and Jake started to talk, "See I told you I would be back again and hope you weren't lonely while I was away."

"I did date a few people but no one was like you. I even date Trevor out there and he was great but I still missed you," Eric said with a tear rolling down his cheek. They sat on the bed and caught up on what's been going on for past year they were apart.

Back outside in the living room, everyone was having a good time and I noticed we were being watched. I walked over to Dante and asked him to check up on the roof for the person watching us. Dante vanished instantly and I saw him sneak up on the person watching us. Dante did his darkness engulfing trick and the person vanished. Dante reappear in the room and told me, "He is imprisoned in my dark cage and we can talk to him later. Don't worry about it and have good time like me," he said and patted me on the back.

"That's good to hear," I told him and went back to the party. I saw everyone having a good time when I just noticed that Jake and Eric were not in the room. I figured they would like some privacy and time to catch up.

The party was going on for a few more hours. Eric and Jake finally came out of his room and join the rest of us. I looked at them as the came into the living room holding hands. I thought to myself everything is falling into place. Just like my friend told me, "Just relax and everything will be shown the way it needs to be." I was standing on the balcony looking over the edge.

When Josh walked up behind me and snapped me back to reality, "Hey friend, how have you been?"

"Busy as hell and just running around like there is no tomorrow. I'm glad I have a chance to just slow down and enjoy the company of my old and new friends but I was done with my quest and then this comes up. I was ready to just relax but this party is helping," I paused and looked up to the sky. "How is your girlfriend doing by the way?"

"She is doing fine. I wish I could tell her that you're alive and well but I guess I can not. It feels like old times don't it. You and me just hanging out, chillen, and not worrying about anything to much. I missed those days," he said and a tear rolled down his cheek as he looked up into the sky as well.

"I missed those days too but I guess living in the past means we miss out on what is going on now. Hey, how about you and I, after everything is all said and done, we go catch up and see a movie. Sounds good?" I said while now looking at him.

He just smiled at me and said, "Yeah and thanks for coming back. It was true I really don't know what to do without my best friend." He gave me a big hug then we went back inside. The party continued to go on till about two in the morning. Most people left and Eric, Jake, John, Mrs. X and I were still there. I said my goodbyes and told them if you need me I'll be live right next door.

The sun rose early the next morning and I didn't get much sleep last night, just was thinking about everything that might happen. I guess this was just the test of my leadership skills and I have nothing to worry about. I know that I was a good leader and was able to make sure that everyone will be alright.

I got up and head for the shower since Dante will be coming over in a few. I hoped in the shower and then got dressed. Just as I threw my shirt on, the doorbell rang.

I walked over and opened the door. Dante walked in and was wearing all black today. "So where are we going to get the information you need to find Anubis?" he asked while taking a sit.

"We are going to see my old friend, Caron. He lives in the cave off the shore of Lake Tahoe. You ready to fly?" I asked.

"Always," he said then we went to my balcony and took off. We landed in front of Caron's cave in a matter of minutes and I yelled, "Hey Caron, you home?"

No answer. I yelled again. No answer. I decided to go in and look around. I forgot how dark it was in his cave and then remembered that Dante had dark vision. "Hey Dante, do you see anything?" I asked him.

He was looking around and then he noticed a small trail of liquid. It was dripping and then he looked up. "Hey Ethan, what does your friend look like?"

"Well he is small enough to ride on one's shoulder, has a green tint to him, and bug eyes that look like they are going to pop out of his head. Oh and his skin is able to lite up in dark places," I replied. "Why do you ask?"

"Well I think I found him, he is not moving," he said. Dante touched my shoulder and force me to look through his eyes. I was able to use his dark vision and then saw Caron on the wall with a message written next to him. It read: *I knew you would come here first, but looks like I beat you to him. Caron said he was sorry but couldn't be able to help any more. I had to kill him or he would give away my big plans. Anubis.*

"I was too late to help him and I figure that he was safe since nobody notices him anyway," I said then fell to my knees. Dante came up to me and sat down next to me. "I didn't want anyone to die. I was careless and now look what happened."

I started to cry. It was not what I wanted; I wanted this to end now so nobody else would get hurt. Basically, I clamed up and was lost in my head. Dante could not snap me out of it, so he picked me up and flew us back to the house. He placed me on the floor of the living room.

He went next door and found John in the apartment. "Hey John, I think I need some help snapping Ethan out of this trance he is in. What happened is that we went to see his friend, Caron but when we got there he was killed and a nice little message was left for us. He just said that he didn't want any one dead then he clamed up. Come quickly," Dante quickly said.

"Ok," John said and both of them went running next door. They rushed in and I was just sitting there, looking straight ahead. John walked up to me and just started talking about anything. He got no response from me.

He got up and walked over to where Dante was at. "I really think he got lost in his head when he saw that. I think we need to get Josh over here quickly. They have been friends since he was young. He'll know what to do to snap him out of this," John said and started thinking where he might be.

The bad thing was they did not know where Josh was at this time. "He must be training some of the ES. I know where the training site is. Follow me," John said and then Dante grabbed Ethan and we all flew out the window.

A few moments later they were outside the big white building with a green door. John went and knocked on the door just to make sure there was no training session going on. A few moments later Josh was opening the door. "Hey guys, what's up?" he said a little out of breath.

"Well Ethan clamed up after he saw the death of his friend Caron. He said something like he didn't want anyone to die. Then he became like this," John said and pointed to me.

"We tried snapping him out of it and nothing worked," Dante added.

Josh opened the door wider and we brought him in and Mike and Trevor where in the room training. They both came down from there flight and noticed that I was not saying anything.

Mike came up to me and just slapped me across the face then yelled, "Snap out of it, if you stay like this how are we going to win against Anubis if you freeze up in battle. I know that I wouldn't be able to handle my friend's death but I would at least not clam up. Well I know I'll fight right beside you till the end but if you do not snap out of it I'm going to kick your ass."

Mike was right, I needed to become stronger and better but I knew deep down I wasn't ready for all of this. I still showed no response from him saying that or the slap. It looked like I was lost and it felt like I didn't want to be found. I knew one thing though that I didn't want anyone else to die.

Josh spoke, "Hey I think I might know what will snap him out of it. What I need is to go inside his mind and help him get un-lost."

"Ok and how are you going to do that?" Trevor asked a little dumb founded.

"I just need to connect with him. I have done this once before but it was with my girlfriend and it freaked both of us out. What happened was that we both were sitting on the couch one night and we're just cuddling watching a movie. Then all of a sudden I was transported into her mind. I walked around for a moment and then meet her self-image. It ran and I just focus on getting out of there. I then woke up with her over my body shaking me. She told me that she thought I was dead. I never did it again because I didn't know how to control it but I'll try it again and hope it will work. If it does not then we will just have to wait for him to come to terms with whatever he's afraid of," Josh said.

"Sounds like that it is our only way to go for now, while you do that I'm going to find the others and see if they might know anything or I just might make a visit to my dad and see if he can help us out," Dante said then flew out the door.

"Well he goes nothing," Josh said then went into a trance and was trying to get inside my head. He made through quite easily since I wasn't really caring who got in. Josh came in the middle of one of my daydreams.

CHAPTER FORTY-SEVEN

JOSH LANDED IN THE MIDDLE OF A RAINY NIGHT. I WAS walking down this stone-paved road. The road was empty and only a few of the street lamps were working but they were flickering on and off. The storm seemed to be getting worse by the moment. Josh caught up with me and tried to stop me but I just pushed him away. He decided to follow me to where I was heading. I stopped in the middle of the road and just let the rain pour down on me. We were both soaking wet. Then I asked shrewdly, "What are you doing following me?"

Josh responded kindly, "I'm worried about you Ethan. You're my best friend and I don't want to lose you again."

"I am following you to find out if you could handle me. Being your other half, I've been here for a long time and now it is time for me to become one with you. If you don't let me help you, you have no chance in the battles that face you in the near future," the voice in front of me rang out.

Josh came running to my side and noticed there we're two of me standing face to face. I was facing my other half. I looked over and saw Josh standing next to me. Then spoke,

"See, even my friends are worried about me. He came in here risking his life to help me out. I don't know if I have the courage or guts to face my fears. The one thing I do know is that as long as I got my friends with me then I'll be able to face it yet if I face it alone it is a whole different ballgame. I know I'm not alone but I don't know if I will be able to protect them."

"Hey knucklehead, I know your tough enough and you're willing to put your life on the line for others but I never thought I hear those words come out of your mouth. I should just beat you up myself right here. I knew you would fight for me until the end of time and I would do the same for you. I know you lost a good friend but you should use it in your fight against Anubis and show him you can not be rattled by that. All I'm asking is for you to come back and don't worry because we'll always be beside you no matter what," Josh said to me.

"You're right, I was being stupid. Anubis can not rattle me. What if I can bring you out? What if he does not come back in time for the fight? What if he doesn't find it?" I asked the other me in low soft voice.

"He will and you should stop worrying everything. It will be fine. Now get your sorry ass out of here and back into reality. People are starting to worry that you'll never come back," the other half said to me.

Josh vanished and came back into his body. "It looks like he was afraid that he wouldn't be able to protect us from Anubis. He seemed like he lost his self since he was spilt into two. His other half talked to him and so did I. It reassured him that everything will work out. He should be coming back with the next few moments," Josh told them.

Back inside my mind I want to talk to my other half a little more. "Why do you need that item to come out?" I asked and still a little puzzled.

"Well it is not really the item that I need. It is what is inside the item. See I locked away all my powers within that item. Once I get my bracelet back, I'll be able to help you out more and show you our full strength. Once we become one again we'll be able to do anything. For now I'll only tell you that because you have people waiting for you to get back. Later my friend," my other half said.

I came back and said, "Ouch." as I rubbed my face. "Thanks for the slap and prep talk, Mike."

"No problem. Anytime you need that I'll be more then happy to snap you back to reality," he said with a grin.

"Well I'm back and now I need to go challenge someone," I said and took off.

They followed me to make sure I wasn't going to do anything foolish. I landed on top of the training building. "Hey Anubis," I yelled out to the world. "You want me so bad then I'll accept your offer. I don't want any of my friends to get hurt so I challenge you to fight, just me and you."

Just then a flash of darkness appeared in front of me and there stood the new Anubis. He was about a good foot taller then me and his skin was a shiny metallic black. "Ok, I accept those terms but it is my chose of time and place. In one week, the planets well be aligned and the gateway to the other world will open. We'll fight at the portal site and the loser will be banished to the other realm forever and they can not step in this realm every again," he said with a little bite and snarl to it.

"Ok, sounds fair. Then one more question," I asked him before we shook.

"What?" he snapped at me.

"What will happen to my team if I lose?" I responded.

"I promise on the title of god that I will not hurt them but I will if they get in the way of my plans," he said.

"Deal, "I said reaching my hand out to seal the agreement.

"Deal with me too," he said and he grabbed my hand forcefully and shook hard.

After we shook hands, he vanished back into the shadows. "Well at least I know you guys are going to be safe, which is what I really care about. Sorry for scaring you guys about everything. So I guess I can start training, who wants to help," I said. They all raised their hand.

Everyone wanted to help me train for the battle to come. Everyday for the next week I was training and practicing and waiting for the return of him. Each day one of my team mates was there for me. They would point out my weak points and then also tell me what I was doing right.

Two days before the battle, Jake came up to me on my balcony. He said, "Hey Ethan, I know that you want to protect us but I see that there is more in your heart then just wanting to protect us. What is going on in that head of yours?"

"Well I do want to protect you guys but it was also for myself. See I know that Anubis is more powerful but I do have something he does not. That something is Will Power. It is strange but I think that is what drives me to do my best and protect everything and everyone that I care about. So deep down I know I'll win against him no matter what," I told him.

"I think I know what your mean. When I was bashed, I didn't care what happened to me, my will power was making me more concerned about Eric's safety which gave me a boost of energy to protect him," Jake told me with some sorrow in his voice.

"I just know this battle is going to be a big one. I'll win and nothing is going to stop me from kicking his ass," I told Jake then walked back inside. Jake followed me inside and we just relaxed instead of training. I think he knew that sometimes training all the time, you'll need to just relax or your body will fall apart. He saw me breaking down so he decided to just let me rest for the night.

The next day I didn't train, instead I went to the mountains and mediated for most of the day. Everyone was wondering where I was. I wanted to just be one with the way of the world so I went into the mountains and just rested all day. I returned home late that night and only one person was up waiting for me. It was Mrs. X.

I knew she would be since she is like the mother of the group. Always watching over her kids and making sure we are not getting in too much trouble. "Hey X, how are you doing?" I asked.

"I'm doing fine, hon. I saw you up on in the mountains mediating. I didn't want to disturb you because I knew your battle is a couple days away. Did you clear your head or is it still messed up as the day I met you?" she asked.

"I went up there so I could figure out some things and just came back with a clear mind. Each time I thought about something it seemed to not be as important as I thought. I figured that it is good to go into battle with a clear mind so I finished mediating and watch the sunset. I bet you have seen some really awesome sunsets?" I said to her.

"Yeah, that is one of the reason I pick that mountain to live on because it was just so beautiful. Plus on the other hand if you want peace and quiet you get it," she told me. "Anyway I just dropped by to make sure you're alright and nothing is wrong. You know me always just make sure the one that helped me does not need help in return."

"I am fine. Just wanted some peace and quiet before the battle and thanks for the talk," I told her. I walked over to her and gave her hug. I went inside my apartment and she left to go home. I fell asleep.

I was awoken to the sound of someone in my bedroom. I looked around but nobody was to be found. I looked out the window and noticed it was just before sunrise. I thought to myself that I must get going to train today and get some good rest for tomorrow's battle.

I flew over to the building and let myself in. Nobody was there, so I started to train myself. After about three hours of flight, fight, and defense training, I decided to just go mediate. I went out the door and lock it. I took off to the one place that always seemed to be peaceful.

I flew fast and landed in the white halls of the peaceful building. "Hey Abe," I said while walking up to him. I walked up to the giant statue of Abraham Lincoln then flew around back and up on to the backside of his hat to take a seat. I just started thinking. I started talking to Abe even though I knew he would not talk back. "I guess I know how you felt during the Civil War and all that. I mean it seemed like you were always cool and clam but I just didn't know how you did it."

I jumped down from his hat and walked around the front side of the statue. The words written on the front was all I needed. I read them and then flew off. It was about six or seven when I got home do to the fact that I was just flying at low speeds this time.

I got back to my apartment and opened the door. The apartment was black and then the lights went on. Everyone from the team jumped out and yelled surprise. I was a little shocked and was wondering what this was for.

"We thought you could use a little fun before tomorrow. It seemed like that is how you work, you get to serious then you just break down. So tonight just have some fun and relax," Jake said.

I looked around the room and then walked inside. I shut the door and then the party got on its way. We all passed out around one that night yet I was the only one that couldn't sleep. I was still afraid that I wasn't strong enough. I walked outside to the patio and was looking up at the night sky. I didn't realize that someone was behind me. It was Trevor.

"Beautiful night," he said which brought me out of my daze.

"Yeah it is. Couldn't sleep?" I asked.

"Yeah, just worried about tomorrow, I mean I know you'll be great but I just hope you don't get to beat up in the process," he paused then looked down at his feet.

"Thanks. As long as you guys believe in me and believe in yourselves we will be alright. Trust me," I told him then went back to looking up at the sky.

After I said that, Trevor went back inside. He fell asleep while I was still watching the sky. I looked up and thought I saw a white streak cross the sky. Then I just thought to myself hope he comes through.

CHAPTER FORTY-EIGHT

THE LIGHT SHINED THROUGH THE WINDOW ONTO THE floor that everyone was laying on. I didn't sleep that night just because my mind was racing around with all possible outcomes. Jake was the first one to wake up. He saw me sitting up and then flashed me a smile. He got up and went to the bathroom. I decided to cook everyone breakfast, so I walked into the kitchen.

I started to make some eggs and few more started to wake up; then I made the toast and the rest of them woke up. We all gathered around the living room floor and started to eat. Nobody said a word all throughout breakfast.

Then Jake broke the silence, "Hey guys, so what do you want to do today?"

"I do not know but I know it should be something fun," Mrs. X said while taking a bit of her toast.

"I know. We should all have a day at the beach," I said while drink some orange juice.

Everyone agreed that would be a great idea. We finished breakfast and then started to get ready for the beach. We hoped in our cars and drove over the mountain.

We hit the beaches of Santa Cruz and had a blast. Eating hot dogs and hamburgers, swimming in the ice cold ocean waters, and just relaxing in the hot sand under the even hotter sun; it seemed like it was the perfect day.

The evening came and we went to one of the beaches down the road. We were all just watching the moonlight hit the water. We built a fire and a conversation started up about anything and everything that was on people's mind. I was looking up into the night sky again and notice that white streak again.

I looked back down at the beach in front of me and saw a dark figure. It started moving towards us. I knew who it was. It was almost time for the portal to open up and to have my battle with the lord of the underworld.

The fire lit up the dark figure and it was Anubis. He just walked straight up to me and said, "It is time and now all this will be mine, once you're gone." Then his long finger pointed at me.

"Will see about that," I told him and start walking towards him.

Just then on the beach, rocks started to form a half circle stretching into the sky. The half circle started to open the portal to the other world. Looking up into the sky, you could see the planets aligned. Just then a streak of dark light came flying across the beach and the other world start to open up.

The other world seemed to look just like ours but it had a darker edge about it. It was trapped within the half circle the rocks made, so I took a guess that we would be fighting in front of it. I made barrier so nobody else would get hurt and trapped Anubis, the portal and me within the barrier. Everyone else was standing on the edge of the barrier which was on the edge of where the beach met the road.

"You ready for this Anubis?" I asked confidently.

"I have been training since that day you banished me into that seal," he answered back.

Then I went flying towards him. I want to test out how strong he got. He didn't move at all. Just as I got close enough to hit him, he took one step to the side and then elbowed me down into the sand. It didn't hurt much but I knew from the side step that he did learn a few more moves.

I got up and felt him hovering above me. "I see you learn the power of flight in that seal. I bet you couldn't out fly me," I challenged him.

"I bet I can," he snarled back.

I uncased my wings and he took off. I took after him. I knew that he was not that good at flight since I was watching him. He seemed to be a little bit shaky and wasn't able to keep full balance. I flew right below him and he tried to kick me but I dodged it. He lost control of his flight and crash into the barrier; falling down the side of the barrier and made a big carter in the sand below. That is when I noticed we had another watcher besides his minions and my team. I didn't notice Anubis getting up so quickly from his fall and was now hovering over me. He punched me in the back and it sent me flying into the barrier. I got a good look at his face as I was sliding down the side of the barrier. I hit the ground with a thud.

He came down quickly on top of me. I used my wings to start a sand storm. It blocked him from landing on me but it was only a temporary shield. I got back up and saw him blow away the sand storm. I made quick dash towards the water. At the water's edge, I dived right into it and transformed. He didn't see me transform into a group of eels.

"What is this hide and seek?" he yelled out loud.

I didn't answer. He walked into the ocean and I sent a shockwave from my body through the water. It shocked him and sent him flying back onto the beach. He landed on his back; he was a little fried and pissed off. I jumped out of the water and started casting a spell. He got up and started sending black lighting bolts towards me.

I just stood there and took the hits. A smoke cloud engulfed me. My shadow vanished and Anubis jumped with joy. The smoke cloud vanished and I was still standing up there and with my hands in the center of my chest. I was standing there in a trance but then the black lighting came shooting out of my hands. It went flying back at him and hit him instead of me.

I went flying over to where he landed. The sand was covering him up and I couldn't see through it. He jumped up and grabbed me and pulled me down to the ground. I hit it with a thud and then he started punching away like there was no tomorrow.

Down on the ground, I was doing my best to dodge the punches. A few of them hit me but I was doing ok. I was digging the sand around his feet to get him to lose his footing. I kick one more time and he fell back into the sand and I got out from underneath him.

Everyone was looking at the fight from outside the barrier. Each cheering me on to kick his butt then they noticed that they were not alone. Starting to appear around the barrier were some of the others that Anubis had under his control. They felt surrounded but they knew they had nothing to worry about because they would not attack till the battle was over. At least they thought that because of what I agreed with Anubis early.

I was catching my breath and so was he. I looked up and noticed that his gang was surrounding the barrier. As I was looking around, he took a cheap shot. He kicked me in the side, just below the rib cage and it sent me flying into the water. I got up and he was on top of me again.

I thought to myself, is it me or is he getting fast by the moment. He kicked me again. This time he sent me flying into the barrier where my friends were. My friends saw me slam into the barrier and then I looked at them and smiled my evil grin. They gave me a weird look like what does he have in mind.

I spread my wings to full and it covered the entire barrier. It confused Anubis. Then my wings turned into needles and all aimed at him. Black and White needles shooting in ever direction. I shrunk my wings and then we all saw that Anubis was like a giant pin cushion.

Then he popped and pieces of him went flying everywhere. I was a little puzzled that he popped. I noticed the ground he was standing on starting to break open. "Nice little trick," I said and gave him a pity clap.

He just laughed as he rose from the ground. "I thought you would like it," he answered with a smirk to kill.

Then we went back to fighting. On the outside, Josh said, "Well it seems like both of them are enjoying the battle and it seems like there are old friends battling again. Neither of them are trying to hurt each other yet but just testing out the waters before they showed off there big guns."

"Well I think each of them are buying there time to something comes up. Seeing each others weakness and then will strike at the right moment," Jake told the crowd.

"Whatever the case maybe it seems to be heating up inside, I'm just wondering why Anubis' gang is crowding the barrier. It makes me worry about if they are trying to break it or find a hole or something," Mrs. X said looking up towards the barriers top.

I was thinking the same thing when I transformed into small bug. Anubis wondered where I disappeared to and then he became the shadows. Inside the barrier became quiet and clam for a few seconds then the shadows covered the entire barrier. He found that I turned in a bug to hide in the sand, since I was the only colored thing in the darkness. A black shadowy hand picked me up and I decided it was time for my next trick. I pulled the multiply trick. I start to turn into thousands upon thousands of bugs. It covered the entire ground and kept going. I started to fill up the barrier.

He pulled back the shadows and then half the barrier was filled with my bugs. I transformed back into myself and there we six of me when I transformed back. "So which one is the real me, I bet you couldn't even hit me," me and my clones said.

"So that is your new trick, to hide and then become many. Seems simple," he said to me with a smirk.

He then started fighting the clones that I made, but every time he killed one it would split into two more. He kept swiping at the clones and in about five minutes of this there were hundreds of copies. Then he noticed that I was just sitting on the barrier. He then went flying towards me; I went flying faster and faster collecting all the clones.

After I rounded up all my clones, I was thinking what I should do to stall for time. Then he came at me with full force, I knew that it was time to stop playing tricks and start truly battling him. The only thought in my mind was would I be strong enough. I turned around a noticed something out of the corner of my eye. The dark figure was still standing there on the cliff side and I wanted to know why he was there.

That spilt sec, Anubis noticed I was distracted and took the chance as his way to get in. He punched me and hit me square in the gut knocking me down to the ground. That one did hurt since I didn't get a chance to stop it. I hit the ground with a thud and didn't see that he was already on top of me and punching me further into the ground. This time he dug his feet into the sand so I wouldn't make him lose his balance. I was blocking his punches but was also becoming buried under the sand. If I didn't do anything to stop him, I would be digging my own grave.

CHAPTER FORTY-NINE

RIGHT BEFORE I WAS COMPLETELY COVERED IN SAND, I saw the white streak again in the sky as I saw for the last two nights. This time it didn't streak across the sky but landed in between Josh and Dante. The light faded away and a person was standing there. "Who the heck are you?" Dante demanded to know.

Anubis stopped punching me and the dark figure looked over at the person that just landed outside the barrier.

"I am Sam, the protector. I was away training and on a quest for the man that just got buried in the sand. It has been one year and now I'm back. I'll tell you more but I need to give this to him," he said holding up the bracelet. It was nothing fancy; it was black string bracelet with puka shells through the middle. Sam turned back into light and went racing through the barrier.

Right where Anubis was standing, Sam went underneath him and through the sand. The sand was glowing, do to the brightness of the light Sam was emitting. "Hey Ethan, I'm back and here is that thing you want me to get. Hope your battle goes well and I'll talk to you later," Sam said with a smile to lite up the world.

"Thanks and not a moment to soon," I said to him. "Now get out of here before Anubis hurts you." I put on the bracelet and saw Sam fly back out of the barrier. Anubis noticed that Sam flew back out and didn't know what it was about. He then started digging for me and found me in a hard case shell. He pulled it out of the sand and placed it near the water.

He was looking at it and nothing was happening. He was walking away and then it started to shake. Just when Anubis turned around the container burst into a million pieces. Standing there was the person that Josh saw when he went into my mind. He stands about 6'1 and had the perfect build not to fat and not to thin. My wings have become metallic black and white colors.

"Who the heck are you?" Anubis growled.

"Me, well I'm his other half. The name is UE. Nice to meet you Anubis but I think we are merged as one now so I guess I'll be finish fighting for him. I warn you that you will lose," I said all confident and cocky.

Anubis got pissed off when he heard that. He went into a flying rage and bolts of darkness went flying all throughout the barrier. I was dodging all the bolts and noticed he was flying straight towards me. He was throwing punches left and right and I was dodging them with ease. I was being back into one side of barrier; I moved to his left and flew above him. While I was above him, I struck him square in his back. It sent him flying down to the sand and made a nice little crater. I didn't worry about Anubis and went over to where I saw the dark figure. He was no longer standing on the cliffside, he was no where to be found.

Anubis didn't care about what I was looking at so he tried to attack me from the back. I moved out of the way and he went flying into the barrier. It shattered the barrier and pieces of it landed in his body. He fell and shards of the barrier, about the size of tires, drove into him when he hit the sand. A shrieking sound came from him. He knew it was over as I was coming down to him; he just started laughing.

"What so funny Anubis? You just lost because those barrier shards will just eat you away unless I take them out," I said to him and started to pull them out.

"You don't get it do you, you stupid puppet," was all he said then he turn to dust. His gang turned to dust as well. I took into the air and felt like I was going to pass out. My wings transform back to the regular wings and I fell from the sky. Everyone rushed over to me and I landed into the sand.

"Ethan, you alright," everyone asked. I didn't response and the only thing I remember after that was being picked up.

A few days later, I woke up and noticed that I was in my bedroom. Laying there I just remember the battle and what he said, "You don't get it do you, you stupid puppet." I also remember the dark figure. I started to get up but was not able to move. It seemed that I was strapped down to the bed. Just then I heard the door open up.

"Hey guys he is awake," the voice said. Before anyone entered the room, UE spoke up in my head.

"Hey I thought you were going to sleep forever. Just to fill you in, we won the battle and then you passed out. I guess your new body was not able to withstand all the power that we were using. It drained it from your body and then you collapsed. You're fine now that we're full merged together. You now look a lot more like me then you do you. Well I'll talk to you later. Oh yeah I forgot to tell you, you did a great job in the battle," he said to me.

"Well so did you," I told my other half.

Just then everyone busted in. I saw everyone's smiling faces and then asked, "What am I doing in these straps?"

"Well, you seem to be fighting while you were knocked out. So we just strapped you in and now to let you free," Jake told me and started to un-strap me.

"Well thanks," I said. "I guess I won since I'm not in the other world. What happen after I passed out?"

Everyone filled me in on what happened and then they all left so I could get dressed and ready for the day. While I was getting dress I looked down at my new body. I really saw no difference but I guess everyone else did. Then my other half started talking again, "Hey I was wondering, who was that dark figure you want me to check out before Anubis destroyed the barrier?"

"Well it was my twin brother, Marko. I have no clue why he was there at the battle. I'm going to go talk to the gods to find out what is going on," I said to him with some concern in my voice.

"You going to tell everyone or just going to let everyone wait?" UE asked.

"I think I'm going to tell them what's going on," I told him.

"Ok, well get out there and let them know," UE said to me.

So I finished getting dressed and met everyone outside. I told them that I needed to go talk with the gods. They didn't seem to mind that I was already off again. I thought it was a little weird that nobody was caring but then I just thought they knew I was going talk to them anyways.

I flew off and in a couple of minutes I was at the gates of heaven. It was if they knew I was coming up because they were waiting for me at the front of the gates.

"Hey guys, just the people I wanted to see," I said to them and trying to hide my concern.

"Well we need to talk about your next quest. We are happy that you found how to unlock your powers. UE is one of the lost ultimate of this realm. Now that we know where he is we can start are real plans," they said.

"What do you mean real plans?" I asked curiously.

"Well to get rid of all the useless human's with powers. Didn't you know that they just get in the way of everything? Always hiding it from the humans is a pain in the butt for us gods. It seems there is always somebody screwing up. The next mission is to get rid of the ones on this list." they said and handed me a list.

I read the list and then said, "I will not do it. They are my friends."

"We are not asking you. We are telling you to do it or your powers and everything will be gone," they threaten me.

"Well, I will not and you can not make me," I told them and started to leave.

"Then we will be taking your powers," they said. They tried to take it back but it didn't work. Just as I was about to leave I turned around.

"Just to let you know, I will stop you from carrying out this plan. That is a promise that I'll keep it," I told them and flew off.

I made it home and Sam was the only one that was at my place. I told him what was up then we spread the word to the rest of the group. We all met up at the training center.

"Well thank you for coming and I would like to let you know now I'll be taking on the gods and probably killing or banishing them from here. I was hoping you would like to help but I will understand if you wish not to," I said to them. The room went quiet for couple of minutes.

Mike was the first to speak up. "I may not understand the whole reason of why they want to destroy us but anything that threats my way of life, I'll take them on. I'm ready to kick some butt." After he said that he walked up beside me and just stood with me. I whisper thanks to him and then looked back to the group.

It seemed to be a hard choice for everyone but Josh stood up and just walked over. Then rest of them started to follow in suit. "Thanks guys, so I guess the plan is to just wait and see what they will do first." I told them a little more details on what they wanted me to do. They didn't like that and I told them to just chill and wait for them.

It was a few weeks after I made that decision to take on the Gods. What they did was strange. They wanted to make a clone of me, all the way down to the bone. They sent down a shadow clone. It looked and acted just like me. The only difference was that it had no personality and it was just like a shadow. It was only half of what I was.

"So this is you big move, to try and copy me. I thought you guys would try something better then that," I said a little disappointed.

"Oh I am not a copy of you Ethan but the one secret that they kept from you," the shadow said. Then the shadow faded away and there stood Marko. "See you were not the only one able to become a God. The Gods kept me just incase you decide to turn your back on the fate that was chosen for you. The only difference is that you have UE and I don't. That is why they waited for you to unleash your other half, so you would have more power to help their plan. You don't want to help them, so I am here to destroy you," he said with some emptiness in his voice.

Then I noticed he had the pitch black eyes again and I knew this time it was not the darkness but the gods controlling him. "Oh I see, so then you would already know that I'll be able to kick your ass," I said with a smirk.

"I am not here to fight you but to make you one last offer. Please don't go through with this, if you decide to go through with this I'll be force to fight you, my brother and I don't want that. See the one thing I know is that the battle of the Gods is not going to be anything like you faced before. Each God will pull you team apart and fight them one on one instead of just one battle for all. I got to go because they are calling me, so please reconsider," Marko told me and vanished.

"Well I guess the first move is not to come after me but then what is there first move. Well I guess that I must do what I think is right and make my final stand," I said to myself.

I called the team together and told them that they took control of Marko and what they would do if we went to battle. They still left it up to me but it seemed that they would stand behind me no matter what.

"Ok guys let go and finish this," I said.

They all stood up and yelled in one voice, "Let's do it!"

We started flying up into the heavens and just like my twin told me every one was being picked off one by one. I looked back and it was only me when I reached the top. I was standing face to face with three people; the two Gods and Marko.

CHAPTER FIFTY

I MADE IT TO THE TOP OF THE HEAVENS AND THREE PEOPLE were there waiting for me: the two gods and Marko. I did notice that my entire team was gone; I thought about them but realized that everyone would be alright. "So I guess this is it guys, me versus you. I just wanted to know one thing," I said to them.

"What is that?" they asked back.

"Why is it that you want to get rid of the people with gifted powers?" I asked them.

They didn't answer me but brought a mirror that showed everything. I knew what they were doing. They wanted me to watch my friends fall and then it would make me easier to beat in our fight. A seat was brought up behind me and I took it. I figured at least they don't make me stand on my feet.

Back at the lowest level of heaven, there were battles that were about to start. It was with Jake and Mrs. X. Each seem to have an opponent that match there skills. There opponents seem to have picked the same battle field so they would duel them together as a team.

"Jake, I thought we would be fighting separate but I like the odds now that we have a small team battle," Mrs. X said to Jake with a smile.

"Yeah I like those odds as well. Even though we don't know each other that well we have meet before. Remember when you were walking in the hall of realms with John, I was the man in white that let you pass. So I guess we need to fight whatever comes out of those clouds coming towards us," Jake said to his new partner.

The next level up was the elemental god's area. So Eric's team of ES had there own fields, each matched up with the color of their wings. Mike was up against the fire god; Patty versus the water god, Stephen versus the Earth god, Damien versus the Wind god. Each stage was set with the two elements, the strength and weakness of that element.

The next level up was Eric and Trevor. The more two powerful ES, it seem that each of there battles areas were far apart and had nothing within it. I saw nothing out of the normal for them. Then I realized what it was since Trevor was Peace and Eric was the good and bad of all things that each stage will be filled soon enough.

The mirror switched to the next stage. John and Dante were on mirror, waiting for something to happen. It seemed like they were pair up like Jake and Mrs. X.

"Hey John, how are you doing?" Dante asked a little concerned for his partner.

"I'm doing fine but wondering what is going on," John said while looking around the area.

"Well as far as I know we are waiting for our opponents to come out and show themselves. We must be on one of the higher platforms since if you look down you can see our teammates below us and above us. Ethan must be at the top with the Gods and Marko. We must win to help the others. I know you're a good fighter but wait till you see me in action," he paused then he went on. "Well let's just worry about our fight first then we can worry about everyone else."

"Sounds good to me," John said then the mirror went off of them.

On the platform below me, was Sam. He was in complete darkness since they knew he mastered the powers of light. It was to battle the darkness itself. The screen went blank then I looked down and saw him. I tried to yell at him but he could not hear me.

I looked back up and then noticed the Gods were not there but Marko was. "Let me guess the Gods are now with you and I'll have to battle you with their powers. I defeat you, I defeat them," I said.

"You were always the smart one knowing everything there is. Yes, you're right. We will not fight till you see your friends fall beneath you then I'll destroy you. Just watch you team fall against the power of Gods," Marko said with an evil laugh.

The mirror went back to the first level. Jake and Mrs. X were wandering through the clouds. "So I guess we are to find our opponents within this mess," Jake said while separating the clouds.

"Yeah, I guess so. I was wondering something Jake?" she said.

"Hmm..." he said while walking into a cloud.

"I really don't know you that well since our tour of the realms but why are you dress in all white all the time?" she asked curiously.

"To be honest, it's real simple. It is the fact that I work in the halls of realms which are absolute black and I lead people through the darkness. I wear the white so people don't lose me in the hallways," he said to her.

"That does make sense," she said shaking her head.

"So I have a question for you," he asked back.

"Go ahead and shoot," she replied quickly.

"Why does Ethan call you Mrs. X," he asked back to her and then stopped in his tracks.

"Well the thing is I don't remember my name after I died on the hill so when Ethan found me, I want to tell him my name but I couldn't remember it. Then he gave me the name of Mrs. X and I guess I liked it," she told him.

"Would you ever want to remember your real name?" Jake asked her.

"Someday but for right now I just like Mrs. X since I like to have some mystique about me," she said. Just as she finished her last word, a shadow appeared in front of them. Then another one appeared right next to it.

"I thought, I heard them over here," a voice rang out.

"No over this way," the other voice said.

Mrs. X looked over at Jake and nodded her head to make him follow her. They moved in silent and then the got to a clearing in the clouds. They poked there heads into the clearing and saw what was making the shadows.

It was two more angels. Their wings were out and they were hovering just above the ground. The difference was that these angels had chains on their wings to keep them pretty much low to the ground. The strange thing was that Mrs. X has seen these angels before. They were the ones chasing John and her in the other realm.

Mrs. X walked over to Jake and whisper to him, "I know these guys. They are the ones that tried to capture John and me in that other realm. They still want me but what do they want with you."

"Well, that is simple my friend. The reason they want me is so they can travel in between realms with out going through me, so if they kill or trap me they can freely move about the realms without care," he said to her.

"Well I guess these must be our opponents. Since it seems they are searching for us. How about we give them a show?" she asked Jake with a devilish grin.

"It does sound like it should be fun to test out these new skills that I have gotten," he said to her. Then he vanished into the clouds. Mrs. X wait on the edge of the clearing while Jake was make his way around to the backside of one of the angels. It was really interesting how he just blended into the clouds. His clothing made him look as if he was one of the clouds.

He made his way to the backside of one of the angel and noticed that the chain was attached to his belt. He reached out and grabbed the chain and started to unhook it from the angel's belt that he was wearing. Successful, he unhooked the chain and then walked back to where Mrs. X was standing.

"Well, I guess the chain they have special powers to contain the power of an angel's wing. I was wondering if you would be able to create a whirlwind because I have a plan to get these guys," he asked her.

She just nodded her head and brought her wings out. They were pretty neat to look at. They had small spirals design on the tips of the wings like fingerprints. She started flapping and created a small whirlwind in front of us.

She flapped harder and it started to grow. She then pushed it into the clearing and it started sucking the clouds around it and it started to cover the clearing. Jake then blended back in with the clouds.

Then Mrs. X noticed that Jake had the chain in his hands and was hooking it back onto the angel's belts. He got the first one hooked and then he was walking over to the next one. The whirlwind was starting to die down. Mrs. X tried to keep it up but was not very successful.

Jake cover vanished and the one that was chained noticed him first. "Hey bro, one of the guys is right behind you," the angel said.

The other one turned around and Jake just smiled at him. Jake stood up fast and then yanked on the chain that he was still holding on to. Then the angel behind him went flying in the air towards him. Jake dropped down to the ground and watched the angel soar over him.

The other angel tried to move but it was too late. They crashed into each other and fell onto the ground. Mrs. X then came out from behind the clouds to join in the fight.

The two angels got back up and got into a fighting stance. Jake still holding on to the chain that was still attached to the angel's belt and the angel noticed it and tried to take if off but Jake yanked it again, sending the angel back down to the ground.

"Hey X, I got a human yo-yo," he said laughing at his joke.

X laughed along with Jake but that pissed off the angels even more. The one on the ground pulled the chain sending Jake to the ground with him. Then X got an ideal and went flying towards the other angel that had its wings chained up. She grabbed him and took him into the air with her.

On the ground, Jake and the angel were fighting for control of the chain. Jake knew that if he could get the chain from the angel that X would be not have anything to worry about. They we playing tug a war with the chain and it seemed like both were evenly matched. Then they both heard screaming and then the chain was hit by a falling angel.

It looked like X dragged the other angel high into the air and tried to see exactly what those chains did. The chains on the wings of the angel do restricted flight of the angel. So she let go of the angel and he dropped like a rock.

It just happened that she dropped him over where the chain struggle was going on. The chain snapped into two pieces. The chain was no longer long enough to tie someone or something up. Jake threw it into the clouds as X was coming down from her flight. The other angel threw his away and saw his friend in a large crater that was made.

The angel knew that this battle was over and he didn't stand a chance against the both of them. He then told them, "I quit. I see you guys are more powerful then we estimated so here take this and leave me out of this war." Then he flew off. The other angel still in the carter, as both of them walked over to see what the angel dropped.

They got to were the angel was and picked up a crystal shard. It seemed like it was piece of a larger whole. Jake put it into his pocket and then turned to X to say, "Well it seemed like that was an easy win, hope the others are doing well." Then they look up and saw a door way and a viewing window. They flew up to the window and they saw that everyone else were in their elemental zones.

The doorway was open and they flew in. As they went into the doorway, it became a hallway were they could watch the other battles but were not to interfere with them. They both wondered if anyone was watching their battle.

"I see that my guardians were right. I trust my team more and more so, even if I'm not there to guide them," I said and noticed that Marko was getting angry. I knew my twin didn't want to fight me; I was just buying my time to figure out how to save Marko and free him from their control. My battle was not with my brother but with the Gods.

He talked back, "Those we weak angels anyway. Your next friends will not beat the four elemental Gods. They have been here since the beginning of time," Marko said to me and then looked at mirror. The mirror changed and had all four them in split screen.

I thought to myself that I hope they remember the one thing they have that the Gods don't.

CHAPTER FIFTY-ONE

THE FIRST BATTLE THE MIRROR TURNED TO WAS STEPHEN'S battle with the Earth God. The stage was half water and half mountains. The Earth god pretty much looked like a giant pile of stones stuck together.

"So I take it you're the Earth God. Well I hope this battle is nice and smooth," Stephen said to the God and then brought out his brown wings.

The God didn't talk but started the battle off with throwing rocks into the water to dry up the water. Well Stephen just stood there watching what he was doing. Stephen then realized that if his opponent got thrown into the water, it would bring him down. Then Stephen made the first attack against the rocks. He flew in low and was looking around to see if there were any openings. Just as he looked around the left ankle, he noticed a crack. That was his opening.

To busy to notice the shadow covering him, a giant fist of stone came crashing down on him. Making a carter into the mountains foundation, it lifted its hand from the crater and you see a small hole in the middle of the carter.

Off to the left of the carter you see the ground being lifted up. Another hand came crashing down right in front of the lifted ground.

The hand lifted up and another carter was created. The lift gravel just stopped and in the carter you see a hole that was just empty. Then the lifted gravel started moving south. The hand smashed the ground again. Same thing happened again and again.

Then the loose gravel trail went over to where the water was. The god lost track of were his opponent left off and then was just standing in the middle of his craters. Then all of sudden the carters started to fill up with the water. The god was surrounded by water filled carters that he created.

Stephen appeared out of one of the carters and flew up. He looked down and thought to himself that it worked and he just made the field just that much small. Now to get water in that small crack on its foot, he went to each carter and sucked up some of the water.

The god was not mad or angry but was more like it wanted to be out smarted. It looked like it had a grin on its face but the battle was far from over. The god was just toying with him; see the one thing Stephen didn't know was that Earth is everywhere even in the water.

Just as Stephen saw his opening to put water into the heel of the God, the God started to shrink. The water went right over him. Stephen was a little puzzled by what just happened then he noticed the water was being drained from the carters. Just then the ground started to crack up and the God reappear just a little bigger then Stephen.

I guess this was when the fighting really started to begin. Stephen then flew down to meet it. They started fighting down on the ground and each was very talented with the solidity of each punch. Stephen threw a punch and it hit square in the chest but Stephen's hand got stuck. Then he tried to loosen it up by putting his foot on the chest and pushing. His foot got stuck. The god started sucking Stephen in and that is when Stephen retracted his wings. The God finished sucking in Stephen and started to grow back to size he started out as. It became more solid and then he went to walk off the screen.

"Ha, ha, ha, it seems Stephen has been swallowed whole," Marko said with a chuckle.

"I wouldn't count on it. You should look again before you talk big," I said and pointed at the mirror.

The god started to shake. Then he started to crumble. The god was falling apart piece by piece. Then two brown wings appear out of the God's back. Then Stephen started flapping his wings and the rest of the God crumbled into small pieces of rocks and since all the water was dried up, the god could not pull him self back together again.

Then Stephen just shrunk back down to his normal size and then picked up a crystal shard that was inside the God. "I wonder what this is but I'll take it with me and when I find anyone else I'll ask them what's up," he said.

"Ha, I knew it," is all I said to Marko and then the mirror showed the next battle. It went to Damien. He was up in the air and his wings were already out and flapping. The sky was a dark gray and it seem like the winds were blowing really fiercely. The clouds seem to be hiding something. Just then the God made his appearance.

Just like the wind it seemed like he was linked into the changing wind patterns. It looked like he was the wind itself. You could only make out a face from the small circles of rough wind in the sky.

"So you're my opponent, you don't look like a good challenge to me," the God said with a smirk.

"Well I'm your opponent and if you want to face me or not I will defeat you one way or another," Damien said and went into a fighting stance.

Damien flew over to where he saw the face and wondered how he could defeat something that is all round him. Then he thought I can also control the winds like the changing of the weather. He then started flying around in a circle and it started moving things around. The god didn't like this and wanted everything to go his way. The god started to counter attack the moment that Damien was creating.

Then the two winds started to collided and that was when Damien struck. He flew right into the middle of the winds and punched the god, knocking him out of hiding. The wind was still stirring and was causing friction in the air. Small sparks of lighting were starting to spark all over the area.

The sparks were becoming more and more like bolts. Then one streaked across the sky. It lit up the area and Damien saw a shadow. It was not his shadow but the one of the God since he went back into hiding. The lighting streak across the sky again and the shadow was moving closer to him.

"Well I guess he ran away since I hit him," said Damien and then the Wind God grabbed him. It sent both of them into a spiral but the strange thing was that they went up into the clouds instead of down towards the ground. The lighting was continuing to streak across the sky. The fighting was being done through the clouds so every time lighting would streak across, you would see two figures in the cloud fighting with fists or kicking or something.

Finally Damien got kicked out of the cloud and the God followed him down. Just as he went flying down, the God almost got hit by the lighting. "That was a close one," the God said.

That gave Damien an idea. He flew up into the clouds and start making the winds force more lighting throughout the sky. The God followed him back into the clouds but when he tried to go in, the lighting block his way. Damien saw that and then kept making more lighting. The cloud got bigger and bigger and soon it filled the entire sky.

Lighting was shooting all over the place. The Wind God was quick enough to dodge the ones coming after him. While that was happening, Damien was inside the cloud forming a lighting ball to catch the God. He was collecting up stray lighting bolts and forming them into a ball. The center of the ball was hollow so anything that got trapped inside it would just be stuck there. Just as Damien grabbed the last Lighting bolt, the god appeared to blowing away the cloud that was covering him.

The god appeared behind Damien and charged towards him. Just as the God got close enough, Damien vanished and appeared behind the God. Damien fired the lighting ball that he was holding and it went straight at the God. The God wasn't quick enough to dodge it and was sucked into the ball of lighting. Since the God was trapped in a small confined space, he just gave up and vanished like the wind. He left inside the lighting ball a crystal shard.

Damien reached into the ball and grabbed it. Then the sky became clear again and he flew off.

The mirror picture vanished from sight and Marko spoke up, "So you think you trained them enough to face the oldest Gods in the elemental world. Even if you trained them for thousand's years they don't compare to the next two battles."

"I bet you'll be wrong. I believe in them and I know they believe in themselves and that is all they need," I said and then look back at the mirror as it went on to the next battle area.

The screen filled up with water. We saw it was a mapped area with small cracks at the bottom. The water was flowing in from the top and going out the bottom. It created small riptides and current flowing through the water.

Patty appeared underwater and started freaking out a little bit. Then she remembered the spell that I taught her for underwater breathing. She cast the spell and air bubble formed around her head. She started to relax when the Water God kicked her in the back.

Since the God saw that see need air to survive then she thought that she could toy with Patty till her spell wore off. She made Patty start bouncing from one end of the area to the other.

Patty was getting sick of feeling like a pinball. While watching the fight, I noticed one thing Patty was doing. She was casting spells while bouncing back and forth and then she stopped in middle of a bounce and then the God went full force towards her.

"Thanks for showing yourself. Now it's my turn to show you how water can be used," Patty said with some excitement and released it.

Five water spears appeared around the God and pinned the god in the center of the area. Then Patty was floating and started to cast her next spell. A water ball was forming up behind her. Patty released the ball towards the God. The God saw it coming and it hit right on top of its head. As the spears unpinned the God, Patty went up to see the damage that was done. One of the spears was still floating inches away from the body.

One of the spears went flying at Patty as she was getting close to the body. She realized that the God transformed into one of the spears. The spear now was aimed right for Patty's head and as the spear got closer, Patty turned into water herself. The spear went straight through her.

The God got angry that someone with less power and knowledge could be that fast of a learner. Basically the screen was all blue with small air bubbles floating up to the top. Every once in a while you could make out the figure of

Patty or the Water God. The battle was going on and on and then Patty became visible again.

"Wow that was a trip, I never knew water could be so much fun," said Patty with a smile.

Then the Water God re-appeared as well. She was drop dead gorgeous. From head to toe, she was all curves. Dressed in all blue she made the water around her dance to her every move.

"Your good honey but this is where it all ends. I'm going to teach you one last lesson before I send you back to where you came from. See the whole God thing is so done with but I know that water is the way life should be. Always flowing and changing and nothing can stop it from achieving its final destination. With that said, it is time to kill you," the God said with wicked grin across her face.

"Well bring it on and show me the true power of water," Patty told her.

She started to do a dance within the water. The dance was moving the water as well as Patty. Then small shards of ice water were being sent from her body and traveling with the current of the water.

Each one was flying straight towards Patty but Patty noticed and started to counteract the water moment with her own dance movements. The ice shards were about dead center, stuck in a battle of who can be as fluid as water.

"You're a good dancer," Patty said.

"So are you," she replied.

"Sorry to say this but it is time to turn up the heat," Patty said. Then she started busting out moves that the God couldn't keep up with and the ice shards started heading back towards her. Then a red aura formed around Patty. It was her passion for dancing that turn the ice shards into little fireballs in the water. She noticed that and tried to step up her dance moves which screwed her over even more.

The Water God messed up and then the fires balls ran straight into her. The fireballs became attached to her ankles and wrists. The red glow around Patty formed in front of her and she finished her dance. The fireball shot from her towards the Water God.

The entire area was then turn into vapors and Patty landed on the ground. Nothing was left of the water field and then a crystal shard dropped down next to Patty. She picked it up and then went looking for an exit.

"Well I guess that is the way of life. Everything vanishes and then starts a new," I said to my brother. Marko didn't say anything. It seemed I hit a cord with the Gods. They were getting upset that I knew my team would be doing great and I had nothing to worry about. The mirror showed the last elemental scene.

Down in the depths of a volcano was where the Fire God and Mike would have there battle. Lava erupted and gasses hissing all over the place and very few spots to step on solid ground in this fiery hell

We see Mike just standing there waiting for the Fire God to show up. Mike was thinking something and staring at the clothes in his hand. Why Ethan would gave me these clothes.

Thinking back about couple nights again Ethan knocking on his door. "Hey Mike how you doing?" he said.

"Not bad so what's up?" Mike asked curiously.

"I just came by to drop these clothes off for your battle against the Fire God. Hope they fit and please remember to wear them because if not you will get embarrassed," Ethan said and then just walked away.

Mike started too wondered why it so important to wear these clothes. He got a shirt, jeans socks shades, underwear and shoes that were in the bag. They fitted perfectly and the shades seem to be just his style as well. Well the good thing is that I don't feel the heat.

Mike put on his shades and saw a fist flying at his head. The shades let him see what wasn't there. He ducked right in time to dodge the fiery fist coming at him. He then backed up a little and stepped into a stream of lava. "Oh shit, my clothes are going to burn up," he thought. He took his foot out and the shoe and pant legs we fine, even his leg and foot did not heat up.

He noticed the Fire God coming after him. "Shit, I have nothing to fight hand to hand with. I can kick him but my fists are doom to heat up if I touch him or anything else," Mike said.

"Ha, ha, ha," the Fire God laughed. "Well I guess then this will be an easy fight to win since you can not hit me."

Mike turned around and started running and was trying to think of what he could do to win this fight and not lose the battle. Running around the area Mike saw a few things that might work. He was throwing fireballs at Mike. Mike was just a little faster then the fireballs and even quicker at dodging them.

He went one time around the area and then grabbed a rock that looked like a giant scoop. He used it to scoop up some lava and poured it out. It made a little lava shield. The fireball hit the shield and shattered it. It didn't work as planned but then he got another idea. He flipped the rock scoop over and was going to use it as a shield.

The Fire God threw another fireball and he hit the scoop and was sent back towards himself. He threw another fireball to block the one coming towards him. Both fireballs slammed into each other. They exploded and bits of flaming rock went flying all over the place.

Smoke filled the area and the shades made it real easy for him to see. Mike's hands fell to his sides and brushed his pockets. He felt something inside them. He reached inside them and pulled out and pair of biker gloves. The fingers were cut off. "Well it seemed Ethan didn't forget gloves, I just forgot to check the pockets," Mike thought.

Mike brought his wings out and flew straight towards the God who didn't have that greatest smoke vision. Mike landed a punch on the backside of the God and now he was in control of the fight. The smoke was still hovering around which made a perfect cover for Mike to fight in.

Mike was punching him all over but not really doing much damage to him. Mike got into the rhythm of each punch he was throwing. He was looking like he was punching and pulled something from inside the Fire God.

The smoke finally cleared from around them and the God was shrinking in size. Mike still punching away and the Fire God was look for a way out. Everywhere he turn Mike was there punching away.

Mike now realizing the Fire God's weakness was using it to his advantage. He was pulling the air from the Fire God and that is one of the key elements of the power of this God. Soon the God was just about the size of a fire ant and Mike just stepped on him. The fire was put out and the arena was now cooling off.

Mike opened his fist and inside his right hand was the crystal from the God. He realized while he was punching he grabbed hold of something. Not wanting to slow down to see what it was he just held on to it till he was done.

Now that the lava was cooling off he started walking around searching for an exit to get out of this area. Then all four doors opened up and each one of them entered the door. Waiting for them was Mrs. X and Jake.

"Well glad to see you guys are alright," said Damien with smile to brighten up the world.

"We watched your battles and you guys fought great," Jake said to them.

"So where are we at?" asked Stephen while looking around.

"We must be in the hallways that link the different levels and battle areas here in heaven. Ethan told me about this place once and then I figured it out when me and X went through our door and ended up here in the hallways. We are heading to the top but we can not go any further till the next battle is done," Jake said and started walking into the next level.

"Well let's follow and see who is next to battle," Mike said and ran to catch up with Jake. Everyone followed in suit and went up into the next level of Heaven.

"Well I see my elementals, were just fine against the Gods of old. So I really think you should stop this and move on from this little game. They will defeat you and when their battles are over I promise, I'll save Marko and defeat you two Gods," I said to them and had a glare to kill.

"Trust me the next one's will be lost in there minds forever and not be able to get out. We are going to play a little mind game, Ethan," the Gods said to me. The mirror went to Trevor standing in the wasteland.

CHAPTER FIFTY-TWO

TREVOR HAD HIS WINGS OUT AND WAS READY FOR ANYTHING to come his way. The wasteland that he landed in was more of a swamp then anything else. The trees blocked out any light getting in and the ground was all mucky and slushy. Trevor started walking towards the direction he was facing.

No noises were being made and Trevor thought that was weird. Here he is, in the middle of a swamp and there are no creatures making a sound. Then he took one more step and started to sink. The solid land that he was standing on quickly turned into mud.

Trevor didn't try to pull out; he just needed to think about what he was doing. It was only one foot sinking and the other one was still on solid land. He looked around to see if he could grab on to anything that was hanging. He did notice a branch that was hanging low and he reached out to try and grab it. He was little to short to reach it. He forgot that he had his wings out and just used them to flap his way out of the mud.

His wings carried himself above the canopy and noticed a city in the distance. He went flying towards that city. In about five minutes, he hit the city limits. There was life there and everyone was to busy to even notice him. He floated down and landed on one of the main streets.

He retracted his wings. "Hey, where am I?" he asked. Nobody answered. He grabbed the nearest person and turned them around. The person turned around and his lips we sealed. Trevor back away from the person and bumped into another one. The lady turned around and her mouth was sowed shut as well. This start to freak Trevor out, he started walking around and noticed there we no signs or billboards or anything.

He couldn't find out where he was. It was slowly driving him mad. He expanded his wings and took flight. He went to the tallest building and stood on the rooftop. He was looking for any signs to help him out. He looked back towards the swamp, but it was no longer there. He took a good look at the city and noticed one thing that was out of place besides the people and the lack of signs.

There was this one building that was smaller then the rest and it seemed like a little mom and pop shop that had one sign. It read open. He flew down to the building and land at its doorstep. He opened the door and went inside.

It was fortune teller's house. The fortune teller was sitting at the other end of the shop. "Come in and sit down and I'll tell you your fortune," said the teller and offered him the sit across from him.

Trevor didn't see any harm in it, so he walked forward and took a seat. The teller started the practice that seemed to be flowing through him. "May I see your palm?" the teller asked and put out his hand.

"Sure, here it is," Trevor said.

Trevor handed his right hand to the teller and the teller gently placed his hand underneath Trevor's, then he started the read. The teller point to the first line on Trevor's hand and said "This line here will tell you about the present. It seems you are lost and don't know where to go. Each time you think about it you get more lost in your head." Then the teller moved to the line right above the one that he was touching and said, "This one tells about what will stand in your way of moving on to reunite with ones you lost. This place is the task at hand; you must solve this puzzle before you get stuck here like the people outside."

"Wow, that is sounding like you know your stuff," Trevor told the teller.

Then a voice rang out, "Who the heck are you, messing with my little world. Be gone from this place and leave my battle alone." The voice vanished and so did the fortune teller. Trevor figured out that the teller was not suppose to be here and was trying to help him out. "Well at least I know that I'm stuck in a mind puzzle and the voice that told the teller to leave was the person trapping me in here," he said to himself. "Hey mysterious voice, why not show your self and fight me like a man. Stop hiding behind these tricks and fight me."

"Now why would I do that? I don't need to test your strength by battling you but to test your mind," the voice said with giggle.

"Well making me wait is not going to help you out and these people without mouths did freak me out at first but I see now that you're nothing but a big fraud that likes to hide," Trevor said while thinking of a way to find out where the voice was coming from.

"Well I'm glad you can see through my disguise but that is not true. I'm here with you. I maybe one of the walking dead that surrounding you or be invisible or maybe just messing with your head, I could have been in the swamp but you'll never find out," the voice said. While the voice was talking Trevor stood still and closed his eyes. He was focusing on were the sound was coming from. In is mind he saw the sound coming from the left of his body. He turned his body towards the vibrations.

"So what is this? A game of cat and mouse, or are we just going to talk all day." Trevor said with his eyes closed and following the sounds waves.

"Well it seems that this cat is not tried of playing with you yet. I think I'll watch you squirm a little more and wait for you to make your move. See in life there is always a right time to do everything and a right way. I know the right way to get rid of you but the timing is still off. Your mind is still strong and I need to weaken that. This is not battle of the fists but a battle of the minds. I know my mind is strong but I also know that your mind is just a little bit stronger. I choose this battle field for you because everyone gets to the point of silence and breaks because it seems that most people are social to an nth degree. So I'm waiting for you to break and want someone to talk to," the voice rang out.

While the voice was talking, Trevor was following the sound vibration and he finished tracking them. Trevor waited till he was finished talking to play one last trick on his opponent. "So what's your name?" Trevor asked and threw his voice so his opponent didn't notice that he was behind him.

The voice answered, "You can just call me, Mastermind."

"Ok Mastermind, I got a question for you. What happens when I win?" Trevor asked with certainty in his voice.

"Well, you will be transported to the hallway, where all your friends should be but I know that they are all dead and the others took them out," Mastermind told Trevor.

"Well I do not believe that and just to let you know you lost your little mind game that we were playing," Trevor whisper in his ear and tapped Mastermind on the shoulder. He turned around and a fist went flying into Mastermind's face, knocking him down to the ground.

The people all vanished and so did the city. Mastermind lost his control over the realm. "This is not over, I'll get your friend, Eric," Mastermind said and vanished into thin air.

The doorway open just like Mastermind said and Trevor walked through it and there was everyone watching his battle with Mastermind. The hallway was a little to thin for everyone to stand next to each other so they lined up since the group was getting bigger. Trevor was happy to see everyone safe and they were happy to see him win the battle of the minds.

"Well one mind game down and one to go," is all I said to the Gods. The Gods didn't reply but it seemed they were getting really pissed off. I was reading into the mind of my brother and he didn't want to play any more.

"Ethan, please help me, I don't want to fight you or continue with this plan. I see why you didn't want to help the Gods," Marko said with a tear rolling down my cheek.

"I promise you that UE and I will do everything in our powers to free you from their control. I'm thinking of a plan as we speak to do it," I told him then the Gods cut off the link between Marko and me. I looked back to the mirror to see that Eric was standing still in the mirror.

Eric didn't like the looks of the area he was in. He knew he would be tested on the balance of life but how would that be tested was the question. Then all of a sudden he was in the middle of a city. It was like he was about to find out how to be the balance of life.

In this city, everything was different. People were robbing people, stealing from stores, beating people up. Basically, the city was in complete chaos. "Tick, tock, tick tock," a voice spoke up over the city ruckus.

"Well I take it you're the one I'm battling but I guess you will not be able to show yourself to the end of this test," Eric calmly said to the sky.

"Bravo, on how quick you figured that out. Yes I am your challenger and the name is Mastermind and soon you will loose your mind," Mastermind said with a sinister laugh.

"Well I guess I need to clean up the city to restore the balance. Oh and just to let you know your hiding spot is very easy to spot since you're the only one that is not doing anything to make this city more chaotic then it is but first to fix the city," Eric said. Then Eric spread his wings and engulfed the entire city within his wings. First trap the people inside.

Next step is to help out the ones that need it. Eric went around the city a stopped the people beating up on people. "Now for the looters," Eric said. Instead of putting them in jail like normal, Eric made them help fix the broken windows or doors that they smashed into rubble.

"Well the last step is not to stop everything because a little chaos in this city will make it balanced once more. Mastermind, I see you moved from your little hiding spot and trust me I'll find you. Now that the city is safe and balanced out again, I think it is time for you and me to have nice long battle face to face. No more mind games unless you want to play these mind games and I'll beat you every time," Eric said out loud.

"Well, well, well I see someone wants to end this faster then I wanted. I think I will just toy with you even more now that you seem to be cocky," Mastermind said.

"Not cocky, more or less, I just don't care about your little freaking mind games. So can we just end this now and move on, I know that all my friends are alright and nothing you can do to my mind will change that. See I made sure that I had open commutation links to each of my teammates and they are speaking to me right now," Eric said and pointed to his ear.

"That is a lie. I don't believe you. Your just bluffing, these areas are built to keep you from knowing anything about the others," Mastermind told Eric.

"Oh yeah by the way Trevor says hi," Eric told Mastermind. That was it, Mastermind cracked. The realm turn completely white and he was standing in the middle of the area. He didn't look like much. He was very thin and short. He was dressed in just normal street clothes. Nothing about him stood out from any other person you would meet on the street.

Eric went up next to him and asked, "So why are you doing this? What are you fighting for?"

"I'm not fighting for anything. I just wanted to prove that I was the best at something. So I trained and trained for years and years. Then one day these two spirits came down and told me that I was the greatest Master of the Minds. They want to help me become the best and promised me all the power in the world. Eric you know the sad part is that I don't even remembered my real name," Mastermind said with some sorrow in his voice.

"Well how about I help you get your memories, I mean it seems that you not a bad person and I know you seem to just be like us. Not really knowing what's going to happen and always wanting to belong. Ethan can teach you a whole lot of things and even help you get your name and memories back. Come on lets get out of here and help save people like us," Eric said and then he extend his hand.

Mastermind reached out and then grabbed Eric's hand. Just then a black hole was formed around the two. Both of them started to fall into the pit. Eric brought out his wings and started flapping and holding on to MM. "I'm not going to let go of you, my friend," Eric said while struggling to get out of the pit.

"Just let me go. The Gods are trying to get rid of me and I don't deserve to live," MM yelled at him.

"That is a load of crap, everyone deserves to live or you wouldn't be created. We are all here for a reason and I bet your reason is it to become the best at mind games and tricks of illusions. I would love for you to teach me how to create worlds once we are done defeating the Gods. So what do you say? Let's get out of here," Eric yelled down to him.

MM looked up and just smiled at his new friend that he made. Just then Eric knew that it was time to get out of this hole and move on to the next level of Heaven. Eric threw him up and he landed on the outside of the black hole. Then Eric flew straight out of it.

Eric landed on the ground and told MM to hop on his back. "Hold on we are going to make our own door of this area," Eric told MM.

"Sounds good," MM said. He hopped on Eric's back and then they went flying up. Eric's wings formed a bullet like shape around their bodies. Then Eric picked up speed and flew straight through the side of the wall.

The mirror went black. "So I see you Master of the mind doesn't work on my guys and it seemed like he switched side as well. I take it you don't like traitors and that is why you opened the black hole. Trying to make them get lost and never find their way out. Well let's see now, your angels didn't defeat mine, the elementals are destroyed, and your Mastermind has switched teams, to me it seems like your losing this war," I said to them with confidents.

"Well it is not over yet, trust me your battle with us will be your end and then we will just take every one of your friends out as well. Just wait and see," they said angrily.

I did notice one thing while they were getting mad at me; that they seemed to lose control over Marko. Just then UE and I realized that is how we can save Marko and get them to fight me without hurting Marko. I went into my head and UE and I started to make a plan for the battle that lay ahead for us.

The smoke cleared in the hallway and Eric and MM were unharmed. Everyone came running up to them. Trevor saw Mastermind and was about to deck him when Eric move in front of him. "He is good for now. He just needs some help to get his mind back together," Eric told Trevor firmly.

Trevor didn't like the idea but went along with it for now. They did intros and then moved on to the next level of heaven. The mirror also moved to where John and Dante were.

CHAPTER FIFTY-THREE

DANTE SEEMED TO HAVE A SMILE ON HIS FACE AND SO did John. The area for an ultimate battle, it seemed like every monster and creature was waiting to get a piece of these two. Both of them had there wings out. John with his angel wings and Dante with his demon wings, they were standing in the middle and back to back so each other knew where the other was.

"Hey Dante, I know they want us dead but I think this is a sign that tells us everyone else is alright. What do you think?" John said with smile across his face.

"I think your right. First the area was clear and we were just standing around waiting then all these guys show up. All I know now is that one of them holds the way out so let's end this quick partner," Dante said and then had a serious look on his face.

The battle begun and it seemed that the creatures in the room were taking turns. The first one to battle them was a just small little sprites and fairies. They seemed to put up and good fight but then Dante sent a spell that trapped all the sprites and fairies in a glass bottle. Dante grabbed the bottle and then shook it up.

The sprites and fairies were mad but couldn't escape. Dante just laughed and got ready for the next wave of them to come. This time they attacked on John's side. They were a little bigger but not as smart. It was snakes. John flew up into the air and then started to cast a spell.

The bad part about John's spell casting is that it took time. He was still a little slow in that department. So the creatures saw an opportunity to hit him while he was chanting. They sent some hawks to screw him up, the hawks started to swoop down onto John but Dante got his back. Dante was fighting off the birds while John was in the middle of his chant.

Just as soon as John was done, the floor to the area was burning up. The floor started to crack open and lava started to spew out. The snakes could not move fast enough and burned in the lava. The next wave of monsters could not get away from the spewing lava that came from the ground as well. Then the dragons came in. The blue ice dragon started breathing his ice breath on the lava and freezing it so the ground was able to fight on again.

The dragon's stayed in the back because they were there to help out the others till they were needed to fight. The next wave of creature was Werewolves. "Oh shit, I don't know how to fight Werewolves," John said.

"You just protect yourself and I'll take care of these guys," Dante told John with a glare in his eyes. Dante started to cast a spell and then the night sky appeared on the roof. The moon started to rise and it was full. The Werewolves stopped attacking and was listening to the sound of Luna singing.

Dante knew that most Werewolves could not resist the calling of the Luna's song. It only comes out when the moon is full and bright. Dante thanked Luna and then he just let her take care of the Werewolves as now they were fighting against the creatures that were left.

"Wow. That was cool," John said.

"Yeah I remembered that the moon can control the ones that were still new or the ones that didn't control their own minds," Dante told him.

"Well you are going to have to teach me how to do that but we can save that for later," John said while getting ready for whatever was to come next.

The stage was set for the next two creatures of night to come out. The first came from the skies and the other from underground. Vampires from above and worms from below, the worms seem to make the ground unstable. The worms broke the ice that was on the ground and were popping up all over the place which in turn made it hard for the vampires to attack us from the air.

That gave John an idea. He went over to Dante and told him the plan to get rid of these creatures. Dante went in the motion and start banging on the ground and John was getting the vampires to follow him. Dante started to feel the ground shake beneath him and leaped out of the way. John flew over the spot and as the worm started to pop up. The vampires couldn't stop in time and got swallowed by the worm.

The worm was happy that he got feed and then went back down inside the hole. The ground stopped shaking and Dante and John figured that the worm was just hungry and needed a snack but they didn't forget about it. The room seemed emptier and the one creature's that still remand were the gryphons, the hydras, and dragons. Since the gryphon' were smart they knew that they didn't stand a chance against this duo. They just flew away and the hydras didn't even have a chance since most of there other creatures they wanted to help were destroyed already.

That just left the dragons. They had just a few dragons in the area. One ice dragon, one fire dragon and one poison one. Dante and John both were waiting for the big guys to come out and battle.

"Hey Dante," John yelled.

"What John?" Dante quickly snapped back.

"Which one do you want?" he asked as the dragons came onto the field.

"Don't care, let's just get rid of them," he said then took off towards the green one.

That left John with red or blue. He picked his favorite color and went after that one first. The blue one was the one he went after. The ice dragon was still a little pissed off that the heat in the room was rising again. So the blue dragon started to freeze every thing in site. John had to dodge some of the ice beams to reach the body of the dragon. John has never fought a dragon before so he really didn't have any clue on how to defeat it.

Dante on the other hand was doing just fine with the poison dragon. Dante turned his hands to flames, so anything he touched would burn. The poison dragon was just spewing his bile all over the place. The one thing about poison dragons is that you could not touch its skin. Dante knew that, so that is why he had burning hands spell on. He final reached the body of the dragon and he just laid his hands on the dragon's body and it went up in flames. You heard the screech of the dragon as it slowly turned into a small pile of green ooze on floor.

John still didn't know how to go about fighting a dragon. Half the area was covered in ice and the fire dragon did not like that. The fire dragon started to heat things up. Then the idea hit John that he could pit the two dragons against each other. Dante came over to where John was and asked with a smirk, "Are you having trouble with your dragons? Cause mine is just that pile of green ooze over there," Dante teased him.

"Nope but I'm going to get rid of both of them at the same time. So just relax and I will take care of the other two," John said and took off.

John went into the middle of the room and was waiting for both dragons to notice him. It took a few minutes for the dragons to notice him but they final did. They both fired there breathes at him and meet in the middle. John vanished from sight.

Both kept breathing their breath and then they stopped. In the middle was to wings one was red as the fire that was on it and the other was ice blue. John turned around and then forced his wings to open up and as he opened his wings, they started firing the flames towards the ice dragon and ice towards the fire dragon. The dragons tried to fight back but John's wing storm was just too powerful. The fire dragon was frozen and the ice dragon melted.

John came down from the air and said, "I told I could take them out."

"Well, I never doubt you and don't forget to get the crystals that your two dragons dropped," Dante pointed to them and then started walking to them.

John picked them up and both went flying out of the room once the door was open.

"Wow, didn't see you guys fighting with creatures of the world. I figured you guys would send gods against them. Well it seemed there is only one battle left and it seems that my team is kicking your ass," I said to them. I looked down and saw Sam just standing there in the completed darkness.

"The darkness of heaven will consume any hope from your friend and his light will no longer shine," the Gods told me.

The mirror went into the darkness of heaven. Sam was just sitting in the middle and was glowing a small light around him self. Nothing was around him. No walls, no roof or ground it was like the darkness had engulfed everything in sight.

Sam just sat there mediating and didn't move from his spot in the darkness. He was waiting for something to happen. Sam thought why waste time walking around and getting lost when the opponent can come to you. Sam knew what was coming and the way he trained for the past year was just training him for this battle and many others to come.

Sam then thought back to the day when Ethan picked him up to start his training. *Hey Sam, hope you're ready to train in the far reaches of the universe. This training will be like no other and I hope you're ready for it. Well let's go.*

Sam opened his eyes and noticed he was not able to see the through the darkness and he was in nothingness. Then it seemed like there was nobody here to talk to or even seem like there was no way out. Sam knew that the best way to solve a problem is just think it out and see what options he had.

Then a voice came out of nowhere. It bellowed through the darkness, "You will lose; you have no chance of getting out of here. Your friends have failed and so will you."

"Well if I'm destined to lose then bring it on. I have been sitting here waiting for something to happen and nothing has. So let's get this done with. I know that you're trying to get rid of my light that comes from within. That is when you will strike but my light within will never go out. With that said let's get this battle done with," Sam said to the voice.

That ticked off the voice and it replied hastily, "Well it seems that time is something I have a lot of but you don't. I guess it is time to show myself to you. The darkness started to take form. It turned into a copy of Sam but it was the darkness within him. "This chamber we are in is called the darkness of Heaven. It looks into the person and brings their darkness to life. I know your darkness and weaknesses. That is how I'll destroy you."

"Well I guess then you know my weakness and darkness, so what. That does not make me a whole but only a half. My weaknesses build up my strengths but I will knock them back down and the darkness within myself only I can defeat. I guess this is my chance to kick its ass or it will kick mine," Sam said to the darkness calmly.

Nobody wanted to make the first move. Then Sam came up with a brilliant plan. He wanted to see how powerful his darkness was. He knew that his darkness was as powerful as he was but since this darkness was not the real thing it must have its limits.

Sam made the first move. He transformed into light and started racing around the room. Darkness engulfed the room again and as Sam's trail of light would touch the darkness it would change to white then go back to normal. Faster and faster Sam went around the room. Sam stopped and the darkness turned back into the copy. "I see that my light trail did little damage to you and the darkness can engulf every piece of light I throw at it," Sam said intrigued.

"Yeah, I'll engulf you as well. Once I drain your light, it will be easy to destroy you," the darkness said to him.

"I see," Sam said then went off to start something else. "So if I lose my light, this battle will be over."

He started to confuse the darkness. The darkness didn't know how to response to that. Then he started to cast a spell. The darkness didn't know what he was doing so the darkness started to attack him.

The darkness was throwing dark energy towards him. The energy bolts went flying by him without even throwing off his concentration. The dark energy made small cuts on his body and in his clothes as well. Then the darkness was getting mad. The darkness was getting annoyed because he was getting ignored. The darkness started to charge up and a big dark energy ball that was forming above its head.

The darkness was making the ball bigger and bigger. Soon it was full and was ready to be shot at Sam. The darkness pointed the energy ball at Sam and fired it. Sam did not budge. The ball came closer and closer. Everyone was watching closely, even the Gods. The dark energy ball engulfed Sam and left nothing but his shoes on the ground.

The darkness and the Gods both were wondering why Sam didn't fight back or even move out of the way. I started to cry a little because I didn't even know the reason Sam didn't move out of the way. The rest of the gang was in shock that something that powerful could exist to wipe something out with one single hit. The door to the top realm opened and there was someone standing right in front of them.

It was Sam. "We just saw you get destroyed by the darkness," everyone said with the shocked looked on their face.

"I think you guys might look again," Sam said and pointed back at the room.

Everyone ran back to the viewing window. They saw my shoes and nothing else in the room. "What the heck is going on?" they asked.

"Well I figured out the only way to get rid of the darkness is to just stop caring about it. See the spell that I was chanting while the darkness was talking was a light/ dark spell. The spell was to get rid of the light in me and switch it with the darkness. So when the darkness was doing the dark bolts and letting them hit me just help the spell get done faster. Then I just told my darkness to get hit by the ball and it would destroy the darkness in the area and we would win. Sorry for fooling you guys but it wouldn't work if any one knew about that power of the light and dark. Well I guess I'll not be able to get my shoes back so shall we move on?" Sam said with a smile.

"Do the Gods know about this and does Ethan know about this spell?" Jake asked me.

"I don't think so, I was taught this spell on a far off planet and they told me not to use it unless it is dire. I think it did the trick and boy will everyone on the next level be surprised." I told them.

CHAPTER FIFTY-FOUR

On the next level, I was down on my knees because I saw one of my friends destroyed by the evil that stood in front of me. I couldn't even move. I lost myself in depths of my mind. Even UE couldn't find me.

"Well wherever you are, I am going to take over your body and fight for you. I'm sure you will not mind," UE said into the depths of our mind. He didn't waste any time after he said that.

"Well you little plan worked. Ethan went into the depths of our mind but I could tell you I will not fall that easy. I'll defend us till he gets back and I promise that I will get revenge for my fallen comrade," UE told the Gods.

UE knew the plan to get them out of the body they were using. Making them lose their control by pissing them off. UE knew that Marko must have been tried as hell since he was being control by two Gods. The first step was to piss off the Gods and second step is to make the body get really tried and pass out. So UE did just that. He started flying around the top level of heaven and was hoping they would follow.

They did take the bait and UE thought he would have some time to go and find his other half. In the deepest of our minds, I sat in the corner thinking of what I just saw. "I don't want anyone to get hurt. Why does this have to be? I really don't think I can do this. I am too weak," I said to myself and then a tear rolled down my cheek.

"Well that maybe so but I believe in you," UE said from behind me.

"It is nice to know someone believes in me but I just don't think I can do this. I don't want to fight anymore. I'm just tried of the whole battles and what happens if I fail everyone since they fought so hard. They'll hate me and then I really will be alone in this world," I said to UE.

Outside UE started just doing some small tricks to divert the Gods and piss them of at the same time. UE knew that the Gods hated when people just try to delay what was really going on. They like getting to the point of things. The Gods sped up the body and then it happened.

Marko's body dropped like a rock to the ground below. The Gods didn't realize that this body was completely worn out. The Gods didn't have a body to use as there puppet any more. They stop chasing UE and retreated back into their little inner sanctum.

UE stopped flying around and went over to the body. UE shook him a few times and he was still alive but needed some good rest. He was so exhausted that his body finally gave out.

Back inside the depths of our mind, Ethan still was sitting in the corner. "Why did I get picked to do this? There got to be a better person for the job," I thought to myself.

"I'm back and the good news is that I freed your brother from the control of the Gods and they retreated for the time being. Now it is time to fix you so we can go and defeat them once and for all," UE told me and put his hand on my shoulder.

"Well I'm glad that Marko is safe but I really think I couldn't do this," I told UE and was looking down at the ground. Then I felt the presence of others around me and my brother. The gang final got up the top level and ran over to where we were.

"Hey guys what's up?" UE said to them.

"Not much and how did your battle go?" they asked curiously.

"Well we freed Marko but Ethan is not able to go on do to the fact that he saw Sam's death," UE paused and looked up and saw Sam standing in the background. UE did double take. "Even through he is standing right there. Wait you're alive, well that is good news and can you help me get Ethan back to normal so we can finish this mess."

"Sure, let's end this mess," Sam said and then walked over to our body. UE grabbed his hand and transported himself and Sam back in the depths of our mind.

"Hey Ethan, I got a surprise for you," UE said cheerfully to me.

"What is that?" I asked while turning around. As I was turning around I saw that he was not alone. Sam was with him. "What the hell are doing alive, I saw you die?"

Sam told him what he did and then asked, "Are you ready yet?"

"I still don't know if I will be able to defeat them," I told the both of them.

Sam walked up to me and just slapped me across the face. "I think you been thinking way to much. I know I been away for one year but I really think you need to just go in there and have fun. Don't take things to seriously because I knew the old Ethan wouldn't worry about the outcome but more if everything was done the way he wanted it to be."

"You know something, your right. Thanks, I forgot about that. Let's go have fun and destroy these Gods," I told them.

"There's the Ethan I know," UE said.

Then everyone left the depths of our mind and I saw everyone just standing around me and Marko. "Hey guys what up?"

"Not much just waiting for you to come to your sense and go kick some ass," Jake excitedly said.

"Time is ticking," Stephen told me.

"Well can one of you guys take care of him?" I asked and pointed down to Marko's body.

"Sure," said Mrs. X.

Mrs. X went and picked up the body and threw him on her back like she was giving him a piggy back ride. Then we all headed towards the doors that await my final battle. We reached the door. It was about your average size door and it seemed to be plain as the door you would find on a house.

I pushed the door open and it creaked like it never has been open in a long time. It opened upon a room that was not very heavenly. No clouds, no big divine light shining in and it seem like I have been here before. I started walking around the room. In the right upper corner there is a queen size bed that was made and seems not to have been slept in for a couple of years. A small layer of dust was on it. In another corner was a small table set up for two. And then the walls seemed to have just been freshly painted.

The rest of the gang entered the room and was looking at everything as if this just completely looked out of place. Then the Gods started to speak, "Welcome to your permanent prison. Hope you like the commendations." Then they started laughing at how easy it was to catch all of us in one simple trap.

"Well just to let you two know, I figured you would trap us and not really wanting to fight, we sought off tricked you," I said. I tapped them on the shoulder while speaking. "See we knew that you guys are to chicken to fight with out the help of your magic, so I figure it was easier to play your little game."

The Gods looked back into the box house and notice nobody was in there. "Where did they all go?" they asked a little puzzled.

I held up a little projection box. I turned it on and it replayed us walking into the place and looking around. "See magic can detect magic so I use some old school tech to fool you guys. Now it is my turn to kick your asses because of putting us through all this bullshit," I told them and threw the first punch.

The White God blocked my punch from hitting the Black God. Then I threw my other hand to punch the Black again and the White protected its other half. "I see you guys protect the other but how long can it last?" I asked then started to kick and punch faster and faster. Each time I was getting blocked by the other.

UE took over while I was making sure the plan was getting ready for the next phase of this plan. I mean how do you beat a God and in this case two of them that protect each other. I did figure out a way.

"You must be getting tried. Your punches and kicks are getting weaker and weaker. Come on and stop toying with us," they said like they started getting bored of this.

"I was not toying with you guys, I can ensure you that," I said with big fat grin on my face. See I back them up to the other side of their little sanctum. Their backs were up against the wall now and had nowhere to go. The Gods felt the wall behind them. The wall behind them looked like it was made out of clouds. I went in for a punch and they moved out of the way.

My hand went through the cloud wall and they did a quick spell of binding. My hand was stuck in the wall and I wasn't able to pull it out. Then the White God went down to my feet and pulled them through the ground while the other did the same spell again. I was stuck with one arm free.

I thought to myself this is exactly what I thought would happen. My plan was working. The White one tried to get my other hand stuck so I would not be able to do anything but I fought back. I was struggling to get free.

"Ha, ha, ha it looks like this battle is almost done. You're going to lose and then we will force your friends to work for us," they told me with evil laugh.

"I don't think so," then I chanted an unbinding spell. My hand and feet broke free and then I start to chant another spell. The Gods didn't know this spell. They started preparing for the worst. They set up counter spells and shields around themselves.

I was almost done with the spell that would either destroy all of us or just them. The spell was called the Ancient. It was lost a long time ago. What it does or at least what the four Ancients told me was that it had the power of the old Gods and can only be performed by someone that was worthy of it. I finished the spell and wait for something to happen.

"Ha, your spell did not work," they said with a laugh.

"Well I thought I give it a shot, it never hurt anyone to try. So how about I just kick your godly asses they old fashion way," I said and cracked my knuckles.

"We would like to see you break through all these protected shields and spells," they said with an evil grin.

I walked up to the shields and with one punch, shattered all there shields. Then I walked through the spells and each one dissolved as I walked through them. Soon I was face to face with the Gods. "That was easy," I said then I grabbed each of them with my bare hands.

They had the look of terror in their eyes. "His eyes aren't human; I have seen those eyes before. They are those of the Gods that have fallen before our feet," they said in terror.

I looked down at the ground that seem to have somewhat of a reflected surface. They did look different, they we like old ancient relics. The color was like a golden brown and looked back up to realize the gods had escaped my grasp. They went into hiding and I was going on a hunt. It seemed that the spell was within me. I felt my power growing with each and every moment. My eyes were now completely golden brown and were able to see what was not shown in full clarity.

The White God was hiding within the clouds. I walked right over him and it thought it was safe to move but I was just waiting for it to appear. It popped its head out of the clouds and didn't see me around. Its body appeared and I grabbed it. The God screamed but nothing came out of its mouth. Then all of sudden my arm became like golden spear. The spell was transforming my limbs into the weapons that can destroy a God.

My arm swung back and then swung forwards and went straight through the body. The gold was spreading throughout the body. Just when the god was completely gold, it burst into golden flakes. I no longer felt the presences. I thought to myself, "Guess this spear like arm is the only way to make sure a God really does die."

My hunt continued for the other God to end this stupid battle. I went walking around the area. It seemed that I was at full power and was not able to grow any stronger. Then I spotted out of the corner of my eye a black dot within the whiteness of heaven. I raised my hands up and call forth the dark clouds. I start to conduct a lighting storm that filled up the place. There was no place the lighting was not striking. It finally struck the other God.

It hit the God but did no damage since it was only nature and Gods can not be affected by nature but it did stun it. I ran quickly over there and as I was running, it felt like someone threw me. My arm was stretched out and ready to spear it. I dove to reach it before it disappeared back into the clouds.

I did reach the God but my spear went straight through the head. Its body disappeared back into the clouds but the head was still out and was slowly sliding down my spear. It started to change into golden color and busted into gold flakes like the other one. The flakes went into the cloud and I started to get up. Still under the affects of the spell, I wasn't able to get rid of the inner demon. It felt like I was being controlled and moved to destroy one more target.

UE and I tried stopping the demon but he was just too powerful. We let him do what he needed to do but then the Ancient demon started to talk with UE and me. "You are the ones that summoned your inner strength what do you seek?" it asked in deep voice.

"You already destroyed the things we seek. Where are you taking us?" we asked it curiously.

"I'm taking you to the site we I fought my last battle with those two that you just destroyed. I'm going to let you have something that belonged to me," it said then teleported us there.

It was a hidden oasis in the middle of the jungle. A peaceful waterfall was flowing into a pond. At the edge of the pond was a shiny object. It was his lost relic. "This is my hidden paradise that those two Gods came and tried to steal my power. I fought them off but they destroyed me. I left behind this small canteen. Inside was the spell to break me free. I put that scroll inside and was once found by one of the four ancients that you found. It was then that I first realized this was not the right time or person to help me destroy those Gods. He told me that he was part of a bigger plan and will help him out," it said to us.

"Well I was the one who found the 365 scrolls and I guess I was the one you were waiting for," I told it.

"Well now I can finally rest, now that my death has been avenged. Thank you Ethan and UE for helping me destroy those two Gods," it said and then vanished. I appeared back into the inner sanctum and fell down to my knees. Everyone came rushing in to make sure I was alright.

"It's over. The Gods have been destroyed and I can go home and rest, it has been a long year. I'm ready to just go home," I told everyone and just looked up into all there eyes. I know I made a difference.

They all laughed at me after I said that. I got back up on my feet and was still a little weak from the battle. "How do we get out of here?" I asked looking for the exit.

"There are two ways out; Go back the way we came or make a new way out through these walls," Jake said to us while pushing on one of the walls.

"I think we did enough damage for one day to the heavens that we should just go back the way we came," Dante said and we all gave him a confused look.

"You mean that you're going to pass up the chance to smash everything in your path?" John said jokingly to him.

"Yep, it just seems that we should leave peacefully," Dante said.

"Well ok, so let's get out of here," Mike said and started walking towards the entrance to the hallway.

We all started towards the door and walked down the hallway. We reached the end of the hallway and the clouds seem to be not as thick. We all started to fly to my home. We got home and said our goodbyes. I thanked everyone for the great job they did and retired to my bedroom. I quickly stripped off my clothes and as soon as my head hit the pillow, I was out like a light.

Everyone quietly left and John and Eric went next door to their apartment. Everyone slept well that night knowing that everything was over. The next day came and everyone went about there business expect for me.

I woke up about one in the afternoon and went into the living room. I went outside on my balcony and was looking at the brand new day. I started to wonder what was going to happen now.

Just then a knock on my door snapped me back to reality. I went over to it and opened it up. There was nobody there and then I looked down. There was a note on my doorstep. I grabbed the note and went back inside. Slowly opening it up since there was no writing on the outside.

It read: *Your destiny is just beginning.*